ASSASSIN'S CREED

THE ENGINE OF HISTORY

The MAGUS CONSPIRACY

KATE HEARTFIELD

T0040241

ACONYTE

First published by Aconyte Books in 2022

ISBN 978 1 83908 167 5

Ebook ISBN 978 1 83908 168 2

Cover art by Bastien Jez

Distributed in North America by Simon & Schuster Inc, New York, USA
Printed in the United States of America
9 8 7 6 5 4 3 2 1

ACONYTE BOOKS

An imprint of Asmodee Entertainment Ltd

Mercury House, Shipstones Business Centre

North Gate, Nottingham NG7 7FN, UK

aconytebooks.com // twitter.com/aconytebooks

For Brent

PROLOGUE

Simeon Price tried to shut out the sound of whispered prayer, and the groaning of the ship. He flopped one arm over his ear, but it was no good. He was, irritatingly, awake.

"Seasick again, Halford?" he mumbled.

The praying stopped. "Not tonight. Can't sleep, is all."

Simeon turned over with some difficulty in his rocking hammock. Private Sawyer Halford was a dark bulk against a line of similar dark bulks, lit up by a single lantern against the wall. The troop deck was stuffy this deep into the night, a stew of sweat and tobacco, iron and wood. Overhead somewhere, a rat scuttled.

"Thinking about what's waiting for us when we go ashore?" Simeon kept his voice low. He'd recently been given the appointment of lance corporal, which was hardly even a rank, but it did mean that he had responsibility over Halford and a few other privates of the 74th Highland Regiment of Foot. Anyway, Simeon liked Halford.

But going ashore was going to happen, and soon. They

had sailed past Cape Town, the captain charting a course that hugged the southern coast of Africa to save time, speeding by steam and sail toward war.

"I suppose so," Halford said. "It was one thing being sent to Ireland. I knew what to expect, or I thought I did." There was a pause, during which they both thought about what they'd seen in Ireland: the houses burned, the children so thin. "But I'd never even heard of the Xhosa before we sailed."

"I doubt they've heard of you either, mate."

Halford might have chuckled or might have sighed; it was hard to tell which in the dark. "At least when my father went off to fight Napoleon, he'd seen a picture of the bastard." He paused, then said, even more quietly, "I've never killed anyone before."

Neither had Simeon, though he'd come close a couple of times in his father's public house back in Ealing. There had been one night in Tipperary when he had expected to be asked to kill women and old men. In the end, they had left the storehouse he was guarding without violence, gone back to their hungry beds, and Simeon had got very drunk. He had no words of wisdom for Halford tonight.

"I'm sorry I interrupted your prayer," Simeon said quietly.

"Prayer?" Halford chuckled. "Oh, no, Price. I wasn't praying. I always recite Shakespeare when I can't sleep."

"Which bit of Shakespeare?"

"It varies. Tonight, it's the sceptre'd isle speech. From *Richard II*."

Simeon was surprised. "Ah, right. 'England, bound in with the triumphant sea, whose rocky shore beats back the envious siege of watery Neptune'... I can't remember the next part."

"'Is now bound in with shame, with inky blots and rotten parchment bonds. That England, that was wont to conquer others hath made a shameful conquest of itself.'" Halford paused. "Maybe not the best choice for tonight, but it was the sea that made me think of it."

Simeon opened his mouth to say he thought it was an excellent choice, when the ship lurched to a terrible stop, throwing him half out of his hammock.

There were shouts from above. Simeon disentangled his arm and stumbled to his feet. The hideous noise stretched on: a sickening crunch, the iron hull tearing open. The floor tilted from bow to stern. Simeon lurched through the jungle of hammocks and ropes, past the bewildered men just waking up. Out to the door and the stairs up to the deck, in his shirt and trousers.

It was a warm night, with cold stars above, the dark water below. The ship was now unnaturally still and lying at an odd angle. HMS *Birkenhead* was a Frankenstein's monster of iron and wood, converted from a frigate to a troop ship, steam coming from its great black funnel and sails furled on its masts, paddlewheels on its sides. There were men shouting up on the forecastle.

"She ran onto a fucking rock," said a passing sailor in uniform, seeing Simeon's face. "There was a light on shore that we thought was a lighthouse – but it must have been a fire. We're on the wrong course. The rock put a bloody great gash in the bow, and we're stuck fast."

"All right," said Simeon, as the sailor seemed to be looking for some kind of resolution, from someone. "Where are we needed? On the pumps?"

"Not yet. They're firing the engines to back us off the rock."

"But won't that bring more water in?"

The sailor shrugged. "Captain's orders. We have to get free, he says. Says the compartments will hold."

As if in answer, the ship came to life and heaved slowly backwards. Shouts from the front, and the bow dipped, throwing Simeon back the way he'd come. As he righted himself, he turned toward the stairs, and saw the water rising, covering the bottom of the stairwell. Those stairs led back down to the upper troop deck, where hundreds of men had been sleeping minutes before.

He slipped and slid down the stairs, into the water, wet up to his knees. The door had swung shut behind him, or he'd closed it – he couldn't recall now. Someone was pulling at it from the inside, and he shoved, and nearly fell onto Private Halford, soaked to the skin and panting.

"There are wounded," Halford said, and pointed back behind him, toward the bow.

Simeon and Halford waded, the ship tilting and throwing them onto each other as they tripped and slid. This deck, which had been built as a gunroom before the ship's conversion, was full of men, all in their nightshirts and frantically crowding to the door that led to freedom. The ship's engines were as silent as death now, and the water as cold. The fires must have gone out.

And all the while Simeon was thinking, There's another deck below this one. Where's the water coming in?

A man had hurt his leg – probably broken – and was trying to keep his head above water as he staggered, the ship still shuddering beneath them and the water as full of waves as though there were wind inside the ship. Simeon and Halford put their arms around the man's shoulders and got him to the door.

Someone yelled, "Lance Corporal Price! You're needed!"

Simeon craned his neck back to see, up on the deck at the top of the steep stairs, a young lieutenant with a frantic expression. Lieutenant Grimes, that was his name.

"The horses," Grimes shouted down. "We cut them free but they're thrashing and kicking up here. We can't get anything done until we get them overboard. It's Bedlam. Look lively!"

Simeon pushed wet hair out of his eyes. "The horses are on deck, but the men–"

"The men, unlike the horses, will stay quiet," the lieutenant snapped.

Grimes was in the 74th Regiment, the same as Simeon. Where was Colonel Seton? Off doing something useful, presumably, which left men like Grimes free rein to issue orders.

Out of nowhere, someone slammed Lieutenant Grimes roughly down to the boards.

The figure wore a cloak, with a hood so close around his face that all Simeon could see was a square jaw, unshaven. Not a uniformed soldier, whoever he was, but he held an axe. He descended the stairs at speed.

"Come on," the figure growled, pushing past Simeon toward the lower deck and the rising water.

"Is he–" Simeon tried to see what had happened to the lieutenant.

"I haven't killed him yet… which might prove a mistake."

Simeon was stunned. Cloaked men didn't appear out of nowhere on Her Majesty's troop ships, and they certainly didn't knock officers down. But there was no time for questions. Whoever the stranger was, he was heading down, toward the muffled shouts and screams.

The water in the lower stairwell was blacker than the sky above. They had to pull themselves down, with the water over their heads. The door to the men's quarters wouldn't open. The stranger beat at the door with the axe, but the water slowed his movement. Eventually he resorted to a kind of scraping and slashing. When the wood of the door split, Simeon pushed his hands in and pulled the door apart, he and the stranger working at it until the door was splintered open and their hands were bloody and there was no air in their lungs. Then Simeon started to black out.

He lost his grip and floated to the middle of the stairwell, and hardly knew whether he was drowning or not. Somewhere, high overhead, yellow light from the ship's lanterns swam in his eyes. His head was free of the water as he grabbed for the steep stairs.

Then the cloaked man was at his side, pushing a coughing and spluttering soldier up into the air.

Simeon was shaking from cold and panic. He seemed to have to think about every breath. But the cloaked man was going back below, pulling himself down the thin stair rail. Who was this bloke, anyway? A stowaway? A paying passenger? A sailor out of uniform?

There would be time to think about that later. Now, every moment was a life lost or saved, and Simeon had enough air in his lungs to do his part.

Simeon took a deep breath and followed the stranger back down into darkness. They found one more man thrashing, trying to get through the broken doorway in a panic. The stranger battered at the door, and this time, it opened. They pulled him out and up.

Their third descent found a man floating limp, halfway between floor and ceiling, and they pulled him out too, pushing his nightshirt off his unconscious face. The stranger rolled him to one side and then the other, shaking him, shouting at him and pushing on his abdomen, but it was very clearly no good. As Simeon and the stranger lay on the stairs, retching and coughing, a dead man lying beside them, the cloaked man gasped, "Go on. You don't want to survive this just to be court-martialed."

A memory leapt into Simeon's mind. It had only been weeks ago, but it felt like years. The hot sun beating down, as all of the six hundred troops on board the *Birkenhead* were paraded to watch a young stoker receive his fifty lashes, punishment for leaping overboard and swimming for the coast of Sierra Leone. Punishment for desertion.

"What about you?" Simeon croaked, his throat aching and tight from their trips under water.

"I don't answer to them," said the man, pushing back his hood. Simeon didn't recognize him: a middle-aged man with light brown skin, sharp cheekbones and a few days' worth of beard on his angular chin. He was panting, his hand to his chest. "But you took the Queen's shilling, didn't you? So go on. There's no one left to save down here."

The stranger stared sidelong at him, as if it were a dare. Beneath the battered cloak, he didn't look any more soldierly. He must be a stowaway, although for what reason, Simeon couldn't dream. And why was he risking capture, not to mention his life, to save the men everyone else seemed to have given up for lost? What would happen to him if he went up on deck?

"I don't know who you are, and for the moment I don't care. I want to know you'll be safe," Simeon said. "Can you make it to the boats? Come on, we'll go together, and I'll make sure no one gets in your way."

The man's face contorted into a smile. "Maybe he was right about you," he muttered.

"Who was?"

"Listen, if you ever find you want to give the Queen back her shilling, make your way to Vienna. You'll find us there. A brotherhood that believes in taking orders from conscience alone. Nothing is true, everything is permitted. Will you remember that?"

Vienna! It seemed as unreal as Fairyland. They were on a sinking ship on the far side of Africa. He seemed unlikely to set foot on land ever again, and if he did, it would be a country where he'd never been before. Even if they survived the night, the 74th Regiment was meant to fight and die for British settlers in their attempt to subjugate the local people. A brotherhood that believed in…? Fairyland indeed.

Simeon wasn't sure what to make of any of the stranger's instructions, except that it was too long a speech for a man to make if he was in danger of dying. He nodded, briefly, not sure what he was agreeing to. The whole encounter seemed unreal, but everything was unreal at the moment: the screams of the dying, the water gurgling and frothing through every crack in the ship, the stink of wet coal and vomit and tar. Lieutenant Grimes was still roaring commands above. He had work to do, and more people to help. The horses would be frantic. And Simeon was, still, a soldier.

Simeon shook the stranger's hand, in thanks and farewell, then scrambled up the steep wet stairs, suddenly dog-tired. The ship was rocking wildly, the mast swinging from one star to another.

There was Private Halford, looking as worn out as Simeon felt. Grimes was nowhere to be seen, for the moment. A few men were running from one part of the ship to another, without any apparent logic to their movements. Others, like Halford, seemed to be stunned, unsure what to do.

"The horses," Simeon said, weakly. "I've got orders to see to the horses."

"Already overboard, and swimming to shore. If the sharks don't get them, they'll be better off than any of us."

"What's next then? The boats?"

Halford shook his head, glumly. "They want us to pump. Fifty men at a go, until they tire, then the next fifty."

"But surely–"

"We got the women and children into the cutter and launched it. That's done, at least."

In the rush to save the drowning down below, Simeon hadn't thought about the officers' wives near the stern of the ship, and their children – there must have been a few dozen all told. A couple of the women had given birth on the journey.

Halford continued, "We tried to get the bigger boats down into the water. Rusted winches and rotten ropes – the boats are no good to us, that's the long and short of it. Can't get two of 'em off the ship with the winches busted, and the third was swamped when the rope broke."

"No good at all?" Simeon was shocked. Dozens of people, maybe hundreds, could have fitted into those boats.

"The rest of us, we're to stay on board and pump out the water." Halford paused. "Do you… do you think that's what we should do?"

Simeon tried to think. He was wet and cold, and couldn't seem to stop his shoulders from shaking.

The ship juddered backward and there was an all too familiar crunch and scream of iron against stone, a crack of wood breaking. The ship tipped backward this time, as water rushed into a fresh hole, this one in the stern.

Captain Salmond strode toward them, the way only a sea captain could stride on the watery deck of a swaying ship. His dark hair was wild, and so were his dark eyes.

"She's going down," he said. "Anyone who can swim for it, do so."

With an aye-aye or two, a few men scrambled to find a place to jump overboard. Halford and Simeon climbed up to the poop deck and clung to the railing. The unbalanced ship was rocking wildly; sometimes the sea was a few feet away, and sometimes it was a great deal further. The prospect of diving was terrifying, but the captain was right. If they stayed on board, the suction of the ship as it went down would pull them under, or they'd be caught in the rigging, and they'd have no chance of swimming to shore or surviving long enough to be rescued.

They climbed the railing as if it were a ladder, and Simeon considered stripping off his wet clothing. It would be a terrible sunburn, on the coast of the Cape, if he made it that far. Instead, he tucked his shirt well into his trousers, to keep the thing from billowing and dragging in the water.

"Beat to quarters!" came a scream from behind them. "Beat to quarters!"

They turned to see Lieutenant Grimes, and all the surviving men, half of them in uniform and half in their shirts, standing as steady as they could on the tilting deck.

You took the Queen's shilling, the stranger had said. Simeon had wanted to become anonymous, to make a quiet living, one man in a crowd. It was either north to Manchester and a factory or off to the army, and the army had seemed less likely to result in injury. He'd wanted to stop thinking, to stop making all the wrong decisions. To stop making any decisions at all.

But under the stars of the far side of the world, on a breaking ship full of the newly drowned, Simeon found himself saying, "The captain's orders were to swim for it."

"And I say beat to quarters, damn you!" The lieutenant took a few unsteady steps to them, and spoke quietly, almost intimately, as though showing the great patience he had for this insubordinate lance corporal. "If these men swim, they'll swim to the two lifeboats out there, which are full of women and children. They'll try to get into the boats, and they'll swamp them."

"Or," Simeon said through gritted teeth, "they won't do that, because they aren't monsters. If they swim, they have a chance."

The lieutenant whirled on his heel and yelled, "Beat to quarters! Stand firm, and stand for Her Majesty! Men, you can be proud of this moment. You have carried out your orders calmly. All has been done with the utmost regularity."

Halford slid down off the rail and followed the lieutenant toward the ranks of men, who were indeed standing in silence, dripping and staring.

"The utmost regularity," repeated the lieutenant, and then the ship broke in half.

It sounded like a cannon and felt like an earthquake. The great black funnel came crashing down, right on top of several men, including Private Halford. Simeon ran forward but as he reached for Halford, the private's body skidded down the rocking deck, coming to rest at the lieutenant's feet. Dead eyes stared up at the officer, blood poured from his lifeless head. Halford wouldn't have a chance to worry about killing a man.

All of the shouts and groaning had stopped. The only men left alive were holding on and staring at each other. The world was silent for a moment.

"Beat to quarters!" screamed the lieutenant again, as the two halves of the ship slipped and groaned, each in its own direction, down toward the sea. Men grabbed for the yardarm, for the masts, for anything. "Beat to quarters!"

CHAPTER ONE

All around the hippodrome, golden gaslights framed the indigo sky. Pierrette loved the early evenings, when humans and gods seemed to be competing for who could dazzle the night. Let them do their utmost; Pierrette was about to give them all a run for their money.

Tonight, she'd perform the troupe's most dangerous and astonishing act. She wasn't exactly *grateful* that the usual performer had broken his collarbone and declared he was done with circus life for good. Still, if this was her chance, she was ready to seize it.

Major Wallin was not convinced, though, even now when the band had started up, and the stands were filled. They were always filled. The new hippodrome in Kensington Gardens was only a few steps away from the imposing Crystal Palace housing the Great Exhibition, filled with wonders from all over the world. There had never been a better place or time to be a performer than London in the summer of 1851. There was so much demand that the hippodrome had several troupes performing. The long oval ring had only just been swept of ostrich dung and chariot wheel-ruts from the afternoon's Astonishing Antiquity performance when a fresh audience streamed in for the horse show.

But Major Wallin, the leader of the Aurora Equestrian Troupe, looked nervous. He stood under the performers' entrance in his crisp blue and gold jacket, a simulacrum of the Swedish cavalry officer's uniform he had worn in his former life. He regarded Pierrette with skepticism.

"You know that I can do it," she said, speaking in French as she always did with Major Wallin. "I've done it a dozen times in rehearsal."

"But everyone will be expecting a man!" Major Wallin scratched one of his graying muttonchops. "Mazeppa is always performed by a man. It only makes *sense* for a man, because the character in Byron's poem was lashed to the galloping horse as punishment for an affair with a countess. You cannot play that part."

"You don't think people will believe I could seduce a countess?" Pierrette put her hand on her hip. Her one-piece costume, which Nell had hastily constructed that day for the Mazeppa role, was the same pinkish hue as her skin.

She was teasing, and he blushed. The Swedish major and his late Italian wife (the Aurora who had given her name to the troupe) had taken Pierrette with them when they left France three years previously, in the wake of the bloody Paris uprising when her parents were killed. Major Wallin had been a second father to her, and she respected his judgment. He was the master of all the horses, and he made every call.

But Pierrette was nearly nineteen now, old enough to know

her own mind, and she knew she could do this and make it the talk of the town. She *needed* to do this. Her destiny lay in the lights, in the air. There was no way the world could see her talents if she only did what every other equestrienne did: the somersaults, the standing on bareback, the vaults. All of it was dangerous and all of it took a great deal of skill, but people wanted more. They wanted drama. They wanted a story. They wanted baying wolves and growling thunder and a galloping horse, foaming and frenzied (or at least made to look like it was – dear old Attila would be fine). She needed an act that would tell make world take notice.

She smiled fondly at the major, and said, "Mazeppa hasn't really been about the poem for years. It's about tying someone to a horse and having that horse gallop into rocks and be chased by wolves and up the ramp. Imagine how our troupe's reputation will soar when people hear that a *woman* has performed Mazeppa! And with my hoop act at the end to fetch my trophy, it will be different to any Mazeppa ever performed."

The major grumbled. "There is something to be said for tradition. We are not mere spectacle. We are artists." But this was a speech he'd given enough times to bore even himself, and he was looking out at the crowd.

"The tradition is that someone performs Mazeppa at the end of the show. Everyone will expect it. And I am the only member of this troupe qualified to perform it tonight."

He'd lost, and he knew it. He sighed, and said, as one last salvo, "I promised your parents I'd keep you safe. Mazeppa is the opposite of safe."

But Pierrette had a salvo ready of her own. She tucked one of her dark curls behind her ear and quoted two lines from

Byron's poem, in English: "'No matter; I have bared my brow full in Death's face – before – and now.'"

The brass band's music went low, the horns quiet and the drums suspenseful. The evening's entertainment began. First up was "The African Hercules," who was really Hugh Robinson from Manchester, riding two horses around the ring, a foot on each saddle. Beside Pierrette, Hugh's wife watched from the wings, her arms folded over her neat blue bodice with its pearl buttons. Nell Robinson was the troupe's accountant and business manager. More than once, Major Wallin had asked her to perform, but she'd said she had seen too many Black women dressed in skimpy furs as "femmes sauvages" to consider it, and always refused to talk about it any more than that.

Then it was the rope dancer, the beautiful and lithe Ariel Fine, billed as "Neither Man Nor Woman But Sprite of the Air," performing intricate steps on a somewhat slack rope, with a balance bar in their hands.

The music took on a military air for Tillie Wallin, the Major's eight year-old daughter, on her pretty mare. She always charmed the audience with her blonde curls, and she could perform as well as any adult Pierrette had seen. The major was so proud of his daughter, and had trained her in the careful maneuvers and jumps of the *haute école* tradition.

Jovita Ferreira, a Brazilian woman who'd left her husband and literally run away to the circus, performed Pierrette's usual act of somersaults, vaults and Amazonian feats.

Then it was Pierrette's turn. Mechanical covers rose up to dim the flames of the gaslights as she strode out into the ring. Major Wallin tied her to Attila's broad back, and there she was, staring up at the darkening sky. They hadn't told the audience there was a change in performer tonight, and whispers went up in the front row as the lights went bright again.

Pierrette Arnaud was about to show the world what she could do.

She was Mazeppa, the poetic hero, condemned to a terrible journey across Eastern Europe. First, Attila picked his way through a course of "rocks" made of plaster. Then out came the dogs to chase him, although they were good friends of Attila's now.

The brass band did its best imitations of wolves and wild horses as Attila raced three times around the ring. The poem, which she had read purely to find an argument for the major, whispered in her mind: *"The skies spun like a mighty wheel; I saw the trees like drunkards reel."*

But there were no trees inside the hippodrome, only a fair few actual drunkards. They were the greatest danger, because the Mazeppa act required the performer to ride quickly up a ramp that they'd put right over a section of the seating, sacrificing a few tickets to create a thrill. Being so close to the audience, there was always the danger of someone pulling at the ropes or grabbing the performer's leg.

It was, in fact, safest to go as quickly as the horse could go, and Attila knew his business. He carried Pierrette confidently on the final run across the dirt, toward the ramp. But he was sweating, and so was Pierrette – even London was hot in July. She could feel herself slipping inside the ropes. If she got tangled in his gait, or he faltered and fell, she could be crushed. Performers had been dragged to their deaths before now.

Out of the corner of her eye, Pierrette scanned for any likely troublemakers in the stands. There was a woman holding an opera glass in her hands, and a man over her shoulder, looking at the woman. A pickpocket, probably, but too far off to cause Attila and Pierrette any concern.

Up, up, and she took her last look at the purpling sky in the center of the open hippodrome. She could not manage the horse at all, not in this position, sprawled on his back with her legs and arms pinioned. But the people were cheering. It was a roar in her ears.

And then Attila reared, Pierrette lurched backward, and the audience gasped.

It was all part of the show. A way for Attila to come to a stop and get his carrot. In the darkness just behind the curtain hanging from the roof that covered the stands, Tillie fed Attila his treat. Major Wallin sliced the ropes, and Pierrette emerged back into her adoring gaslight, stumbling because her character had been broken and was waking from a faint. And stumbling because she'd just been untied from the back of a leaping horse.

She had three breaths to recover her equilibrium so she could perform the last part of the act: receiving a trophy from a beautiful woman. The audience reacted first to Pierrette staggering, free and alive, and then across to the beautiful woman in question, who was Jovita in a new costume, lowered in a hoop that hung from a high crane that the apprentices had wheeled out into the center of the hippodrome. Jovita was high in the air, out of reach. But there was a series of hoops on cranes, and Pierrette would swing on each until, dangling from her knees on the last one, she would catch the trophy as Jovita threw it, in midair.

Another hoop descended from the roof over the stands, at the base of the ramp.

Her heart beat with joy as she staggered down the ramp. She loved this part.

Off to her right, the woman with the opera glass now had four men around her, and they were all turning to her. She was nearly obscured by their broad shoulders and bowler hats. Four men. That wasn't pickpockets.

Focus, Pierrette ordered herself, and ran down the ramp toward her hoop. At the last moment, she leaped up, caught it in her hands. Now she had to get the hoop moving. A series of climbs and twists, hanging from the hoop, as it started to swing. Then on to the next hoop, and the next. Finally, she dropped to her knees, keeping her eyes on Jovita and the trophy. The final moment was nearly here.

And the man behind the woman with the opera glass now had his gloved hand over her mouth, and she was wriggling, her eyes alarmed, her arms restrained, no sign of the opera glass now. They started moving her through the stands, but backward, and nobody around her seemed to be paying any attention – or they didn't care. *Help her!* Pierrette wanted to scream. The woman would be out of the audience altogether in a moment, taken by these men for who-knows-what purpose.

All eyes were on Pierrette. Except her own. If she was the only witness, well then, so be it. She was the only one who could help.

Instead of turning to catch the trophy, Pierrette leapt back to where she'd started, hoop by hoop, and then dangled from her knees over the audience, as they reached up to her, unable to touch her, shouting their praise. She was almost low enough. She could do this.

She swung the hoop sideways, again and again, back and forth, turning it into a pendulum. A little more, and she'd be nearly over the abducted woman.

Down to her ankles, looping her feet to hold herself steady, she reached down and grabbed the woman by her arms. It never would have worked if it weren't for the fact that the men around her were so startled by this phenomenon that they slackened their grip and ducked as though from an aggressive seagull.

Under her wide green skirt and yellow cape, the lady was a tiny, bony thing. Even so, the weight was too much, and she made it worse by kicking and squirming. Pierrette's ankles were screaming. Her body was contorting in all the wrong ways. A few more seconds was all she had. As the hoop swung backwards, its arc shortened now, she dropped the woman onto the ramp where she and Attila had galloped a few moments before. Pierrette dropped beside her, skinning her knee and jarring her wrists. But the lady was sprawled face first.

Pierrette glanced up at Jovita, still high in her hoop, frozen in a dramatic posture, the trophy forgotten in her hand. Her eyes were wide, and her other hand gripped the hoop so hard it was rotating.

Everyone in London, these days, knew that it was pointless asking for help from the police. Most of them were in cahoots with various gangs and criminals, and there was no telling which ones were the good ones, at a glance. Anyway, there were no bobbies to be seen in the hippodrome that night, good or otherwise, but there were four men who seemed determined to get their hands on this woman.

So Pierrette took the woman's arm and whispered, "Run," and lifted her to her feet.

She didn't need to say it again. The scrawny lady ran like a frightened cat, gathering strength from who knows where, her skirts in her hands, and her heeled shoes slipping on the runway, down into the ring, across to the performers' entrance, and out of the hippodrome.

And whether out of some performer's instinct for a dramatic ending, or because she didn't seem very likely to get to safety on her own, Pierrette ran with her.

They tore past the rope barrier that kept people without tickets from getting close enough to see inside the hippodrome. People milled beyond those ropes, out for the evening in the shadow of the Great Exhibition. Men and women, some well-dressed, but most with worn shawls and patched coats, some with children on their shoulders, little dogs yipping on leashes.

The lady ran into the crowd, tripped, and collapsed in a heap of bottle-green poplin.

Pierrette snatched up the lady's bonnet just before a dachshund could, then helped her to her feet. The people around them were murmuring, gasping, smiling, confused – a mixture of reactions on every face.

Someone said, "Is it part of the trick?"

Pierrette turned and smiled at the man. "I'll get my trophy yet, by gum!"

At that, everyone around her laughed. She knew her English was a bit accented, and that was probably part of what they were laughing at, but that didn't matter. She was who she was, and she would use all of it, with every audience, until they shouted her name, stamped their feet, whistled and clapped.

Pierrette glanced behind. There was a man in a bowler walking toward them with purpose, but whether it was one of the abductors, she couldn't say. And there was a roar from the crowd back in the hippodrome, but in reaction to what? Maybe Jovita and the others had found some way to make it all look intentional. Maybe Pierrette's performance wouldn't be thought a total disaster. All the same, Pierrette wasn't looking forward to seeing the look on Major Wallin's face.

Cursing herself for not leaving well enough alone, Pierrette ducked down by the lady on the ground. "Come, just a little further."

She pulled her to her feet one more time, and they walked over mostly green rolling ground toward the Crystal Palace. In the evening it was lit like a fairy palace. Pierrette had been inside three times already, and had seen a lump of rock billing itself as the Koh-i-Noor, to which she had said, if *that* was a diamond, *she* could be anything she wanted. Tonight, she had no desire to pay the shilling admittance, or to walk through the crowds in her skimpy flesh-colored maillot.

But there was a line of hansom cabs on the road on the far side of the Crystal Palace.

She asked the lady, "Have you got money? For a hansom cab, I mean. As you can see, I have no pockets at the moment."

The lady grimaced, as though she was in pain. She had probably hurt herself in the scramble. She was older than Pierrette: in her thirties, at a guess, and very thin.

"There's no need," the lady said, her voice clear and

determined. "I'll have no trouble reaching my house on foot – it's just on the other side of the park."

Pierrette frowned. Hyde Park could take a half an hour or more to walk through. She couldn't let the lady walk alone, but Major Wallin and the others would wonder what had happened to her.

As if in response to the frown, the lady said, breathlessly, "No, you've done enough. I'm quite used to walking on my own. Thank you for your help tonight. You will call on me, won't you? I'm the Countess of Lovelace. Ada, to my friends. I think it's right that you and I should be friends. That poem you performed tonight. Mazeppa. It was written by my father."

Pierrette had met people before who thought they were Napoleon, or Wellington, or both at once. But she believed Ada. There were the clothes, for one thing.

But also, there was the man in the bowler, again. Walking in a straight line toward this corner of the park, with his coat flaring, his eyes on them.

"I won't let you walk through the park alone, Lady Lovelace," she said. "The show is finished for tonight, anyway. We must hurry."

Pierrette imagined the map of Hyde Park in her head: a great green rectangle in the midst of London. The Crystal Palace, home of the Great Exhibition, was in the middle along the southern edge. That was on their right now. Beyond it lay busy, bright streets, which might be safer. But if Lady Lovelace was trying to get to the northeast corner, it would be much faster to go diagonally through the park. That meant crossing the bridge over the Serpentine, the lake that cut the park in half.

She pulled Ada to the left, urgently, taking a gravel side-path.

As they approached the Serpentine, Pierrette looked back. There was the shadowy man, and he'd been joined by another, loping along beside him like a hound.

"*Bande de salauds,*" Pierrette grumbled. Then louder, to Lady Lovelace: "Who are these men and why are they so persistent?"

"Creditors," Ada said, out of breath. "I assume, anyway. I do have rather a few debts, you see. I have a wonderful plan – I can guess the horse races – but it hasn't quite worked out. Or I suppose it might be…" She broke off.

"What?"

"Or they might be someone else," Ada whispered.

At the near end of the bridge stood another two men in bowlers, just at the edge of a circle of light cast by the nearest gas lamp. In the hippodrome, the thugs had counted on the crowd's attention being on the performance. Here in the open, they'd be looking for darkness and isolation.

Pierrette took Ada's hand and hurried her toward the path that led to the bridge. They fell in behind a group of three school-aged children following an irritated governess. The children glanced at Pierrette, in her pink maillot, but the governess seemed too flustered to care. They were so terribly late and their poor mother would be so worried, her posture announced.

Past the men and over the bridge. One of the children ran toward the wooded shore, eager to make friends with a pair of swans. The governess groaned, lifted her skirt and ran after her charge, with the other two following.

They were alone and exposed again.

Pierrette glanced behind to see four men now, matching their brisk walking pace. They crossed a broad road, the earth packed hard. Pierrette considered taking it north, but there were only occasional carriages on it at the moment, and it was lined with trees that would cut them off from public view. Besides, on the road, they'd be easily bundled into a carriage.

They struck out on the footpath leading diagonally across the park. Here the land was open, but it was so dark now. The pursuers were still behind them, and she could see two more men approaching on the path ahead, little more than dark shapes.

She looked frantically around. Toward the south, on another path, a couple was strolling arm in arm. Would they help, if she called for it?

Pierrette pretended to stumble, crying out. Lady Lovelace stopped, but Pierrette waved her concern away. It was a test. The couple on the other path paused, but didn't change course or even turn their heads. The selfishness of some people! The men were closing in.

"This way," Pierrette whispered, and grabbed Lady Lovelace by the elbow. By the time the men were almost within grabbing distance, they were passing the couple. They settled in front of them, still close enough that the man's pipe smoke billowed around them, and slackened their pace.

Before long the odd procession – Pierrette and Lady Lovelace in front, the irritated couple behind, and four men trailing them – passed two more men in bowlers. They might have been the men who'd been approaching on the other path. For a moment, Pierrette wondered whether they might attack all four of them, including the oblivious couple. But the thugs simply touched their hat brims and sneered.

The end of the park at last. Ada was walking steadily, one

hand on Pierrette's arm. Park Lane was bright and busy, and Pierrette didn't chase after the couple when they took the first opportunity to leave the path. Once there was no sign of the men in the bowler hats, Pierrette risked slowing down for a moment to rest. People walked all around and past them: a sea of silk, felt and beaver hats in all states of repair; shawls smelling of oysters, jackets smelling of beer.

"I used to ride out in the park," Ada said with a wistful glance behind them, after they'd caught their breath. "Nearly a decade ago now, when I was healthier. Caused quite a scandal, as I rode with friends – men, I mean. But my husband couldn't always go riding with me, and I enjoy riding so much. I'm very good at it. Oh, but of course, not anything like you! Your performance really was marvelous. The demonstration of the principles of motion. I have been wanting to see someone perform Mazeppa since I was a girl."

They walked on. Pierrette's nerves calmed as they approached the Marble Arch, newly moved to the north-east corner of the park that spring. There was a police station occupying a few rooms inside the Arch, and though Pierrette had no intention of involving the police in anything, it might keep Ada's pursuers at bay.

Besides, this corner was brightly lit by the gas lamps of Park Lane and Oxford Street. They dodged the wide skirts of fashionable women. A man in a shabby top hat was gesticulating to a crowd, shouting about the glories of Britain's Empire.

Now that the danger had passed, Pierrette stifled nervous laughter at what she'd done. She had picked up a lady from the audience, and deposited her in Park Lane, all while wearing her costume, which was starting to feel very chilly in the night air.

Major Wallin would be beside himself. Had poor Jovita come down from her hoop?

After they passed the Marble Arch, Ada lifted one of her bird-thin hands and pointed at one of the tall, dignified brick houses. "Home. William – my husband – is out tonight, but Mother's there. She'll be frantic, of course, once she learns I am not resting in my bedroom as she thinks, but she always forgives me.

"You must come and see me, my Mazeppa." She looked Pierrette up and down in her pink maillot, and said, "But perhaps not tonight."

Chapter Two

The daring rescue of a woman from sinister ruffians was all well and good, but it was not exactly a satisfactory ending to the night's performance. The *London Evening News* suggested the whole thing was a stunt, meant to draw attention to the "woman question," whatever that was, by "providing a display of sisterly compassion as a more fitting victory for the equestrienne, who, it is said, was not long ago an urchin of Paris." Altogether, the newspapers said, it would have been better to leave well enough alone. Yes, of course, it was all well and good to showcase female talents, but don't call it Mazeppa!

Major Wallin, vindicated, hired a male equestrian from Mr Batty's circus to do Mazeppa. Pierrette was back performing her original act with Jovita.

Pierrette smiled in the ring but scowled backstage. An *urchin*, they'd called her! She had never been anything of the kind. Pierrette Arnaud was the child of Parisian musicians, who had been passed over for positions at the Paris Opera due to some slight that Pierrette never fully understood, but that made her father's mustache quiver, and his cheeks go red, even years later.

It wasn't Papa's own talents he mourned; he was only a passable trumpet player, or so he said. But his wife, he was convinced, could have taken the world by storm with her bowing. No one could bring Vivaldi to life the way Marie Arnaud did. The spotlight was her due. She should have graced every stage in Europe. Instead, because of a petty weasel who always went unnamed, Madame Arnaud had to be satisfied with making the wolves howl and the raindrops jump on her cheap violin. They played in the orchestra at the Paris Hippodrome, and counted every penny.

When the riots began in June of 1848, the Arnauds had gone to the barricades, and asked Major Wallin to look after their daughter, if anything should happen to them. Pierrette, who was fifteen at the time, believed fervently in the cause, as her parents explained it to her: everyone should have the right to work so that they could feed themselves and their children. Not starving to death seemed the very least anyone could ask. She would have fought for it herself, but her parents told her to stay with Major Wallin, to look after him and Tillie. Her parents were killed by police fire at the barricade on the rue Soufflot and buried in an unmarked grave.

Pierrette decided that not starving was too little to ask for from the world after all.

Major Wallin had left Paris with the Aurora Troupe, selling their horses and buying new ones in England. They'd played for a few months in Brighton, traveled to Manchester for three nights only, then spent months with no work at all. Then at last they got word of the new hippodrome going up next to the Great Exhibition, and the world seemed brighter.

A week after the Mazeppa debacle, Pierrette received an

invitation to a soiree at number 6, Great Cumberland Place. She was not very sure what one wore to a soiree in a grand house in London, but Jovita said she was clearly being asked because of who she was, and so there was no point in being anyone else. Armed with that logic, and a yellow silk dress borrowed from Nell, Pierrette walked through the park once more.

The house was tall and terrifying. A butler opened the door, taking her coat and hat. There was a room full of people, all of whom looked more comfortable than Pierrette felt. But there was Lady Lovelace, smiling at her. She sat Pierrette down and told her again that she must call her Ada. Her dark hair was parted on either side of her face, with dark ribbons tying it up, and she wore a simple, loose dress with a flowered border at the collar.

"Do you know," Ada confided, leaning on the arm of her chair, "I completely forgot to ask your name the other night, and the newspaper didn't print it, so I had to send someone to find out. It's quite terrible, of course, what they wrote about your performance. It was a triumph, and would have been recognized as such, if it hadn't been for me."

Pierrette couldn't quite disagree with this. "But are you safe from your… pursuers now?" she asked softly.

Ada winced. "There is no longer any danger. They won't hurt me. I've given him what he wants. One doesn't always have a choice."

As Pierrette tried to decide how to respond to this, or to ask who "him" referred to, Ada took her arm. Her host had a feverish look in her dark eyes. "I've decided that the world must know, must understand, how important your work is. We are coming into an age in which all the old snobbery must break down, and what was considered mere entertainment will be understood as art. And as science, for that matter! It's all one, if you ask me. Come and meet Mr Ruskin."

John Ruskin was a man of about thirty, with fine sideburns and a rather red nose, lounging by the unlit fireplace with a glass of port in his hand, and talking with several other gentlemen.

"Ruskin," said Ada briskly, addressing him by surname only in a very manly fashion, "this is Pierrette Arnaud, an equestrienne whose performance I had the good fortune to see. It combines a mastery of angles and velocity with a grasp of the sublime. Never before have I seen anything like it. It reminded me of music."

"I shall have to witness it," Ruskin said politely.

"But more than that," Ada went on, "her art must be painted. Your opinion is respected. Your reviews are courted. It is you, and only you, who can establish the equestrienne as a suitable subject for painting."

"Oh, I don't know about 'only me'," Ruskin said, with a self-deprecating laugh.

But after that, everything changed.

Although the search for the Rescued Lady died down, the crowds at the hippodrome were fuller than ever. They included several young men with sketchbooks, because word had spread from Ruskin to his artist friends, and they all wanted to capture the remarkable form and movement of Miss Pierrette Arnaud. A letter from Ruskin even appeared in *The Times* about the shifting ideal of the Muse, mentioning her by name.

Major Wallin separated her act from Jovita's, which Jovita didn't mind at all, as she said with a smile that she'd rather warm up the crowd than be upstaged.

"God knows I don't want to be famous," Jovita said with a laugh. "And I certainly don't want any drawings of me in the newspapers."

But Pierrette did want to be famous. Desperately. And she could finally glimpse it.

Pierrette had three proposals of marriage that summer, including one very persistent and unwelcome suitor who ultimately had to be run off at the point of Major Wallin's rifle.

She became a regular guest at the house on Great Cumberland Street, and sometimes it was only her alone with Ada.

At others, though, Ada's friends were there. Some of them smiled at Pierrette's accent, but she didn't care. She met scientists and philanthropists and various dissipated cousins. She met some of Ruskin's protégés, including several alarming young artists and their models. She liked Lizzie Siddall, who seemed as out of her depth as Pierrette felt; she'd been a girl in a hat shop before one of Ruskin's painters had decided that she would make a good artist's model. She didn't much like the modeling, Lizzie said, but she was learning how to write and paint and draw, so it had turned out to be a good bargain in the end. Everyone in Ada's circles seemed to be bargaining for something, with someone.

And sometimes, when Pierrette came to the house at the appointed time, Ada's formidable mother, Lady Byron, told her Ada was indisposed. It was the truth: Ada had always suffered from poor health, but that summer, she was in constant pain, clutching her side and grimacing when she thought no one was looking. She had become somewhat gaunt and ate very little.

At the end of July, Ada invited Pierrette out to her country house in Surrey, to watch the imminent eclipse of the sun. Major Wallin assured her she should go, that absence would make the audience's heart grow fonder – so long as it was no more than three days. So, Pierrette said yes. Ada even sent a carriage, and Pierrette felt like a girl in a fairy story when it drove into a courtyard dominated by turrets and ivy-covered walls. This was Horsley Towers, a seemingly never-ending building project that kept Ada's husband busy. Pierrette had never seen anything like it. It was surrounded by thick woods dotted with tracks, little bridges, and unusual grottos and shelters.

Inside the enormous Great Hall, a portrait of Lord Byron in Albanian dress stared down at them.

"When I was a girl, that painting had a green velvet cloth covering it at all times," Ada confided as they sat, petting one of the house's dogs. "I never knew my father. He left England when I was a baby and died when I was eight. The great poet. Really, I think I must be very like him. I have a terrible imagination and it often gets me into trouble."

They watched the solar eclipse from a tower room that Ada's husband had built especially for her to explore her scientific studies. There were piles of notebooks and dusty old treatises lying everywhere, and Ada confided that she spent hours in this room writing letters and chuckling to herself. She corresponded with every great scientist in Europe, she said, and some of the bad ones, too. She showed Pierrette all of her papers. She was most proud of her published commentary on Charles Babbage's design for something called an Analytical Engine. One evening, she talked excitedly about how the Engine could solve any problem that humans could imagine, using punched cards and rotating drums.

"But where is it, this Engine?" Pierrette asked, frowning.

"Oh, it's never been built," Ada said, as though that were unimportant.

Pierrette was as dazzled by Ada's talents as Ada was by hers, but sometimes she wondered what it was all *for*. The world was full of problems, and if a machine could solve them, why not build it? Ada and her friends seemed to be both fabulously wealthy and perpetually short on funds, both incredibly powerful and unable to achieve any task. There was no doubt of Ada's genius. If she were healthier, less distracted by horse races, less annoyed by constant family squabbles and society scandals, what wonders could she achieve?

Perhaps Pierrette could help Ada's career, just as Ada had helped hers. She had a practical mind and Ada listened to her. But there was so much Pierrette didn't understand; her own schooling had been so basic. She listened to Ada's rapturous explanations, and even when she didn't grasp a concept, she was always inspired to learn more.

In the evenings, they had dinner with Lady Byron and two of Ada's children: Anne, who was nearly fourteen, and Ralph, who had just turned twelve.

"My oldest boy, Byron, is away at sea," she said. "He writes me the most alarming letters about his exploits. But I suppose I deserve what I get for naming him after his grandfather. Do you know, when they brought my father's body home to England and they took me to meet the ship, I didn't quite understand what it was all about, and I thought he'd been the ship's captain. There were many things I didn't understand, in those days."

She went quiet, after a prim glance from her mother. Pierrette thought of the gossip that the rope-dancer Ariel Fine had told her: Ada had a cousin who was really her half-sister, the product of Lord Byron's incestuous affair with his own half-sister. His exile from England had been to escape that scandal, and his creditors – a problem he shared with the daughter he'd never known.

"Ships have carried so many of the people I loved away from me," Ada said, more brightly. "But they always come home again, one way or another."

As the winter of 1851 drew on, the Great Exhibition closed, but the hippodrome did not. Major Wallin consulted with the troupe, and they were all happy to stay on for another season or two. Nobody was very eager to return to France just then; the president, Louis-Napoleon Bonaparte, had just seized total power, overruling Parliament and putting down all opposition. Another Christmas in London seemed prudent and would grant a little more time to decide where to go next. In the coldest months of the year, the open-air hippodrome closed. The horses rested and so did their people.

As winter turned to spring, Ada Lovelace's health worsened. By the summer, Pierrette was performing again, but Ada wasn't well enough to attend. She couldn't leave the house on Great Cumberland Street at all, not even to go to the country.

The crowds were smaller at the hippodrome now that the Great Exhibition had ended, but there was still enough business for the Aurora Troupe to sell tickets four nights a week. They always ended with Mazeppa, ably and traditionally performed by Benjamin Silver, the handsome equestrian Major Wallin had hired after Pierrette's one and only interpretation. She had to admit it had been a good decision. She was making her own name, with her own tricks, and soon she would create something that would make Mazeppa obsolete.

As the summer ended, Lady Byron pulled Pierrette aside one day as she left. Ada's mother had never particularly approved of her friendship with this French performer, and usually ignored her visits. But on this day, she told Pierrette that Ada was dying. Her family would be around her now, to nurse her. She needed rest and quiet. Pierrette would understand.

Pierrette replied she would do as Ada wished. And every time she came to visit, Ada made the young woman promise that she would come again soon, that she wouldn't abandon her. Pierrette made that promise, every time, and kept her word.

Ada was so small near the end that she hardly seemed to disturb the bedclothes. At least the days of her writhing and shouting were over. Pierrette had witnessed a little of that, when she'd kept her word to come visit but Lady Byron, the patient's anxious mother, had ushered her out. She had witnessed the strange bed made of a rubber sheet stretched over water, designed in an attempt to relieve all pressure on Ada's aching body.

At the end, Pierrette's friend lay still, in an ordinary bed with white sheets. Her thin hands picked at the edge of the coverlet. Her jawbone was a knife. And her dark, deep-set eyes, when they were open, had universes in them.

"Do you know that there was a time when I could see… everything?" she whispered.

Pierrette leaned closer, to hear better. "Can you not see now?"

Ada lifted her small, birdlike hand. "I see what's before me. But there was a time when I could see everything that is, was and will be. I understood it all, Pierrette. My great work – no one even knows – no one can yet know–"

She stopped. Pierrette placed her hand upon the cold fingers. "We know. And no one will ever forget."

Ada winced as though this hurt her. "My husband is not here."

"He'll be in to see you soon, I'm sure."

Lady Byron didn't tell Pierrette anything, but the chambermaid did. And the chambermaid had heard something disturbing, just a few nights before. Ada had asked to see her husband, who stormed out of the house a short time later, telling an astonished, hand-wringing Lady Byron that her daughter had just confessed something so hideous that he could not remain in her presence. Could not bear to be under the same roof. It was hard for Pierrette to imagine what could make a man flee from his dying wife, and harder for her to forgive him. The chambermaid thought it must be an affair. Or possibly something to do with the gambling debts. But surely neither of those would have come as an unforgivable shock to the man who'd married Byron's daughter.

Ada whispered, "I don't have anyone left I can trust. Nobody who understands. All my papers – my letters – I wasn't expecting to die. Not quite yet."

Her words were coming slowly, with heavy breaths in between them, but Pierrette sat patiently. The people of London could live without a performance from her tonight.

"I burned my correspondence with him," Ada whispered.

Ah. The lover? Pierrette waited.

"But I can't burn the notebook. It might be needed. To undo the harm I have done."

After thinking for a moment, Pierrette asked gently, "What notebook? What harm?"

The thin eyelids closed and fluttered for a long time. Then Ada said, so softly Pierrette could hardly hear: "I have been... corresponding with a great scientist. I don't know his name. He signs his letters 'Magus.' I have helped him to understand his own ideas, just as I helped Charles Babbage with his Analytical Engine. But this collaboration... this is no calculating machine. This is a horror. It will change the world, and it will take many lives when it does."

Despite the fire casting dancing shadows on the wallpaper, Pierrette shivered. "Ada, my dear friend, you are not responsible for every scientist who designs a new machine."

"I'm responsible for this one. He must be stopped. There's only one person I know who can do it. Will you find Simeon for me?"

Pierrette's mind went through the names of the gentlemen who came to Ada's parties, back when she had parties. "Simeon?" she prompted.

Ada took a long breath, gathered her energy. "I was very ill as a child. For years. Measles. Then paralysis. Terrible pain. I couldn't go out. Couldn't ride a horse or see my friends. I had no brothers or sisters. Or rather, none that I knew about, then. I was alone. Then the summer I was sixteen, I got better. I was so happy to be... back out in the world. I fell in love with one of my tutors. I made mistakes. We used to meet in the greenhouse, and kiss, and... Mother suspected. There was a boy living with us, six years old, named Simeon Price."

"Ah. So this Simeon, then, is younger than you? I don't think I've met him."

"No, he is far away."

She said nothing further for a long time, and Pierrette thought she might have been sleeping. She was just about to slip out and let her rest, when Ada said, in a stronger voice, "He was a publican's son. One of the students at my mother's school in Ealing. But too bright. The schoolmaster couldn't teach him. My mother took him to our home as a project. He was sharp. Noticed everything. She demanded that Simeon tell her what I was doing, and with whom. But even at six years old, Simeon had honor. He kept it all to himself. Mother sent him away. Denied him his education. Did everything she could to punish him. But he never broke my confidence. Mother found everything out anyway, of course. I was so angry that I ran away to my lover's house. Caused myself... no end of problems."

She paused to catch her breath. She was looking to the side, into the fire. "My husband didn't mind about it, you know. He didn't care about scandal. Convention. Any of that. He didn't mind my odd behavior. He could forgive almost anything, back then."

"Did you ever see Simeon again?" Pierrette asked, to break Ada's melancholy.

Ada turned to Pierrette, and her eyes refocused. "Years later. By chance, at a scientific demonstration. At last, I had a chance to thank him properly. We became friends. Rode out in Hyde Park together. Quite unsuitable. He had endured his terrible father in Ealing, then ran away to London. Did whatever work he could while educating himself in the evenings. I don't think anyone has ever understood my strange brain as much as

Simeon did. Not Babbage, not Faraday, not Brewster. But then my health took a downturn once more. By the time I was better again, he'd joined up."

"Joined up? So he's in the army, then."

Ada nodded. "He was on the HMS *Birkenhead* when it went down in February."

"I'm sorry."

"I'm not," Ada said, earnestly. "Now Pierrette, please, I'm very tired–"

"I'll go."

"No, no, not yet. Please. In that bookshelf, if you find the pale blue notebook, open it. There's a letter inside. Yes, that one."

Pierrette did as Ada asked, and a single sheet of worn, cheap paper fell out into her hand. It was covered in gibberish; she couldn't make it out.

"That's code. Flip it over, you'll see."

On the other side, in Ada's handwriting, was the decoded letter.

My oldest and dearest friend,

You will by now have heard terrible news concerning me. Keep this as secret as any we ever kept, but I want you to know it's all right. I've given up one brotherhood to seek another, and perhaps, one fight for another, but I think – I hope – this fight may be a better one. I'm convinced it can't be worse. One day I hope we will all be free, whatever that might mean.

What I want to say is – don't worry about me. I'm far away, and I will be quiet for a long time, I expect, but the world can't get rid of me that easily.

Pierrette read it twice. "It isn't signed. You think this is from your Simeon?"

"I know his handwriting. I never thought he was dead. It didn't seem possible. And then this came, a month ago, with no postmark. Just arrived among our letters somehow."

"A month ago!" She looked at it again. "Not dated, either. You think he wrote this after the shipwreck?"

"He refers to 'terrible news', doesn't he? I think he's alive. He didn't know, you see – I never told him about my condition, in my letters." She turned her head again and faced the wall. She whispered, "One day we will all be free."

Pierrette sat on the bed, gently, the letter still in her hand. "You said Simeon could help you with this theoretical project of yours."

"Not help me with it," Ada said, impatiently, almost angrily. "Help me put an *end* to it. He'll understand it. He always understood. And he is a soldier now. He can fight, which I never could. Simeon will know what to do. You must give him that notebook when I've gone. Promise me, Pierrette."

"But I don't know where he is."

"Find him, then!"

Ada writhed, clutching her side. Pierrette stuffed the letter into her pocket. She fetched the bottle of claret laced with laudanum, but Ada knocked it aside. She said, in a voice like a violin string tightened to the point of breaking, "Find Simeon."

Chapter Three

Simeon Price did not want to be found. As far as the British Army knew, he had died a year ago. In June of 1852, a man calling himself Jack Straw arrived in Egypt from the south. He wore a dirt-colored cloak over a much-repaired shirt, and trousers that had long since faded from their regulation colors. If he could have forgotten that his name was Simeon Price, he would have.

He reckoned there was only one person in England who would mourn him. Certainly not his father or his older brother, but Ada would weep. All Simeon wanted from what remained of his time on Earth was to do no harm, and as far as it was in his power, let no harm be done, but news of his death would cause Ada unnecessary sorrow.

So he wrote her a few lines, and gave them to a homeward-bound British officer whose bags he carried in Cairo. Written in the old code that only he and Ada knew, just in case. It seemed very low odds that the letter would ever reach its destination, but he had done what he could. He put England out of his mind. Simeon Price was dead – long live Jack Straw.

The name had come out of his mouth unbidden one day, and almost made him laugh, and almost made him cry. All around the wreck of the *Birkenhead* in those terrible seas, men had been clinging to whatever they could: bits of wood, pieces of mast, even bundles of hay, fodder for the horses. (Simeon had heard a rumor in Bagamoyo that seven of the horses from the ship had survived and were living free in a herd somewhere on the South African coast.)

On one of those bundles of hay, a young private named James Boyden had been perched, bobbing on the waves. A friend of his called out, "Hey, Jack Straw!" and everyone smiled through their tears and terror for a moment. Simeon had no idea whether that young man, the original Jack Straw, had lived. Simeon hoped that if he had, he too, had taken his chance to resurrect himself.

He spent several weeks in Alexandria, doing whatever jobs he could with the intention of saving up enough money for a passage to Athens. Simeon had received a better education than any other boy he knew from Ealing. He'd learned German, French, music, history, mathematics, composition and elocution, before Lady Byron had exiled him for keeping Ada's secrets. But those skills wouldn't do him much good now. He didn't relish the idea of answering to a master for a clerk's wages, and besides, who would hire him, looking as he did? The same went for any job as a messenger. His only paying employment had been drilling as a soldier – no good to him now – and pouring pints in his father's public house, which came with too many bad memories. But he was able to haul things, and clean things, and through those talents he was able to feed himself and put a little money aside, bit by bit.

Truth be told, he wasn't looking forward to taking ship again. But he couldn't forget the mysterious stranger who had mentioned Vienna, and a brotherhood that believed in the supremacy of conscience. He considered going overland, up through the Levant and Turkey, but then he became irritated with himself for being afraid. So he bought his way onto a merchant ship and stayed belowdecks the entire time, where he didn't have to see the dark water. Even so, he woke up several times every night, believing he'd heard a hideous crunch.

Simeon arrived in Vienna wearing a new-to-him greenish coat he'd picked up in a street market in Sarajevo, and a battered Greek fisherman's hat. When it rained, he wore the dun cloak he'd acquired in Bagamoyo. He'd let his beard grow on the journey and patched his boots with newspapers. He was quite sure that his own father would not have recognized him had he passed him on the street, which suited Simeon very well.

A childhood spent in a pub had given Simeon the ability to listen to conversations without seeming to be listening, and to say things that nobody would remember the next day. It took him several weeks of bringing up "brotherhoods" and "conscience" and listening to much drunken philosophy, before a medical student told him about an Irishman who had had the most infuriating argument with him a week before.

"He was trying to convince me that nothing is true," said the man, tipping back his nearly empty beer glass sadly. "I won the argument – really, how could one not? But the thing is, I haven't been able to stop thinking about it since. Maybe he's right. Maybe you're not real."

"Maybe I'm not," said Simeon with a grin he hoped disguised his interest. "Who is this Irishman? Does he drink in here?"

"Never seen him in here, no. I had a game of chess with him in a coffee house in the Graben. Said he lived nearby. His name was Kane. Not like the one in the Bible, though. K-a-n-e."

Simeon stood at the door to a grand apartment block at one end of the Graben, in the heart of Vienna. He had asked around a little more, and he knew the name to ask for: *Oscar Kane*.

"Would you like to leave a card?" the doorman asked, looking him up and down.

Simeon's German wasn't good enough to leave room for politeness. "Do I look like I have a card?"

Frankness was apparently not among the qualities that the doorman valued. Simeon considered loitering in the streets nearby until Kane emerged, but he had only the vaguest idea what the man looked like. The doorman hadn't been wrong about Simeon's appearance; he was still wearing a jumble of cast-off, ill-fitting clothes he'd earned by his work on the long journey. He needed a barber, he smelled, and he only knew the origin of seven of the nine stains he could see on his frayed shirt and jacket.

As the door closed, Simeon said, "Tell him one thing, please." He switched to English, to be sure he got it right: "Nothing is true, everything is permitted." Back to German: "tell him that. I'll wait."

He only had to stand outside for a few minutes, listening to the pigeons cooing and the carriage wheels rolling and wondering what he had done with his life. The doorman returned, gestured for him to enter, and let him walk through the marble foyer to the staircase.

Two flights up, a man stood in an open apartment door, waiting for him. Simeon had half been expecting the stranger from the *Birkenhead*, but this man had lighter skin and a bulkier build. He might have been forty, or close to it. He wore a neat brown goatee and mustache, and a fancy crimson and gold striped waistcoat. His right hand was perched on the handle of a gentleman's cane – no, it was a blackthorn stick, knobby but gleaming.

"Jesus, your own mother wouldn't recognize you," he said with an Irish lilt.

Simeon stopped walking. "My mother's been dead ten years, sir. You must be Oscar Kane."

Kane looked at him, as if puzzled, then switched his stick to his left hand and put out his right. "I am indeed."

"I'm Jack Straw."

"Are you indeed? And what brings you to my door, Mr Straw?"

Simeon paused. "I met a man a while back who spoke of a brotherhood of conscience. What he said interested me. He said I should come to Vienna. So here I am."

"Ah, that's it, is it? Well, you'd better come in."

Kane's apartment was like nothing Simeon had ever seen – Turkish carpets scattered on the wooden floor; red walls punctuated with heavy old paintings. The far wall looked like a choir screen in a church; a circular staircase led to a sort of balcony made from the same carved, dark wood, and under it a medieval fresco gleamed. A narrow doorway led into a second room full of bookshelves.

Kane gestured for him to sit in an overstuffed brocade chair near to the heavy marble fireplace.

"This man you met," he said without further preamble. "Where was this?"

Simeon paused, picking his words carefully. "In Africa. He was helping people. I don't know his name. But he risked his own life to save the lives of strangers, of ordinary men who were worth less than animals to the men who ordered them to go to their deaths. Whatever creed was driving the man, it rang true to me, as nothing ever has."

"The man you met was an Assassin."

Simeon opened his mouth to protest, then remembered the man saying, *I didn't kill him yet, which might have been a mistake.*

"He told you about a brotherhood of conscience, you said. Well, being guided by conscience means making decisions. Sometimes to take a life, and sometimes to save one. You say the maxim he spoke rang true to you, but its first words are 'nothing is true.' A man guided by conscience learns to be comfortable with paradox." Kane looked away into the distance for a moment. "Many people take lives. Criminals. Soldiers. They all have their reasons. Sometimes, death is necessary, to protect the innocent. To preserve life. And by life, I don't just mean survival. I mean freedom."

Simeon was uncomfortably reminded of the day he had joined the 74th Regiment. He didn't know what Kane's connection was with the stranger on the *Birkenhead*, but he knew a recruitment speech when he heard one. Had he traveled all this distance just to be lectured about the necessity of violence? He stood up, abruptly. "Thank you, Mr Kane, for answering my questions."

Kane didn't move. He smiled up at him. "Mr Straw, you have

guessed that I am also a member of this brotherhood. Have you not?"

Simeon nodded.

"I was born into it, you might say. My parents were Assassins, though I barely knew them. Despite what you might think from my comfortable home here, I came from poverty. I was orphaned young and grew up in the hands of the Church. I was a smart boy. I managed to get myself an education. And then the potato blight came. I don't know whether you know what it was like in Ireland, during the famine."

Simeon did know, very well. The faces of the hungry crowd swam before his eyes, and he felt sick again, as he always did. He'd hoped the whiskey would cauterize the memory forever but instead it had only made it sharper and brighter. He didn't remember being drunk in the pub that night, but he remembered everything before it and everything after it with sickening clarity.

"You were there, weren't you?" Kane said, softly. "And what did you choose to do, I wonder? Did you 'protect the innocent'?"

Simeon said nothing.

"I made my own choices," the other man continued. "Took it upon myself to facilitate some redistribution of wealth. I made some enemies and found it prudent to leave Ireland. So I went to Germany, where my mother's family lived. But I found things there much the same as home. There were riots over the cost of food, and what little I had ran out. There was nothing I could do to protect people from starving, from being beaten, imprisoned. Me and my knife and my shillelagh." He held up the blackthorn stick, which gleamed in the light from the window. "That's when I knew I had to be smarter. I made some investments, in the railways. I came south to Vienna and obtained a patent for a manufacturing process. What you see here is what I have built up, myself, in the last two years, from nothing. And I am going to use it, Mr Straw. I am going to use it to protect the innocent from the bastards who give the orders."

Simeon nodded, slowly. This he understood, though he was still uncertain. These references to a Brotherhood of Assassins – it seemed odd Kane would speak so openly about such things with a man he'd just met. "Why are you telling me all this, so openly?"

Kane was smiling. "A man who finds his way here from Africa, just to ask me a question, is a man I should like to get to know better. And a man with secrets of his own is the sort of man I trust. You'll be under no obligation, Mr Straw, but you are welcome to stay here with me for a while so that we can learn from each other. Everything I have is at your disposal: my books, my home, whatever you need. I'll answer any questions you have. What do you say?"

No harm could come from learning, from asking questions. But no education came without a price.

"What do you ask in return?"

Kane paused. "My friend – the man you met in Africa – would not have told you to find me unless he thought you would be an asset to the Brotherhood. Let's find out. But in the meantime, I need a sharp man to help me with my business. I buy and sell industrial products: tools and parts of all kinds. If you don't mind carrying messages and taking notes, you may find it interesting work. I'll introduce you to some of the most fascinating people in Vienna. Call it an apprenticeship, if you like."

Simeon had one more question first. "Your friend – the man on the ship. Did he survive the wreck? Is he here in Vienna?"

"You'll find we aren't easily killed. But no, he's not here at the moment. You'll have to wait a while yet to meet him properly."

That was a conversation Simeon wanted to have. After all, he'd thrown his old life away for the faint hope of a life with a better purpose. Here was a man who might be able to give it to him, or at least tell him whether it was all a mirage. Simeon swallowed and said, "If you're going to introduce me to people, I suppose I should get cleaned up."

Kane laughed. "My valet is out for the day, but if you'd like to go upstairs, you'll find a washstand, and I'll have the housekeeper send up hot water. You can shave and wash. But you've at least three inches on me, so the clothes may be a more difficult matter."

While Kane went to speak to the housekeeper, Simeon walked up the carved circular stairs to the churchlike balcony. He found it was a kind of corridor. At either end, there was a room with a bed and a washstand. In the middle of the corridor, a door opened to a room full of laboratory equipment: glass beakers and bottles and metal devices. Simeon stepped inside. There was an outdoor balcony off the room, and hanging from the ceiling near the French doors were half a dozen cages. In each cage was a pigeon, and he realized he'd been hearing them all through the conversation with Kane, but had assumed they were outside.

"My messengers," Kane said, standing at the door. "Since the uprising here a few years ago, the emperor's minions read all the mail, so it became useful to find private ways to conduct business. The birds are a marvel, really." He was holding a pitcher. "Hot water."

After Simeon had washed and shaved – right to the skin everywhere, to keep it simple – Kane brought him a towel.

"That looks like it fits your hand," Kane said.

Simeon looked at the pearl-handled razor he was holding.

"Feel free to keep it. It's yours."

"That's very generous, but–"

"I insist. It shaves well, and besides, any apprentice of mine needs to be able to protect himself. You have a knife? A gun?"

"I sold my knife, somewhere in Greece, for boots."

"We'll find you something that suits you, but in the meantime, keep that in your pocket. A slice across the throat is quick and quiet, and you could do worse."

When Kane had invited him in, Simeon had wondered for a moment if he had an obligation to tell the man he'd be harboring a deserter. But it seemed he was willing to harbor whatever Simeon was prepared to become.

CHAPTER FOUR

The tailor looked at Kane, then looked at Simeon, took a step back and looked at them both. There was no name on the grimy storefront, squeezed between a tobacconist's and a bookshop just beside the old city wall, but Kane insisted that Janos Libenyi was the best tailor in Vienna, the only man Kane would trust to make his waistcoats. Not only that, but he could use the business. As a Hungarian who had fled when the emperor brutally put down the rebellion there, Libenyi had lived through a difficult few years, and needed friends.

Inside, his shop consisted of a desk and some shelves and papers in the front, and a table in the back with scissors, needles, pins, all neatly contained in bins. Bolts of fabric lined the walls on racks.

Libenyi counted on his fingers. "Two shirts – two collars – one waistcoat – one jacket – three drawers – two vests – and two pairs of trousers."

"That's right," said Kane. "How long?"

"Two weeks." Libenyi addressed Simeon. "I don't use a

machine for anything. All hand stitching, as God intended." With a cock of his head to clear the black curls from his face, the tailor said, "A military man, weren't you?"

Simeon froze, not looking at Kane. "What makes you say so?"

"I know the look." The tailor beckoned him closer and lowered his voice. "I sewed the uniforms for the Hungarian patriots in '48. That was when the emperor executed the generals, may God bless all martyrs." The tailor put the money into a box and locked it with a key from around his neck. "What name shall I put on the order?"

"Jack Straw."

The apprenticeship began with several long talks.

Kane explained that the history Simeon had learned – wherever he had learned it – was wrong. Well, not exactly "wrong", Kane said, but far from the whole picture. For millennia, there had been hands in the darkness, shaping the course of humanity with a well-placed blade. The Brotherhood of Assassins stretched back to ancient Egypt, even beyond. The creed that guided them was deceptively simple: never shed the blood of an innocent, hide in plain sight, and never compromise the brotherhood.

"We take no comfort in absolutes and rules," said Kane. "For us, every situation presents a difficult set of ethical and practical considerations. We know there is no such thing as a perfect world or perfect understanding. And that's where we differ from the Templars."

Every time Simeon got used to the wild version of history Kane was teaching him, it got wilder. "The Templars? The medieval order of knights?"

"Oh, they are so much more than that, and an organization far, far older than you might think. The struggle for freedom has always been matched by a struggle for order. The Templars are trying to shape the world, to perfect it. They'll stop at nothing to achieve their goals. They try to control industry, government, science. All imperfections, they believe, must be brushed aside. And what are humans but imperfections?"

Simeon remembered young Lieutenant Grimes on the deck of the *Birkenhead*, mouthing the words "utmost regularity" as the ship went down. The terrible faith that man had. That kind of faith killed thousands with the stroke of a pen or a bellowed order. If a single blade could have stopped that man's voice, many lives might have been saved. If a single blade could have stopped a ship full of frightened Private Halfords from going to the Cape Colony in the first place, the world would know peace.

It was a tempting thought.

"But if no one can know anything, how can you act?" Simeon asked. "How can you take a life, never knowing whether it was the right thing to do?"

"We don't ask whether it's right. We ask what the consequences will be. And then we take those consequences on ourselves, come what may. Which means that we don't take any life lightly, because we know we'll live with it." Kane paused, pulling a pipe out of his waistcoat pocket. He sat tapping it for a while. "It isn't an easy life, Mr Straw. You'll be in danger for the rest of your days, and those days may very well be few. But you'll know that the only conscience you followed was your own."

Simeon didn't just want permission to do whatever he wanted; he wanted to build something bigger than himself, working with equals, in a community of mutual respect. He wanted that – but he couldn't quite believe it was possible. "Then is there no structure to the Brotherhood? No hierarchy?"

"We help each other, and we take each other's guidance. In some places, we form councils to guide our activities and defend ourselves against the Templars. If you join us, you won't be alone. You'll share what you know with your Brothers, and you'll take their advice. But you will not be a mindless cog in an uncaring machine. That I can promise you."

"Are there other Assassins in Vienna?"

"Of course. And I'll introduce you, when the time is right."

Kane offered his spare room to Simeon, but Simeon preferred to stay in a garret he'd found for a very cheap rent, in a dark alley near a pokey bridge, with medieval buildings crowding all around it. All the same, Simeon was at Kane's nearly every day, because the job of being the man's apprentice was constant and varied. Part of the role seemed to be simply to help Kane maintain his business, which was a mix of natural philosophy and enterprise.

The natural philosophy was conducted in the third-floor laboratory, filled with Leyden jars, bell jars, copper wiring, and various other bits of equipment. Kane was interested in the potential of electrolysis to separate metals from ore, and he sold various devices for achieving this. The factories that used his machinery were mainly outside the city, but the owners were a mix of nouveau-riche and nobility, so the work of selling the equipment happened in salons, while the work of finding out how well it was working, what the factories needed, happened in taverns and noisy, grimy offices. Simeon was happy to do the second part and leave the first to Kane, who seemed to enjoy it.

There was always somewhere for Simeon to go. When a message couldn't be tied to a pigeon's leg, Kane sent Simeon. Nobody trusted the mail in Vienna. Sometimes it seemed half of the people in the city were bustling from one person to another, to convey some information they didn't want to put in writing.

Another of Simeon's tasks was to take deliveries to people whose names he did not know. The deliveries were usually in crates, and given the contents of Kane's laboratory, he guessed that they were usually weapons. Sometimes he wondered whether the people he delivered them to were Assassins, and he came very close to asking or dropping a hint, more than once. But every time, he told himself that this could be a test – of discretion, or of patience. With Kane's taciturn driver waiting in the carriage, Simeon handed over the crates and took the money.

When Simeon wasn't running one of these errands, his task was to read.

Kane's many books stretched across every wall of the little room on the first floor of the apartment. Simeon had never owned any books himself. He said this out loud one day, and Kane declared his astonishment.

"Not even as an adult, once you had a little money of your own?"

"I walked into Vienna with the clothes on my back."

"But before that."

"Before that – no. I had some friends I used to borrow books from, but none of my own."

"Ah, I see. And did you ever have anyone with whom you would talk about ideas?"

He thought of Private Halford, mumbling Shakespeare, and the talks they might have had. He thought about Ada and wondered whether she had received his letter.

"Not for a long time. I didn't have the most orthodox education, Mr Kane."

Simeon told him about the schoolmaster in Ealing, and about working men's lectures he'd attended in London. He didn't mention Lady Byron by name, but said he had had a short stay in the home of a liberal activist who turned him out for bad behavior.

Kane was very interested in all of this. Simeon told him he was grateful for the friends who'd helped him learn, and before long he found himself talking more about Ada, though again, not by name. Kane never pressed him, but he was a good listener, and Simeon found himself talking about things he hadn't properly thought about in years, or ever.

Kane gave Simeon a pile of books to study: medical textbooks, anatomy books, herbals, and combat manuals, some of them hundreds of years old. At unpredictable moments, Kane would demand that Simeon demonstrate how to get out of a hold, or show him six of the most efficient knife strikes. Sometimes he made Simeon walk across the laboratory without causing a single floorboard to squeak or hold his breath for a set number of seconds. It was not much like his army training.

On Sundays, Simeon learned philosophy. Sometimes this had to do with natural laws and took place in the laboratory.

"At its root, the Brotherhood is about learning how to build the world by breaking it apart," said Kane one day, wiping mineral oil off his hands with a rag. "We begin with the molecules, and we move on to the men."

As the summer cooled into autumn, Simeon learned to hone what Kane called his power of observation. In Vienna, there was a great deal to observe. Just outside Kane's door, the Graben was walled with fine stone buildings with windows that shone in different hues according to the time of day, and full of people, milling around the baroque plague column that rose in gray and gold in the middle. There were ladies with parasols and working men with their hats pulled down over their brows. After dark there were the "Graben nymphs" plying their trade with the gentlemen, pulling up their skirts to reveal beribboned stockings.

One of Simeon's lessons involved perching on an iron-railed balcony high above the Graben every day for a whole week, taking notes on a dozen people who he recognized from day to day. What time they walked through, what they wore, what they carried, how quickly they walked. He then had to follow them, and to find out who these people were and where they went every day. One was a woman carrying on an affair; one was a man going to his job in a bank.

When Simeon had successfully identified all twelve of them and handed over his notebook, Kane took him to church.

It was the end of November. Inside the cold stone stairwell, the 353 steps to the top of the spire of St Stephen's cathedral turned, turned, up and up. Simeon hated the smell of damp stone by the end of it. His fingertips had traced the carved names of visitors from across centuries to keep him from getting dizzy. And his legs ached. It must have been even worse for Oscar Kane, more than a decade older, but he just trudged in silence ahead of Simeon.

From a little chamber at the top of the cathedral, all of Vienna lay before them. Squat rooftops arranged in squares, with roads and rivers meandering through, all the way to a deep blue horizon where low clouds sat like hilltops, gilded by dawn. The cathedral itself was more colorful than anything else in the landscape, with its steep roof tiled in green, white and red, in a zigzag pattern that didn't help with the dizziness.

They were all alone at the top, at seven o'clock on a Tuesday morning. After Simeon had looked out of each of the tall, narrow windows, Kane opened one somehow, and gestured that Simeon should go out through it.

Simeon peered out. There was no balcony beneath it, no railing. "I don't understand."

"See all those lovely carvings? You can grab on to one of those well enough. Just be careful what you put your weight on. Don't rely on any one of your hands or feet and keep your body close to the wall. The limestone's eroded in places."

Simeon wasn't in the mood for Kane's brand of wit. He'd been so patient, for months, doing everything his teacher asked, so he could learn more about the Brotherhood. "I don't understand what you're training me to do."

"I'm welcoming you *home*, Straw. This is our city – up here. We members of the Brotherhood have to see the way birds of prey see, and there's only one way to teach you that. Now go on. Out the window, then get yourself down to the ground. I'm taking the stairs, and I'll meet you at the bottom."

The window was narrow, and Simeon winced at the thought of going to Libenyi to ask him to sew up tears in the new trousers he had only recently sewed, but he managed to squeeze through without any rips. Still clinging to the window frame, he slid down to sit in the crook of a carved stone outcrop. He felt like a boy sitting in a tree. On board the *Birkenhead*, he'd watched the sailors climbing the rigging and thanked his stars he was a soldier instead. Now here he was, out sitting on a church spire at dawn, for no reason other than he'd been told to do it by a man he'd known for a few months. Simeon was still taking orders, somehow, no matter how many times he'd told himself he wasn't.

But he was learning, and all learning required humility, Kane said.

It was strange, how different the view could be – could *feel* – from outside the steeple, rather than inside it. The wind carried the first of the day's carters' calls and shopkeepers' greetings up to him, reminding him oddly of the call to prayer in Cairo. A city waking up. Pigeons – ordinary birds, not Kane's flock – walked along a ledge below him, completely unfazed by his presence. He could see not only the bright tiles but the dirt that stained them, even though it had rained the night before. Nothing seemed to be damp, though, which was probably a blessing from the perspective of a man who had to get down the side of a church.

Getting down. Suddenly the uncomfortable stone outcrop seemed like a place Simeon never wanted to leave.

He dared, though, moment by moment. He turned, and grabbed on, and let his foot find something solid. And then again, and again. Anything would serve, so long as it was lower down, although twice he had to go up and sideways until he found a better path. By the time he dropped to the cobbles, his hands were raw, his legs were shaking, and he had tears on his face from the wind and weariness.

Kane put one hand on his shoulder. "It wasn't pretty, but you earned your breakfast."

At breakfast, there was a newspaper, with news from all over Europe, and in it was the news of the death of Ada, Countess of Lovelace, philosopher, writer, and daughter of Lord Byron.

CHAPTER FIVE

A few days before Christmas, Kane told Simeon that they were going to a party, and that he might need a gun.

Simeon took it. A short, squat pepperbox with a burl wood grip and six barrels. It sat well in his hand.

"It loads well, and never chain-fires. You know how to shoot, Mr Straw?" Kane asked.

"I know how to shoot."

That evening, the carriage pulled up to a tall door flanked by marble columns, rising to statues of knights holding large shields emblazoned with crosses. Three stone steps led to a heavy door, where a footman admitted them to a gleaming vestibule. Everything seemed to be made of marble, like a mausoleum. But there was a long crimson carpet, upon which several dozen people stood, posing and preening.

Simeon felt uncomfortable in a black tailcoat and trousers, white waistcoat, white shirt with a stiff collar and a folded necktie. But he couldn't fault Libenyi for the tailoring. It fit him beautifully, as did the new patent leather shoes Kane had bought him. He had a stack of visiting cards, and a shining top hat and an ebony cane with a pleasant silver handle. All in all, Simeon felt like a man in a costume – or worse yet, in a form of uniform, fit for a gentleman, complete with the gun in its holster beneath the tailcoat. Self-conscious inside this unfamiliar uniform didn't help him feel like he was blending into the crowd here, even though every other man walking through the vestibule was dressed in the same black and white, with only a flower in the lapel here and there to differentiate them. It was no wonder that the toffs all wore such varied mustaches; there was no other way to tell them apart. Maybe that was why Kane loved his dazzling waistcoats.

Simeon cringed at the sight of an old gentleman with two drooping tufts of white beneath his nose, but it wasn't the unruly mustache that gave him the shivers. It was the military uniform, glittering with medals.

"This is our host," said Kane at his elbow. "Baron von Haynau."

The baron looked at Kane with an odd expression, like triumph. Maybe a man with that many medals on his chest always looked triumphant. "So, you received my message," he said in perfect English.

"Received, and understood, and here I am," said Kane, pleasantly. "May I present Mr John Straw? He's an Englishman, newly arrived in Vienna last year."

Simeon kept a straight face, but was amused by Kane's apparent assumption that Jack Straw's given name must be John.

The baron turned a pair of watery eyes their way. "Ah, your new apprentice! We have heard about him. I think you will find

Vienna a more civilized place than your London, Mr Straw.
And the women more beautiful."

The ladies in the room were, unlike most of the men, a riot
of color. Dresses in sage green, lemon yellow, rose pink, with
feathers and beads everywhere. The baron had turned his
remark to the young woman beside him, a slim brunette in a
deep crimson dress that was drooping off the shoulder, pinched
at the waist. She had been talking to someone else, but seemed
to sense she was being shown off.

"Countess Konstanze von Visler," said Kane, gallantly, and
said in German: "I had hoped you would grace us tonight."

"Jack Straw," said Simeon, putting out his hand. She
responded with hers, white-gloved, and he raised it nearly to his
lips, as Kane had told him to do. She had a champagne glass in
the other hand. They stood across from each other, with Kane
and Baron Haynau on the other two points of the compass.

"I have the feeling I was being discussed," she said in Bavarian
German, with an easy smile.

"In the general, not the particular," Baron Haynau said
pompously. "I was explaining to our Englishman that the
women of Vienna are not only beautiful, but the very model of
womanhood."

"Well, I am only a woman of Vienna by adoption, but I
shall take the compliment," said the countess. "And what *is* the
model of womanhood?"

"Virtuous ornaments to the home," said the baron, as though
he'd been thinking about it.

Kane said, very smoothly, "But it seems that ideal is not
universal throughout the Empire. I heard that the uprising in
Hungary had as many women as men in the ranks."

"There are always women in mobs," the baron retorted. "The perversion of the ideal. It must be rooted out and cleansed wherever it occurs. When women mirror the sedition of their men, they will be flogged as though they were men. As indeed we did, in Hungary."

"You flogged women?" Simeon asked in English, uncertain he'd understood the German words. He remembered a sunny day off the coast of Sierra Leone, the deserter caught, the lash ripping red lines out of his back, his broken gasps.

"*Fifty* lashes each," the baron boasted. "It put an end to it. The worse the disease, the stronger the curative. *Pour encourager les autres*, as Herr Voltaire says, eh? We didn't have any more trouble with the women after we made it clear there would be consequences. After that, we only had to hang the generals."

"Fifty lashes," Simeon repeated, unbelieving.

"There are some languages that everyone speaks," said the baron, looking at Kane.

At the baron's shoulder, a short man with a blond brush mustache, holding a monocle in one hand, joined the conversation in German. "The women could take a great deal more than you might think. God gives them tolerance for pain, for childbearing, you know, and the women of Hungary – well, they are no better than she-dogs, some of them." He smiled at the countess.

"Oh, they clearly survived," the baron added. "Why, we know of one in Vienna, don't we, Mayr? Mr John Straw, this is Karl Mayr, my lawyer and right-hand man."

Mayr shook his hand. "Delighted to make your acquaintance, Mr Straw. We've heard what a help you've been to Mr Kane. It seems you have a head for his kind of business. You must come and see me in my offices. I'm frequently away – the baron keeps me busy – but if you leave your card, I'll call on you whenever you suggest."

"Mayr," the baron said impatiently, "I wanted you to tell them about the Hungarian girl."

Mayr swallowed with evident anticipation of a story he wanted to tell, tucking his monocle into his pocket. "Oh, she was a red-headed thing with the most striking eyes – a strange color. Would have been burned as a witch in our grandfathers' day. Anyway, I would have recognized her anywhere. She was a terror in the mobs, and even after her lashing, we had evidence that she was still at it, though we never caught her again. Incorrigible. But once we restored peace, wouldn't you know, she and her brother came to Vienna. They all do, to make a penny, of course. They fight us and then they try to take our money."

"What happened to her?" Simeon asked. His German had been just about good enough to get the gist of Mayr's story.

"Nothing. Her brother has a rathole where he mends shirts, in the shadow of the old city wall."

"I thought the walls were slated to be demolished, to make room for the new avenue," said the countess.

"Oh, they are!" the baron said with glee. He turned back to Simeon. "We – my friends on the municipal council, I mean – are turning Vienna into a model of the modern city. Wide roads, clean buildings, beauty and progress. But we have to clear these medieval jumbles out of the way. Mayr here is the man in charge of getting all the paperwork signed and sealed."

Mayr stepped in closer, as though he were telling them a secret. A yellow silk scarf hung around his neck. With evident pride, he said, "Once I told the little Hungarian tailor we recognized his sister, he was all too eager to pay whatever fines I invented for him. We'll make sure he's no richer for coming here to bleed us, the parasite."

The little Hungarian tailor in the shadow of the city wall. Libenyi, it had to be Libenyi. The man just trying to make a living, now that the army whose uniforms he'd sewn were no more. The humble fellow who'd made the very clothes on Simeon's back.

Simeon's nails were making little wounds in his palms. He smiled the smile he'd learned in the pub in Ealing, the one saved for the customers who'd get the flattest beer. "I can see I have a lot to learn about Vienna's civilization."

"Oh, you mustn't think we're all bloodthirsty old soldiers," said the countess, managing to convey to the baron that she was teasing, and to Simeon that she wasn't at all. "Come, Mr Straw. Let's go through to the ballroom. It's getting too crowded here anyway. Do you dance?"

"Very badly."

"But he *is* learning," said Kane, nudging Simeon's elbow encouragingly.

"I will dance with you, but just one moment, please, countess," said Simeon, and he stepped aside so he could talk to Kane alone.

"She's a useful woman to know," Kane said quietly, when they were out of earshot. "I'd never ask you to dance with her without good reason. Believe that everything I ask you to do is part of your training."

"I do believe that," Simeon said drily. "And I assume you had a reason for introducing me to that whiskery bastard."

"You hadn't heard of Baron Haynau before now?" Kane asked.

"Should I have?"

"His reputation is spreading through Europe. He had to run from a mob in Brussels – simply because people heard stories of his brutality. The flogged women, and other things. The people will see justice is done, given a chance. He went to London last year or the year before – you caught that remark of his? – and tried to visit a brewery. The draymen horsewhipped him, and he barely escaped with his life."

"I wish they'd finished the job," Simeon said.

"Funny you should say that," Kane replied. "Go on, go and dance."

Simeon walked with his companion into a vast white and gold ballroom, on a floor of veined marble. Dance had not been on the curriculum at Lady Byron's school, and the only dancing Simeon had learned from behind the bar in Ealing was how to duck a right hook. But as a reluctant ten year-old, he had learned the basics from Ada, who found his first efforts hilarious, so then he kept at it to make her laugh. He remembered the steps: up, over, together, up, over, together. He remembered how he and Ada had giggled over her father's satirical ode to the dance: *Round all the confines of the yielded waist/The strangest hand may wander undisplaced.*

After a surreptitious check of how everyone else was holding their partners, he put his hands where they ought to be.

The countess shifted her right hip forward, closer to his, with an indulgent smile. She smelled of bergamot and lemon, and there was a small red silk flower tucked into her dark hair, the same color as her dress. "I had to practice the waltz a lot a few years ago, when I was a debutante," she confided. "My aunt helped me. Do you know the main difference between the English waltz and the Viennese?"

Simeon shook his head slightly.

"It's faster," she whispered, and the music began. They whirled, the other couples in the room a blur of color, the lights from the candelabras blinking and flickering in the corners of his vision. Turning, turning, like the stairs of St Stephen's cathedral. Every few turns, he caught sight of the violins, their bows jumping. He felt trapped inside the circle of his own arms, and hers. At least they were going too quickly to talk.

He wanted to leap through one of the plate-glass windows, go out into the dignified stone terrace, out into the gardens, out into the night. To leave the name of Jack Straw behind and to give his eyes some relief from the bright whirl of this room.

Finally, finally, the dance came to an end. He feared the countess would want to enjoy another turn around the floor. Out of the corner of his eye, he saw Kane, walking into an anteroom with Mayr, the lawyer. There was something odd about the way they were walking. Kane looked almost beaten, subservient. It was a posture he'd never seen in Kane before, and there was something unsettling about it.

"I think my employer needs me," he said, and bowed, still dizzy. He didn't wait for the countess to say anything, but strode off toward Kane.

He stopped dead in the doorway. The room contained a large desk, covered in papers, and behind it was Mayr, yellow silk scarf in his hands, wrapped around Kane's neck. Kane was on the ground, his legs thrashing, a horrible gurgling sound coming from his throat.

Simeon fumbled for the gun, pulled the trigger. A terrible, soft click. Nothing came from it.

He lunged toward Mayr, who had his back turned just enough that he didn't see Simeon until he was almost at the desk. Simeon grabbed a gleaming metal pen with his left hand and plunged it into Mayr's ribs from behind.

It wasn't a killing blow. The wrong angle, and even with all Simeon's strength behind it, it didn't go that deep. But it bled, and it made Mayr release Kane, who scrambled to his feet and flailed backward with his hands at his neck.

Simeon scrambled over the desk, shoving the wooden chair aside. Mayr had doubled over, but his hand was inside his jacket, reaching for a knife or a gun. If someone came in now, it would be the gallows for Simeon. He needed something quick and quiet. Out of the corner of his eye he saw Kane crumpled against the wall, watching him.

Simeon grabbed Mayr's hair from behind, pulled his head back, and with his right hand, he reached for the razor in his waistcoat pocket, flipped it open, and slid the blade across the man's neck.

The man crumpled, pulling Simeon down with him.

"Shit," Simeon whispered. "Shit, shit, shit." He eased Mayr down to the floor as he died, until there was only the sound of two men breathing.

He rushed over to Kane, who had his hand raised, pointing back at Mayr. "Take his blood."

Simeon twisted to look at the corpse on the floor, and

grimaced. Kane had told him it was tradition to take something stained with the target's blood. A white feather, in the old days. A handkerchief was popular now, but Simeon hadn't brought a handkerchief.

With his left hand, the less bloody of the two, he pulled his visiting card case out of his tailcoat pocket and opened it. They were plain cards, with nothing but his name on them: his false name, Jack Straw. He brushed the card against Mayr's bloody neck for a moment until it was stained, then put it back in the case with the others.

"Shall I get you to a doctor?" he whispered to Kane, checking his neck. There was a red line, but it wasn't as bad as Simeon had feared.

Kane was already standing and breathing more evenly. "No need."

"What do we do?"

Kane went to the window and opened it. He gestured for Simeon to follow.

In a small street behind the house, Kane's carriage was waiting. The evening was damp, and a few drops of rain fell as the carriage started to roll, off into the gaslit streets.

"What the devil was that all about?" Simeon asked. He was shaking, from cold or something else.

Kane took a moment before answering. "Mayr and I were in that room to sign some papers. A business deal, to make peace. They know I want information on the weapons they're manufacturing, and they think I'm desperate to get it. But I have my own ways of getting that information. I just wanted them to think they had me."

"Baron Haynau and Mayr," Simeon said, putting it all together. "They're Templars, aren't they?"

Kane nodded once, slowly.

"And they know we're Assassins."

He'd said "we" without thinking, but didn't correct himself. He might not have been inducted into the Brotherhood formally, but he had just killed a man. He could still feel the rhythm of Mayr's final breaths in his own body.

Kane looked out of the window, which was fogging as the evening cooled. Outside, the rain picked up pace; the glows of lamps refracted and swam as they went past. "They thought we were weak. Tonight, we've shown them otherwise."

Simeon closed his eyes, to think better. He saw the room, the man with the silk scarf, Kane in his final throes. A scene. A scene for his benefit?

"The gun you gave me…"

"It's a piece of shit. Get rid of it."

"Did you know it would not work?"

Kane paused, then said, "You need to learn to kill quickly and quietly, Simeon. To move in the shadows, as we always have. But that kind of killing takes a strong stomach. Guns are for cowards and soldiers. I needed to know whether you could kill like an Assassin."

Simeon exhaled, angry, confused. "You manipulated me."

"No, I put my faith in you, and you proved me right. Mayr would very likely have succeeding in killing me if you hadn't come in."

"A terrible chance to take."

"Haynau will cover it up. We've embarrassed him, by getting into his house by his own invitation. That's the kind of man he is. You don't have to fear the police, not for this."

"And why not kill Haynau himself, rather than his lackey?"

Kane put his pipe in his mouth and lit it. "You know your Shakespeare, don't you, Straw? The first thing we do is kill all the lawyers."

The carriage rolled through the streets. Simeon's hands were still bloody, and he had nothing to wipe them on. He stared at them.

Kane said gently, "You saved many lives tonight. Haynau is a killer. You heard him brag about it, for Christ's sake! He may have retired from the army, but he can kill through the law itself, with men like Mayr doing his dirty work. You made a choice to protect the innocent."

"I thought I was protecting you."

"Exactly."

That didn't follow, but Simeon said nothing. He was out of words, and exhausted. The movement of the carriage made him feel sick.

"As for Haynau," Kane said, looking out the window, "we will deal with him in time. The baron is very well protected, with friends at court. Many Austrians consider him a hero. The law will not touch him, no matter who he murders. If he's assassinated, the emperor will take it out on the people. There would be reprisals."

Kane smiled terribly at Simeon. "He will die, mark my words. But not in a way that will bring unwanted attention."

Chapter Six

Simeon found Mayr's bloodied fountain pen in his own pocket the next day. He hadn't realized he had kept it. Stolen a pen from a corpse.

Private Halford had gone to the bottom never having killed a man, but Simeon couldn't say the same. If there was a Hell, then he was very likely bound for it. But he didn't care. He had always preferred consequences to rules, and now at last he had found others who felt the same way. Or at least, one other.

He found Kane in his laboratory, talking to his pigeons. He showed Kane the pen, and said he was not quite sure what to do with it. Kane took his crooked pince-nez out of his pocket for a better look.

"It has an interesting mechanism. And look – the iridium tip on the nib. I've seen pens like this in Birmingham. Gorgeous devices. I don't blame you for taking it. But I don't recommend its use as a weapon. Unless you'd like me to add a proper blade to this one. Now there's a thought. Get ahead of the Templars for once."

Simeon put the pen back in his pocket. "Why do you say that? What do they have that we don't?"

"They've made knowledge their priority," Kane said, looking past Simeon at a table piled high with pieces of twisted metal, glass jars crusted with only the devil knew what, and loose sheets of paper bearing his scribbled notes. "And until we are ready to fight like with like, we'll always be outmatched. I've argued this within the Brotherhood for years, but I think, at last, we're on the cusp of change. A new consensus."

Kane opened a cage and put his big hand around one of the birds before gently drawing it out. He regarded it for a moment, like a friend, then pulled a tiny roll of paper from his waistcoat pocket and slipped it into the little tube attached to the bird's leg. Kane was a paradox: a man who loved science, but was afraid to communicate using anything but birds. A man who dug for the future in the dirt of the past. A man who had connections in every world – including that of the Templars, it seemed – but who seemed solitary all the same. He spoke of the Brotherhood with fierce love, and also with frustration.

"You've mentioned the Assassin's Councils," Simeon said. "Did a council sign off on Mayr? Will they want a report?"

Kane opened the window and pushed the bird out into the Vienna sky. It caught the wind in a flutter and was gone, off to deliver one of Kane's many messages to someone, somewhere.

"Let me worry about that," he said lightly. "There's something else I want you to do today. Go and let Libenyi know what you've done, and why."

"Libenyi! The tailor? Why the devil does he need to know that?"

"Because we need to liberate the city, not just rid it of tyrants who'll return in new form every year. We need the people to know who they have to thank for lifting the boots off their necks. Mayr was delighting in hurting Libenyi, and now Mayr is dead. Don't you think he deserves to know?"

Simeon had read in a newspaper account that one hundred and ninety-three people had survived when the *Birkenhead* went down, though four hundred and fifty were presumed dead. Some of those one hundred and ninety-three owed their lives to a man in a cloak whose name they'd never know, and they'd never know his reasons. It was partly that anonymity that had drawn Simeon to find the Brotherhood. The idea of stepping out into the light, demanding acknowledgment, made his guts squirm.

But Kane was his teacher, and Simeon was humbling himself to learn, so Simeon went down to the tavern where he knew Libenyi went after work.

The Nachzehrer Cellar had a painted sign over the door of a shrouded figure, with the only parts visible being the long, grasping hands. It was the only indication that the door, on an otherwise quiet, small street with no gas lamps, led down to an old tavern.

It was pleasantly dark, lit by candles in iron sconces in the walls. There were no windows, just a spread of tables against a long bench, and a wall of casks. The narrow stairs led up to the only door, the one with the sign over it. Simeon noticed the fact that there was nowhere to get away from an attack here. And then he noticed himself noticing it. His training had changed him, and it hadn't even been a year yet.

The best thing about the Nachzehrer was that it was quiet

and extremely unfashionable. The leather on the bench was cracked and faded, the wax dripped down the sconces, and the tables all wobbled. Though the beer was good, it looked like a place where down-at-heel men went to feel sorry for themselves, which wasn't so far off the mark. The barman had a tendency to slip into the back room when he wasn't needed, which was almost always. And there were no other patrons at the moment. Simeon had hoped to be the only one, as he waited for Libenyi to come in after his day's work. All the same, he wasn't disappointed to see Josef Ettenreich, another regular in the tavern, sitting alone in the far corner.

Ettenreich was the most gentlemanly butcher Simeon had ever met. He had a very fine waxed mustache and wore very trim, very white shirts under a dark jacket. As the son of a tavernkeeper, he was able to talk shop with the barman, and frequently got a free round out of it.

Simeon went to the bar for an amber lager, then slid into the chair opposite the butcher, telling himself not to care that his back was to the door.

"Your German is getting better," said Ettenreich. "You asked for your lager properly."

Simeon grinned. "I didn't know I used to do it improperly."

"Eh, you used to be too formal about it, that's all. You're more relaxed."

"Well, I'm more relaxed when I'm in here, I suppose." It was true; he was slouching down over his glass, letting himself just sit, for the first time in weeks. "But my German's not as good as you think. I don't know what to make of the name of this place, for example."

"What, the Nachzehrer? It's a body that rises after death.

Something like a vampire. This was a plague pit once," he said, tipping back his lager.

"What, the cellar?"

"This whole area. So goes the story, anyway. Ah, Libenyi!"

Simeon turned to see his friend the tailor walking down the stairs with a glum expression. It was an excuse for Simeon to hop over to the other side of the table, next to Ettenreich, with his back properly to the wall.

Since he'd last spoken with these men, he had taken a life. Somehow, he felt it should be written on his face, on his hands. When Simeon had washed the blood off the inside of his coat, from where his hand had brushed it as he took out his calling cards, Kane had found it funny to walk past him quoting Lady Macbeth. "'Will all great Neptune's ocean wash this blood clean from my hand? No, this my hand will rather the multitudinous seas incarnadine, making the green one red.'"

Whenever Kane quoted Shakespeare, which he did frequently, it made Simeon think of Private Halford, who had never killed a man. But Ettenreich must have seen his share of blood and knives. And so had Libenyi, for that matter, in the uprising.

The barman brought over a glass for Libenyi, whose foul mood seemed to have made itself felt even in the back room. It hung in the air like a miasma.

"Bad day, Libenyi?" asked Ettenreich.

"I had the misfortune to read a newspaper," Libenyi grumbled. "I don't know how they can print such damned lies. Or at least, if they're going to write about Hungary, hire someone who's been there, at the very least."

Ettenreich nodded. "Every good writer in the country is

terrified since the emperor revoked the constitution. Write what the emperor wants or face a prison cell. So we end up with lies."

"At least some people have the guts to speak the truth," said Libenyi.

"And who would that be?" Simeon asked.

Libenyi looked around, as if there were a chance of anyone else darkening the door of the Nachzehrer. Then he leaned over the table and whispered, "There are people who are organizing. Holding meetings. You'll see some better publications before long, mark my words."

Organizing. That didn't sound like the Brotherhood. Probably Libenyi was talking to radicals.

"Just be careful, my friend," Simeon said. "You don't want to give anyone an excuse to get you out of the way."

"They don't need an excuse," Libenyi said darkly. "They're building a road through my shop, so they tell me."

"What!" Ettenreich wiped beer off his mustache. "Who is?"

"The city council. That odious lawyer, Karl Mayr, has been haunting me. And he may be a thug, but I believe he's got the law on his side."

"They'll tear down the whole damn city before they're done," Ettenreich said, shaking his head. "Fixing what isn't broken."

"And not fixing what is," agreed Libenyi, making a fist on the table. "But it's no good. It's over for me. They'll take my shop, I know they will. But I've been hanging on, paying their so-called fees, to stall the eviction long enough to give me a chance to find a new place I can afford, which doesn't seem to exist. Meanwhile they take every penny I can give them. By the time they're through, they'll take my livelihood, they'll take everything. They might as well take my life too. I hoped to provide for my sister but she's going to get married to a respectable Austrian she doesn't love, and who am I to argue? It's better this way."

"What way?" Simeon asked, but Libenyi said nothing, and took a large swig of beer.

Simeon moved closer to Libenyi, and spoke quietly. "Listen, when it comes to Mayr, you don't have to worry about him anymore. I'm sure the city council will still tear down your building, but you'll get a reprieve from paying his bribes. They won't evict you, and I'll help you find a new place. Starting tomorrow morning."

Libenyi frowned. "What do you mean, I don't have to worry about Mayr?"

Simeon looked down, traced a circle in the moisture the glasses had left on the table. "He's dead."

"Dead!" Libenyi nearly shouted.

"Shh," Simeon said. "I don't think it's common knowledge yet. At some point they'll have to announce his death in the newspaper, I'd wager, although who knows what they'll say about it."

"Then how do you know, Straw?" Ettenreich looked at him with shining eyes.

He took a deep breath. "There's an organization. No, not an organization. There's – as Libenyi says, there are people who want to change things. People who take action, and take the consequences. I'm one of them. I... He's dead. By my hand. There. Now you have a secret you can trade, if you ever need to barter with the police."

The two men stared at him in shock. Libenyi said, very seriously, almost childlike, "I would never use such a thing against you."

"No, I didn't think you would. I'm sorry. I just did not know how to tell you."

Libenyi shook his head, smiling, his curls bouncing. "No, no, this is exactly what we need! This is the beginning of something! We need action, not words!"

"Well, we need to be careful," Simeon cautioned, keeping his voice low. "We mustn't draw attention. Nobody has any reason to suspect me. Just believe me when I tell you that I'm here to help, and so are my friends. If it ever seems like the city is under the control of people who want to grind you into dust, believe that they don't have as much control as they want you to think. Believe that there are people who weaken their control, people who just want ordinary people to have freedom to live their own lives."

Ettenreich and Libenyi just stared at him.

Then Ettenreich said, "You've told us to be careful, but are *you* being careful, Straw? Do you know what you're getting into?"

"No, that I do not," Simeon said honestly. He thought for a moment. "But that's what makes me think it's the right thing to do."

Libenyi stood up, pushing back the little chair. "Well, this calls for another round. On me."

Simeon shook his head, laughing. "You've just been telling us about how Mayr was bleeding you dry! Let me. Kane pays me well."

Libenyi looked disappointed, but he sat down again. "Someday, I'll repay you, my friend. That is a promise."

CHAPTER SEVEN

Kane had a habit of leaving Simeon notes in his apartment, while Simeon was sleeping. The morning after his talk with Libenyi and Ettenreich, he woke slightly worse for wear, with one such note resting on his chest.

> *Carriage will fetch you at eleven o'clock sharp. Dress:*
> *day formal. You will find an appropriate suit in your*
> *wardrobe.*

It was one of the many paradoxes of his training that Kane expected Simeon to do as Kane instructed, but also to question his own feelings and reasons for it, constantly. Were all Assassins this way? Simeon wanted to find out. He wanted to meet the mysterious "council". So far, his Brotherhood was a group of two.

The dove gray frock coat and trousers in the wardrobe fit perfectly. Kane had said that he preferred a frock coat to a tailcoat, when he could get away with it, because the higher cut of the tailcoat in front made it difficult to conceal weapons. Libenyi must have made it to Kane's order, with the measurements he had on file. The tailor could keep a secret, it seemed.

Kane's black carriage was current and stylish, but not remarkable. His driver was a young Irishman – a distant cousin of Kane's, he had been told – who had an uncanny knack for memorizing maps, but didn't speak a word of German.

It was relaxing, rolling through the streets of Vienna, the wheels and hooves cutting pleasantly through a thin blanket of snow. Maybe the truth was that some part of Simeon took comfort in being told what to do. If his actions weren't his own, he could keep his mind and his will away from the gaze of the world. Safe. But at the same time, something in him railed against that instinct, the way men fought to survive in rising waters.

The driver took them through the city walls, and across the open space that surrounded the fortified central city known as the *glacis*. It stopped in front of a dignified white house, with evergreen boughs wrapped around the front columns. When he handed one of his cards (from the unstained side of the stack) to the footman, Kane himself came down the hallway. His coat hung open to reveal a sky-blue silk waistcoat, embroidered with tiny gold stars.

"Come into the conservatory, Mr Straw," Kane said. "The countess is just about to make a demonstration."

"Good morning to you too, Kane. Do you mean Countess von Visler? Is she here also?"

"This is her house." He paused, then said quietly, "A young woman with brains and an independent streak can be very useful to us. You might try to seduce her, if you like. That could prove convenient."

Speechless, Simeon followed his teacher into a wide room with tall windows on either side, and dark wood bookshelves lining the far wall, broken by a fireplace in which a fire crackled and glowed. The floor was nearly entirely covered by a pale patterned carpet, and dotted here and there with round tables, each of them displaying an item under a bell jar. The effect was inviting, like a museum – much less jumbled than Kane's library and laboratory.

A half-dozen men and two women were gathered around one of the tables, with Countess von Visler among them. She wore a dark navy dress; in truth, all of them were dressed very soberly, other than Kane, who had never worn a sober waistcoat since the day Simeon met him. She looked up and gave Simeon an appraising smile, as though she was well aware his suit had been ordered for him, well aware he had been summoned. In this company, two things stood out: her youth and her height. She couldn't have been more than twenty, and she was tall. When they'd danced the other night, he hadn't thought about anything other than where to put his hands and feet. But seeing her standing in a group of five men, all gathered around a table, she was roughly the same height as all of them. She was certainly taller than Kane, who strode over to the little group and requested the countess to carry on with what she was saying before the interruption of Straw's arrival.

As Simeon approached the little knot of people, he caught a glimpse of what was on the table. It looked like a piece of artillery for use by toy soldiers: a mouse-sized iron contraption consisting of a trestle and a long barrel, slimmer than a cannon's.

On one side, a slim, flexible tube ran from the side of the barrel.

The countess picked up this tube between two fingers. "This is the key, to connect the drill to the boiler. Do you see? It took a great deal of trial and error to get the material right, so that the steam wouldn't lose its power on the way to the drill."

"What about safety?" one of the women asked. "The steam, and the recoil?"

"This is safer than anything the miners use now," the countess said. "Mining is a dangerous business. This device will save lives and reduce injuries. I don't know whether you've ever watched two men wield those enormous hammers while a third man holds the drill, his fingers exposed. It's taxing and difficult when they're drilling sideways or even upwards. With a steam-powered rock drill, the men stand behind it, and they are perfectly safe. Not only that, but this drill can do in a day what it used to take an entire town's worth of men to do in a week."

He could see why Kane, with his hunger for innovation, seemed fascinated by the countess. Ada would have liked her, too. But, like Ada, she seemed too eager to believe in her own ideas.

Simeon asked, "And where do the men work, after this machine comes to their mine?"

The countess looked at him. "Ah, always the objection to any innovation. We want things to roll on the same as they have always been, don't we? We can't imagine a world in which people have more leisure, more freedom. But machines won't ruin us. After all, someone has to build the machines. Humans will be free to use their minds, once we're freed from banging on rocks like apes to get the metal we need." She looked at

Kane, and added, "As I have told your mentor, there were those who needed to be persuaded even within my uncle's company."

Kane said, "The countess hit upon a brilliant method of persuasion."

Her eyes twinkled. "Mr Kane was very impressed with how an empty-headed nineteen year-old heiress turned out not to be so empty-headed after all, when I told him what I did. No, don't object, it's true. I will tell you, too, Mr Straw. It was very simple. I let them see the consequences of their cowardice. I identified a seam that would be difficult and time-consuming to get at in any traditional way, and I let them try their methods to get it. After the inevitable accidents with black powder, I suggested an alternative."

Uneasy, Simeon glanced at Kane, whose expression was inscrutable. Kane had said that the countess could be useful to them. She seemed more dangerous than useful.

Kane said to the countess, "You promised us a demonstration, I think?"

A smile broke across her face. "Indeed I did. And this is where I tell you all, gentlemen, that we are demonstrating two devices at once: my mechanical drill, and Mr Kane's new power cell, which I am trying to convince him ought to bear his name."

She opened a cabinet on the underside of the table and lifted out a glass jar with a bulbous bottom that made it look a little like an electric arc lamp. Simeon had seen jars like this one, in various conditions, in Kane's laboratory: some holding a blue liquid, some with no liquid at all, some blackened, some cracked. This one had a clear orange-red liquid inside that reminded Simeon of fresh blood. The lid of the jar had three tubes of metal sticking out of the top, the one in the middle taller than the others.

"It is much more reliable than a voltaic cell," his teacher explained to the admiring audience. "And one can use it intermittently, simply by removing the zinc from the solution of potassium bichromate and sulfuric acid."

The countess depressed the plunger – that was the tallest of the metal tubes. Then she carefully set the jar on the table near her model drill.

"If you'll be so kind as to bring me that lump of granite," she said, gesturing to another table, where a large rock sat alone. One of the men picked it up and brought it to her. She set the drill in front of it and connected the wire to the jar.

Simeon had to admit it was impressive. A thin iron rod, needle-sharp at one end, drove into the granite, over and over. Every time it rebounded into the mechanism, the mechanism sent it back.

After about a minute, the countess disconnected the wire, and they all clapped.

"You can see the dent it's made," she said, and they could: a small divot in the rock, with no muscles flexed. Just the chemicals in a jar, driving a machine.

"The larger model is steam-powered," Kane added. "But I believe that electrical current can be reliably harnessed to power machinery. And in fact, many of our experiments with power cells have suggested methods for using electricity itself to separate ore from rock."

"Is there anything electricity can't do?" said one of the women, a gray-haired lady with a soft face and violets embroidered on her collar. Just then, a gong sounded from out in the hall.

"We can't eat it as yet," said the countess with a smile. "But lunch is served."

Kane and Simeon held back as the others went to lunch.

"You weren't impressed?" Kane asked quietly.

"If electricity can drive an iron bar into rock, it can drive an iron bar into human flesh too. Is that why you wanted me to see it?"

"Christ, no, you cynic. Weapons aren't the only things that interest me. The countess comes from an old family with a respected name, but her parents left her with no estates, after some scandal. She's had to build her own business up, using her wits and connections. The family history reminds me somewhat of Lord Byron and his clever daughter."

"Yes," Simeon said casually. He didn't want to talk about Ada. He never wanted to talk about Ada. His friendship, and his grief, were private. "So, the countess herself is what really interests you. She's too young for you, Kane."

"She interests me greatly, but not in that way. The Templars have a massive practical advantage over us. They understand the value of science and industry. Of money. Of investment and innovation. We are, by nature, somewhat solitary, somewhat old-fashioned, I know. But we can't let them get ahead of us. I monitor their achievements and learn from them. That is the role I play in the Brotherhood."

The import suddenly dawned on Simeon, and he took Kane's elbow to hold him back. "Wait. You don't mean – the countess is a Templar?"

"Well, she's from a Templar family. Didn't I tell you? Didn't you guess?"

Simeon shook his head. "I don't suppose I thought you'd invite me to take lunch with our sworn enemies, no."

He regarded the slightly dowdy assemblage of natural philosophy enthusiasts walking in front of them and wondered how many of them were Templars too.

Kane raised his eyebrows. "This is what 'hiding in plain sight' looks like. We learn from our enemies. We strike only in the right time and place. They watch us, and we watch them, and when they strike at us, we strike back. And they know this, so they don't strike at us when they're weakened or rattled. Right now, since Mayr's death, they're very rattled indeed. And the countess is young enough to have the good sense to be more interested in advancements in science than in pointless brawling."

Simeon shook his head. Pointless brawling? He'd slashed a man's throat. It mattered.

"So, it's a game," he said. "And who's winning?"

"That's impossible to say until the final move, isn't it? Come on. I can smell the roast beef from here."

But Simeon was reeling as though he were back on board a ship in a storm. As they came out into the corridor, he walked faster, leaving Kane behind, catching up with the countess just as she was entering the dining room. He caught sight of a gleaming table, with silver covered dishes.

He looked at her, and she looked at him. Her eyes held not a hint of suspicion, but maybe she was just a consummate actress. A Templar. A member of the age-old order that killed Assassins and was ready to sacrifice ordinary people in the service of their greater good. If Assassins believed that nothing was true, Templars believed that the truth was as sharp and singular as the point of a drill. She was his enemy, just as surely as Mayr had been his enemy.

And eventually, the day might come when Kane decided it was time to strike, and he would send Simeon here to this house to drive a knife into the countess's delicate throat.

Simeon needed clarity. He needed to think. He turned to the right and coughed a request to the doorman for his hat and coat. Ignoring Kane calling after him, ignoring the silent, curious stare of the countess, making no polite excuses, he walked out into the snowy afternoon.

Simeon felt better once he was out of the house in the clean, cold air. He wished he'd brought a scarf, and his top hat did little to help his ears. But no matter. He could breathe freely out here and think more clearly.

The countess lived on a wide street that easily accommodated carriages passing each other in both directions. Out here beyond the city gates, the streets were busier than Simeon would have expected, with men and women walking briskly, the smell of hot pies in the air. It was snowing softly, which might have been the reason so many pedestrians had their collars up, their hats low and their faces taut.

However, Simeon suspected it had something to do with the sound of soldiers shouting drill commands a few blocks away. His butcher friend, Joseph Ettenreich, had told Simeon that it had not been so common to see soldiers in Vienna, back in the old days. Ever since the uprisings five years ago, back in 1848, there were always knots of them around every corner, and the emperor took any excuse for a parade.

Simeon was somewhat grateful for the military activity, as it told him in which direction he could find the glacis. Part of the ring of open ground around the central fortified city was a drilling ground. If he walked that way, he'd find the city walls, and then home – or the closest thing he had to a home. He didn't even particularly mind that the drill blocked his way, so he had to walk around them. It gave him more time to walk and think.

It was natural to have doubts, Kane always said. In fact, it was required of an Assassin. But what was he doubting? Kane's judgment: certainly. His own morality: absolutely. The creed itself: well, no, not when it came to it. He didn't doubt that. He did believe that the world was a place in which something could be true one day and false the next. He was not the same man he had been the day before, a year before, a decade before. He was a collection of thoughts and experiences and sensations, all informed by his life history. If that was wisdom, then he would use that to make his own judgments.

But other aspects of the creed were more difficult to countenance. Never shed the blood of an innocent: who was innocent? So far as he knew, Countess von Visler was guilty of nothing worse than putting some miners out of work. Very likely, if Simeon were ordered to kill her, he could rationalize it by making a list of her sins. But the terrifying thing was the sheer number of people in this city – in every city – of whom that would be true.

As for the rule to never compromise the Brotherhood, well, perhaps he already had, by leaving so abruptly today. Was loyalty to Kane the same as loyalty to the Brotherhood?

Simeon climbed a stone staircase and emerged on one of the city bastions. The soldiers below were a moving sea of men whose names didn't matter, bright colored uniforms marching amid the falling snow. They stood upright in their uniforms and their drums beat a melancholy rumble. Military music drifted up, slightly out of phase somehow, but maybe it was Simeon who was off kilter.

He walked along the edge of the bastion, looking down across the green and brown belt of the glacis to the low and scattered suburbs beyond, to where the snowy sky hid the horizon. Other people were strolling too, watching the drill below. He had decided he should change course to avoid a small clump of people up ahead of him, when he spotted a man running past him, toward the crowd – and recognized him.

It was Ettenreich, the butcher. Always so sleek and dignified, it was strange to see him running flat out. Simeon looked behind him to make sure he wasn't being chased, but there were no obvious pursuers. Even so, Simeon picked up his own pace. Ettenreich was running for a reason.

Then the reason became clear, and Simeon fell back again, relieved. There was Libenyi, up ahead. Ettenreich must have spotted his friend and was just jogging to catch up with him and say hello. Libenyi had his back turned and was standing with the half-dozen people Simeon had been trying to avoid. He'd assumed they were watching the drill down below, but he saw now that they were looking further along the bastion, at something Simeon couldn't see.

Something was wrong… very wrong. He'd been learning observation under Kane's tutelage, yet he'd failed to observe something. Simeon put his hand around the knife in his coat pocket and strode toward them.

When Ettenreich caught up with Libenyi, the tailor didn't greet him. He just waved him away like he would an irritating fly. Had they quarreled or something? Now Libenyi broke with the little crowd and strode off, and Ettenreich was staring after him, dazed or baffled.

Simeon caught sight of two uniforms – two military men, standing up ahead of the little watching crowd, alone. Gold braid and high hats. They were studying the drill below.

No, they were reviewing the troops. That young man with the serious face was the emperor.

The young and hated emperor, walking out on the bastion, a single aide at his side.

Libenyi strode toward them like a man with a purpose. He drew a knife. Tiny snowflakes fell.

Simeon was running now, trying to stop Libenyi from stabbing the emperor, here in plain view of dozens of people. There was no way Libenyi would emerge from this situation with his life and freedom. A moment. That's all Simeon had. If he could distract Libenyi – pull him down – there was still time.

A woman saw the knife and screamed.

The scream alerted the emperor, and both he and the aide standing next to him turned. Libenyi leapt forward, his knife high, and stabbed Emperor Franz Joseph in the neck.

CHAPTER EIGHT

There was blood on the emperor's collar, and on the hand that he raised to the wound. Blood splashed on the snowy ground too. The aide standing beside him pushed the emperor to safety and Simeon tried to do the same for Libenyi, barreling into him like a rugby player, but Libenyi just stumbled and dropped the knife.

Then there were people all around them, and after a moment's confusion Libenyi was on the ground, blood coming out of his temple. Ettenreich held Libenyi down, twisting his arm behind his back while looking up at the crowd, as if to show them that Libenyi was no danger to anyone. And Libenyi made no sign of resisting. Simeon pushed the little crowd back. He swore to himself that the first one to land a kick or a punch on Libenyi would have to deal with him, and he could see Ettenreich making the same resolution. But nobody moved.

The aide in the greatcoat and military hat who had been standing beside the emperor walked the few steps to them. He looked at Ettenreich holding Libenyi down and said, "Good man. You've done the empire a great service." Then he knelt beside Libenyi and hissed, "Was there poison on the blade?"

Libenyi's face was down on the snowy ground. He said nothing for a long time, then, weakly: "Long live the Hungarian republic."

The aide grimaced and stood up, drawing his saber.

"Look at what he used," Simeon stalled. He pointed at the knife on the ground. It was, pathetically, an ordinary kitchen knife, the kind used to chop vegetables, with a plain black handle. Newly sharpened metal gleamed on both the cutting side and the top of the blade, suggesting Libenyi had given it a double edge himself.

The aide looked at Simeon dubiously, then knelt and picked up the bloody knife by the handle.

"I see no poison on it," Simeon said.

The aide said, "The doctor will be the judge."

Simeon turned to see who was helping the emperor – or whether he was beyond help. But he was already back on his feet, with a group of soldiers around him. They must have run up the bastion stairs when they heard the commotion.

Emperor Franz Joseph was a young man, in his early twenties, much the same age as Simeon. But the emperor looked even younger. His boyish face showed no fear, no hatred, only confusion. He held a bloody handkerchief to his neck. That stiff collar might have turned the blade just enough. But truth be told, Libenyi had struck like a man who wasn't sure he actually wanted to kill. Simeon recognized it, the hesitation at the last moment, the slight adjustment of angle, the weakness in the blow. It was almost a mirror of the business with the fountain pen, the day he had killed Mayr. But unlike Simeon, Libenyi would not have a second opportunity to finish the job.

More soldiers came and dispersed the crowd, taking Libenyi away in shackles.

Libenyi's sister looked like him. She made Simeon a cup of tea in the small apartment she had shared with her brother. She folded up a pattern book with a pencil and pins inside it, clearing the little table so they could rest their cups. There wasn't much else in the room: a screen, with a bed on either side of it, and a bookshelf with works in various languages. A violin case leaned against the wall – Libenyi's, or his sister's? He had thought he knew the man, but it was all superficial. Shared grumblings about taxes and police and the price of bread.

She stared at Simeon with large hazel eyes. "But what will they do with my brother, Mr Straw?"

"Try him, I suppose. Not that there's much question of his guilt."

"And then?"

Simeon said nothing. She knew well enough what it meant when a man stabbed an emperor in front of witnesses. Janos Libenyi would hang.

"I don't understand," she said, shaking her head. "Why would he do this?"

"I was hoping you would tell me."

She looked at Simeon, this stranger in a gray suit who had brought her the news of her brother's arrest for attempted assassination. He wished he could give her a concrete reason to trust him, but every time he tried to say that he was a friend, that he would do whatever he could for her brother, it sounded hollow. So, he just waited for her to make her own mind up.

"It was nothing new for Janos to talk to radicals," she said. "He'd been going to meetings since we came to Vienna, despite my worries. I tried to tell him we should stay quiet, not attract notice. I tried to tell him that the Hungarian dream was over. And to be honest, I think he agreed with me, for a long time. After a while, he attended the meetings the way some men attend church, to say the words and promise himself that a better life was coming. A way to get through the day. Do you know what I mean?"

"I do."

"But then–" She paused.

"Then?"

"He met someone new. I don't know the man's name. I don't think he was one of the radicals. Janos was excited. He kept telling me that Vienna had men of action in it after all."

Simeon went cold. Surely Janos hadn't been inspired by Simeon himself! "When was this?"

"Oh, some months ago."

This was a relief, albeit a confusing one.

"So he's been planning this for months too?" Simeon asked.

"I don't know. At first, it was just some vague talk about a visionary, a great leader. A few weeks ago, he said this brilliant man had a plan for him – for Janos. A plan that would make life better for all of us. I thought it was a scheme of some kind, a job at the best, a shady deal at the worst. I couldn't have imagined that he meant… this. But what else could it have been?"

Simeon nodded, thinking. "And he kept the details from you, and he told me nothing about it at all. Miss Libenyi, the police will come and talk to you. They may even arrest you. Tell them the truth, but protect yourself above all. That's what your brother wants, I'm sure."

"My brother clearly doesn't care what I want," she said, her face like stone. "I will make my mourning clothes."

Simeon didn't have any mourning clothes himself, and with Libenyi in jail, it would be a little more difficult for Kane to acquire him some. In any case, he didn't intend to mourn. He intended to break the tailor out.

On that snowy afternoon on the bastion, Simeon's fears had not been for the emperor. If Kane had come to Simeon and made a case for the young ruler's assassination, Simeon would have listened. The revolutions that had spread across Europe in 1848 had touched every part of the Austrian Empire. There had been revolution in Hungary, a war for independence in Italy, and unrest in Vienna, enough that the imperial family had to relocate to keep itself safe. Eventually, the former emperor abdicated – he had mental and physical health conditions, and either his advisors thought he was incapable of bringing his empire to heel, or they feared that people wouldn't believe him strong enough even if he were. The emperor's nephew, Franz Joseph, had been given the throne. He quickly set about tearing up the constitution that had been dangled in front of the rebels, using force to subdue every city and town under his thumb.

It was arguable that the world would be a better place without Emperor Franz Joseph in it, but Simeon wasn't being called upon to judge whether the consequences of that assassination would be worth its costs. Not right now, anyway. He only cared about Janos Libenyi, a good and brave man who had plainly been encouraged – manipulated, even – into attempting the assassination. And attempting it in the most ill-considered way, without any training or support.

And now he would hang for it.

Kane didn't mention Simeon's abrupt departure from the countess's luncheon. When Simeon arrived back at the laboratory, fresh from his conversation with Libenyi's sister, Kane put a bottle of cognac and two glasses on the table, pushing a pile of his notes to one side.

"You've heard," Simeon said.

"The whole city's heard, yes. They're having a mass of thanksgiving for the rescue of the emperor. Bells and drinking songs. I'm sure Johann Strauss will have a new composition in honor of Franz Joseph by the end of the week. And where have you been?"

"Wandering and talking to people."

"Find out anything interesting?"

"Given myself a bad headache, that's all." Simeon took a swig of cognac and thought for a moment, regarding Kane appraisingly. "You'd tell me, if the Brotherhood had its hand in this. Wouldn't you?"

Kane smiled. "I don't blame you for asking, but if the Brotherhood decided the emperor had to die, we wouldn't send a wild-eyed tailor out with a cheap kitchen knife and tell him to lunge at the man in broad daylight in the middle of the street."

"No, I didn't think so." Simeon rubbed his hands through his hair, as if he could push his headache away. "It's just that Libenyi mentioned something to his sister about a man who made him promises, who may have encouraged him to try something like this."

"Did she say who this man was? What he looked like?"

Simeon shook his head. "She doesn't know anything about him. I'll ask Libenyi himself, though."

"And how do you propose to get an interview with a man in jail for treason? In a city under martial law?"

"He won't be in jail when I ask him the question."

There was a moment of silence, as Kane weighed what Simeon was saying.

"You intend to do something rash."

How could Kane keep his cool detachment, knowing a good man's life was at stake? "He'll fucking hang otherwise."

"Yes. When people clumsily try to murder the emperor in front of witnesses, that tends to happen."

Not in England, Simeon thought. Queen Victoria had survived five assassination attempts, and all the men had been punished with hard labor or banishment to the penal colonies. She seemed almost to take pity on each of her attackers. But England had largely escaped the waves of revolutions, and maybe its monarch could better afford mercy. Emperor Franz Joseph didn't seem like the sort of man who'd be inclined to take such chances.

"You know Libenyi too," Simeon said. "This doesn't bother you?"

"It bothers me a great deal. But I'm a practical man, Straw. I may not weep and gnash my teeth, but I'll make sure his sister has an allowance for the rest of her days. Does that meet with your approval?"

Simeon, chastened, said, "That would be very welcome, thank you."

"And, of course, I am going to help you break him out of jail."

The prison was five stories high, a pallid block broken only by narrow windows. Simeon and Kane stood on the roof at night, looking down at the gaslit courtyard below. Timing their movements with the clanging of a nearby church bell to disguise any sound, they had rigged a long cable from the roof of a nearby house, hooked a box of equipment onto it, and guided it over the street and courtyard to the prison roof. Simeon was in front and Kane behind, fussing over his wires and jars the whole time.

Simeon checked the gun that Kane had given him (with promises that this was a good model this time). A gleaming black Adams revolver, faster to fire than anything Simeon had shot before, loaded and ready. Guns were not just for cowards and soldiers, Kane had acknowledged, handing it over. They were also for emergencies.

Kane leaned backward, his hands on his hips, groaning. "I advise you never to turn forty, Straw."

"I'm doing my best. I may not reach thirty if tonight goes badly. What do we do with all this?"

"It stays on the roof. I descend on the rope, as far as the window. And you, Straw, will perform a rite of passage common to every Assassin. You are on distraction duty."

Simeon had spent two nights drinking in the tavern nearest the prison, until he had bought enough rounds for one of the guards to learn which window led to Libenyi's cell. It was on the third story, so Kane wouldn't have far to go. He'd be hooked to a wire around his waist, and carrying two cables, connected to a metal tube about the size and shape of a blunderbuss. He called it an arc gun, but it wasn't exactly a gun. When Kane hooked the other ends of the cables to a half dozen of his power cells – the same kind that the countess had used for her demonstration – the gun produced a blinding light, an arc of electricity jumping between two carbon rods affixed into the far end of the device.

Kane assured Simeon he had no intention of using his arc gun on humans, at least not that night. He would use it to cut the bars on Libenyi's window, by melting them near each end. It would be quick, he said. Much quicker than a file, or a hammer and chisel.

But not much quieter. Which meant that Simeon had to disguise the noise, and make sure Kane's activities didn't attract attention.

Kane wrapped a rope around the equipment box and a nearby chimney until he was satisfied their tools were secure. Then he set the plungers in his power cells. With the unconnected end of the cables in one hand, and his arc gun in the other, he gestured that Simeon should look in the box.

Simeon leaned over the edge and pulled out three stiff paper tubes, with twists at either end. "These are smoke bombs?"

"Yes, to my own design. I've added a bit of a kick, to make sure there's noise. A bit of percussion, you might call it."

Simeon cocked his head. "So, they're grenades?"

"No, nothing like that. Well, a little like that. But not likely to be lethal. Now, tempting though it is to clear the guards right out of the building with this, the last thing we want is guards milling out in the courtyard where they might see me hanging halfway down the wall with a bright light in my hands. So let it off on the street on the furthest side of the building, if you could, to draw their attention that way. The main thing is just to create enough noise and confusion."

Simeon nodded. "When?"

"What time do you have now?"

He pulled out his pocket watch and tilted it until it caught enough light from the waxing moon. "Six minutes past midnight."

"Good, I have the same. At a quarter past, let the first one off. Wait a minute or two between each. That ought to buy me enough time."

Simeon didn't bother with a rope. He walked carefully to the opposite side of the roof, where the jail wall was an easy enough jump, and the street was just beyond that. This building hadn't always been a prison; it used to be a convent, attached to the nearby church with the convenient bells. The only signs of its present purpose were the guard boxes at the gate, the lampposts inside the courtyard, and, of course, the bars on all the windows.

The prison was on the far side of the glacis, in a suburb. All the same, it was a fairly busy thoroughfare in the day. At midnight, in a city where a man could be arrested for breathing, it was quiet. There was a bookshop, closed up, and a legal office (very handy for the prison, no doubt), and a few other offices with brass name plates but no indication of what sort of work their occupants did. A few streets down was a tavern with a sign that Simeon could just barely make out in the gaslight, but it seemed tranquil: no one was loitering outside. No fights or deal making.

Who would the distraction bring running? Guards from the prison, probably. Police, if there were any nearby. Maybe a few people from the tavern.

Simeon checked his watch, waited a minute, put it away again. Then he pulled a box of matches from his pocket, drew a deep breath, lit the bomb, and tossed it down into the middle of the empty street.

He'd expected a simple bang, something like the little black powder packets the boys back home had used to play pranks on unsuspecting old ladies. Instead, whatever devilry Kane had put into that tube made a continuous racket, a repetitive series of loud bangs and rumbles like the engine room of a ship.

It took less than a minute for the guards to come running: four of them, all with their pistols out. Half the entire street was filled with reddish smoke, and they slowed as they approached, looking for danger. They didn't look up. Simeon sat on a chimney, dangling his legs, watching the shapes of the men below.

They found the smoke bomb just as it went quiet, and Simeon could hear them grumble to themselves.

For just a few seconds after the smoke bomb stopped, he heard a raspy growl from the direction of the prison. Kane at work.

The second smoke bomb fell a few houses north of the first, as Simeon trotted along the center line of a roof. He ducked behind another chimney as the guards turned again.

Simeon went through six matches trying to light the third smoke bomb. The wick wouldn't take; it shriveled away to nothing, and then he tried digging it out but there wasn't anything to dig.

The guards were joined now by two of the new federal police, the hated gendarmerie, nearly indistinguishable from soldiers in their morose unforms. After a brief conversation, the guards walked back toward the prison, and the gendarmes stayed as the smoke cleared, on guard for another disturbance. But there wouldn't be another disturbance. Frustrated, Simeon set the inert smoke bomb to one side and considered his options.

It was possible that Kane and his device had already had enough time to cut through the bars. Maybe he was waiting on the prison roof with Libenyi right now.

Or maybe Kane needed every second those smoke bombs could give him – or more.

There was nothing for it. He'd have to create another distraction some other way. A noisy distraction, and he only had so many bullets. Simeon slid down the roof. He had already been thinking of the rooftops as a refuge, as the city above the city, as Kane had taught him. But he was needed below. He hung carefully before dropping, landed on a garden wall and then jumped right into the circle of light cast by a streetlamp.

He sang at the top of his voice: "Oh a soldier and a sailor went walking out one day. Says the soldier to the sailor, I mean for to pray, for the rights of all sailors and the wrongs of all men, and whatever I pray for you must answer 'Amen.'"

Nobody joined in. The gendarmes advanced on him, one from either side of the street. They had clubs in their hands but half-amused expressions on their faces.

"Come on then, my lad," said one in German. "You've had enough."

Simeon took a deep breath and sang even louder. "Well then, first of all, let us pray for some beer. Amen, said the sailor, may it bring us good cheer! And if we have one cask, then may we have ten! Let's have a bloody brewery, said the sailor, Amen!"

The gendarmes were nearly at him now. They'd seen his face and heard him singing in English. All right then, bugger it. Simeon may have started out pretending to be drunk, but as he sang the song he'd learned back in the army, he lost all desire to be anything but deadly sober.

He stepped backward, out of the light, away from his pursuers – almost dancing, he was moving so quickly. He couldn't remember all the words correctly, but he made up his own. "Now pray for the lawyers who plead for our cause, who take our hard earnings and give us hard laws, if they get one beating may they also get ten, let's have a bloody bloodbath, said the sailor, Amen."

Simeon's voice was becoming hoarse. As the two gendarmes lunged for him, he stopped, and ran forward. Then left, toward the front of the jail. He pulled his revolver and kept singing, fairly screaming now. "Now pray for the gendarmes who send us to jail, yes, pray for those bastards whose souls are for sale–"

As he ran, he glanced to the left, up to the window where Kane should have been long gone. But he wasn't. He was still there, with his blue light just visible in the smoky gloom. Simeon faltered, and now two guards were running into the street–

"If they take one bullet may they also get ten, to the devil with gendarmes, said the sailor–"

Someone pushed him face-down into the cold cobblestones. He wriggled into a position where he could shoot at the man on his back. He squeezed the trigger, winced from the noise, and felt the man shudder, and roll off him. He could hear the policeman swearing – not dead, then. As Simeon struggled to get off the ground, another man's knee to his back from behind knocked the breath out of his ribs and the gun out of his hand.

If they had locked Simeon into the same prison where Libenyi was, he might have had some idea whether Kane had succeeded. Instead, he spent a sleepless night pacing a tiny cell in an anonymous police station, tucked into an old stone gatehouse out at the edge of the city. It was pitch black in the cell until dawn came, and even then, very little light came from the narrow window.

Simeon must have shut his eyes at last, because he opened them to see Kane standing at the open cell door, with a guard just behind him.

"You're free," Kane said, brusquely. "Come on."

They walked out of the station, into the bright cold morning. Simeon blinked. His head still ached from the knock the night before. There were carters and carriages on the road, everything hideously normal. The buildings were low and scattered, but the center of Vienna sat on the horizon.

"They nearly got me too, I'm afraid," Kane said. "I had to run, and they kept after me all night. Couldn't get here sooner. Come on."

Simeon whispered, "Libenyi?"

When Kane said nothing, Simeon stopped walking. Kane stopped too, and said very carefully, "By the time the gendarmes gave up the chase, there was nothing I could do. It was too late."

"Bloody hell." Simeon's throat closed. *Too late.* It was difficult to imagine those dark eyes flashing no more, those curls never bouncing again in time to the tailor's animated conversation. Those quick fingers, that brave heart. All for nothing. All his hopes, and plans, and his fight to survive. His move to the heart of the empire that he viewed as the oppressor, because he couldn't see any other way for him and his sister to live.

"Where did they do it?"

"Not far from here. The Spinner on the Cross – the old tower on the hill. A traditional place for hangings."

"I want to go there."

"Straw, there's no point drawing attention to ourselves… not that that worried you last night."

"I was trying to buy you time. It didn't work, did it?"

Kane shook his head. "Not your fault," he said tightly. "The damned thing kept going out, starting and stopping. Shorted out eventually. I really thought it would work. It made a dent, but I couldn't bend the bars in time, and then… well, it is done. Besides, they'll have cut his body down by now. Come on. My carriage is a few streets away – couldn't have it waiting near a police station."

Kane's ego had seemed endearing once. His utter confidence in his own ingenuity, his careful management of social ties, his cultivated reputation. Now it just worsened the terrible taste in Simeon's mouth. If Kane hadn't insisted on relying on his inventions – if he had less confidence and more courage – maybe Libenyi would still be alive. It wasn't enough to simply stay one's hand from the blood of an innocent. One had to put one's hand in harm's way. To protect them.

As though he were reading Simeon's thoughts, Kane said,

"He knew the consequences of his actions. He did what he felt he had to do. I hope it brought him peace."

"I've seen men hanged," Simeon said. "Nothing peaceful about it."

Chapter Nine

Pierrette had seriously considered leaving the troupe a few months after Ada's death. She couldn't find any mention of Simeon Price anywhere, except for a few people who had known him in his younger days in England, and those people were all sure he had perished on the *Birkenhead*. One weekend, she tracked a lead to a pub in Ealing, and met with a most unpleasant man who said his son Simeon was definitely dead. He seemed to think that she was asking because Simeon had done her wrong somehow. He wouldn't believe that she didn't want any money from him. She just wanted to find Simeon. But Simeon was well and truly dead. All the evidence pointed that way.

And maybe the Magus was dead, too, or had had a change of heart, as Ada had. Maybe the mysterious weapon was as ephemeral an idea as the Analytical Engine that Ada and Charles Babbage had been trying to convince someone to finance. If some scientist had developed a terrible new weapon, surely the world would know it by now?

The only thing that couldn't be explained away was Simeon's letter. If it hadn't been for that scrap of paper, Pierrette would have given up altogether. Instead, she convinced Major Wallin it was time to travel.

In truth, he wasn't that hard to convince. After two years in London, the shine had come off the hippodrome in Hyde Park and the crowds had thinned. France was still uncertain; not content with cementing his power, the president had recently made himself Emperor Napoleon III. Then, in October of 1853, France and England went to war with Russia.

Major Wallin made his choice. He took the troupe by ship to Rome, where they played for three weeks in a marvelous open-air hippodrome, and Pierrette felt like a gladiator, even though their act was, by design, extremely French. ("One doesn't give the audience what they already have," Major Wallin said.) The following March, after a successful run, the troupe went north to Brussels by caravan. It took the animals several days to stop being skittish on arrival in any new city, and the humans had to learn the dimensions and foibles of every new theatre and hippodrome too.

After Brussels, it was Berlin. Wherever they went, Pierrette searched for Simeon's name in the agony columns, death notices and crime stories of all the newspapers – after Ariel had finished combing them for reviews of Aurora performances for the company's scrapbook. Ariel also took a keen personal interest in the debate in the newspaper columns over what word ought to be "the epicene pronoun". The Sprite of the Air even had an American correspondent who was considering "thon", though the performer seemed to favor a simple "they".

But the newspapers were no help to Pierrette. Spending a

few weeks in a strange city, while performing, didn't leave much time for looking for Simeon. So, Pierrette decided that the best thing to do was advertise. Not in the newspapers, though – any notice would surely get lost in that sea of gray.

Instead, she called out for Simeon every night in letters of fire.

By the time the troupe came to Vienna that May, she had almost forgotten the origins of her most popular act, the Flying Flame.

Major Wallin had originally learned his trade in the old Vienna circus, in the vast suburban meadow they called the Prater, now an area full of bright shops and coffee houses and performers of all kinds. That building had been demolished in 1852. Two years later, the new Circus Renz, owned by the German family that was coming to dominate all circus life in Europe, went up a short walk away, in the middle of Leopoldstadt, on the north side of the Danube.

The Circus Renz reminded Pierrette of a fairytale castle, its entrance flanked by two towers topped with flags. It seemed circular from a distance, and had a domed roof, but the building itself had twelve sides. Its stands could accommodate more than three thousand people. Inside, hanging from the center of that dome, was a chandelier, with more than a hundred and fifty gaslights. Everything inside the circus was dazzling, warm and bright, the world outside was blossoms and sunshine, and the Austrian officers in their crisp uniforms were all over the place.

The Renz company had its own haute école performers, including several women, all of whom dressed like ladies going out for tea, in long skirts and stylish top hats. As much as

Major Wallin might have liked to make a name for his troupe in that tradition, it was clear that their own show's niche was in acrobatics, in tricks, in what Major Wallin called, with resignation, "stunts". Hugh Robinson was in the best form of his life, able to support both Jovita and Pierrette on his shoulders while he rode at a gallop. Tillie put a pretty bay pony through her paces. Jovita vaulted from one horse to the other in a way that made one marvel at the freedom of the human spirit. Ariel somehow managed to make it seem as though they were about to drop off the rope, and that gravity had no pull on them.

Hugh and Ariel had combined their talents, in an act that never would have been developed if Major Wallin hadn't made a strict rule that knives could never be thrown right at anyone, and there would be no wheel of death in an Aurora performance. Since Hugh had taken up knife-throwing and was very good at it, this created a disagreement, which at one point got heated when Hugh accused Major Wallin of being afraid that audiences wouldn't want to see a Black man with a knife in his hand. But Ariel had come up with a way to show off Hugh's skills that Major Wallin agreed to, and peace was made. At the end of their act, Ariel hopped from the rope to the top of a perfectly smooth wall, and then mimed a good show of not being able to get down again. Hugh reappeared, and threw knives perfectly positioned to make a staircase – or at least a staircase for someone as nimble as Ariel.

It was a comedy act too, because Hugh only had four knives, so after every set of four, Ariel had to pull out the top two, balance, then throw them into a hay bale, where Hugh would collect them. After the last set of knives, Ariel would pretend to slip off, only to land in a handstand on Hugh's shoulders.

The crowd loved it. But Pierrette was the star. She was the Flying Flame.

The year before, they had finally dropped Mazeppa when it stopped getting ovations; tradition was one thing, but audiences were fickle. By then, they had a new glory. At the end of every show, Pierrette rode out on a black horse, dressed all in red. She cracked her whip (nowhere near the actual horse) and it blazed, and the audience gasped. As she passed each of her colleagues, they handed her a new prop – a fan-shaped frame with six wicks, a staff with fire at either end – and she lit the new one and extinguished the old, all while jumping through lit hoops set up at intervals.

Then she grabbed each of the hoops, danced in and around them, threw them to the ground, and grabbed up her fire wand.

With this, she wrote names. They were random, although sometimes she caught the names people yelled out to her, and sometimes she obliged. First names, surnames, sometimes both. Charles. Ted. Mary Roberts. She'd throw in an unusual name from time to time, to add to the impression that there was some strange link she had with the audience. After all, if Charles and Mary had seen their names, it seemed only reasonable that there must be a Jabez or a Clementine. And sometimes, she got lucky, and a Jabez or Clementine let out a hearty cheer.

She mixed up the names and tried to match them to the city they were in, so in Rome there had been Carlos, Karl in Berlin. But one name never changed. The final name, burning in the air as Pierrette's arms tried to keep up with the weight of her staff, was always Simeon Price.

Nobody in the troupe knew why she'd chosen that name, and

she knew they'd taken bets on who this Simeon was and when he would turn up. But she didn't mind. And they all cheered her on, as Pierrette clearly loved the act, and so did audiences. She'd had more than one burn, but nothing serious. It kept her on her toes. She always said Tillie was in more danger than she was, in her full skirt and passing so close to the gaslights that ringed the performance area. Pierrette's sleek red costume wouldn't go up as easily.

As for the wooden circus building, well, they kept sand and water buckets handy. And Pierrette knew her business. She was careful. Careful enough.

After their fourth night in Vienna, as all the performers were backstage removing their makeup, they heard loud voices at the backstage door. It was Mrs Robinson and Major Wallin, arguing with someone in English.

The argument turned to sharp yells as a young man burst into the dressing room and demanded to see the Flying Flame. Pierrette stood up, wrapped in a black robe, a gift from Herr Renz, who had traveled.

"You aren't allowed back here," she said calmly. It wasn't the first time a man from the audience had come searching for her, or Jovita, or even Tillie – disgusting creatures. "You must leave."

"I want to know why you're spelling out the name of Simeon Price," he demanded, in better German than hers.

This question didn't slow down Major Wallin at all, and he grabbed the interloper's arms and bent them behind his back. Of course, the mystery of why she always spelled that name had spread outside the circus as well as in. But Pierrette's heart sped up.

"Major," she said in French, as calmly as she could manage.

"Please show this man into the tearoom. No, it's all right. You can stand outside the door."

The tearoom had a little cast iron stove, a kettle, a set of china cups and saucers with scenes from Aesop's fables painted on them, and a teapot to match. The teapot belonged to Nell Robinson. There were several shabby chairs, a table with a red and orange Indian cloth thrown over it, and several lamps and candles.

The room was mainly used for talking down performers who had what the Aurora Troupe had come to call "the tinky-onders." This had been coined while they were in London, when Major Wallin had kindly tried to explain the condition to a performer from another troupe. Major Wallin had taken refuge in the Swedish word for "overthinking," which apparently sounded something like "tinkyonders" to the poor Briton suffering from it. It was a state they all feared: the moment when you became hideously aware of precisely where your body was and what it was doing, which happened the moment before one suddenly became unable to continue moving it in the way one wanted. The performer's body could turn into a rock in midair, and everyone was at risk.

Pierrette offered the chair to the stranger and stoked up the fire, then put the kettle on the stove.

When she turned back, he still hadn't sat down. He was glowering at her. A broad-shouldered man in his mid-twenties, with sandy hair, a bit long. Dark blue eyes. Impressive sideburns but otherwise clean-shaven. He was dressed in a clean frock coat, with black and gray plaid trousers and waistcoat, and a simple tie.

"Are *you* … Simeon Price?" she asked in English, crossing her arms and glaring back at him.

"Tell me why you spell out that name." He spoke slowly, as though uncertain whether she'd understand. Making an assumption based on her accent, most likely.

She tried not to sound petulant as she responded, "I spell out a great many names, sir. I can read and write, and by the way, I've been speaking English since I was quite young."

He nodded an acknowledgment. "But always that one name at the end, a mystery that half of Vienna finds fascinating. A friend of mine, a very sober-minded butcher, saw your show two nights ago and has concocted a romantic tale about it. He was telling all this to me this evening over a glass of beer and imagine my surprise when I heard that name. A name my friend the butcher has no reason to know. And neither does anyone else in Vienna. And I'd like to know why you do."

"I know it because my friend Ada, the Countess of Lovelace, asked me to find a man by that name," she spat back.

At that, the young man sank into one of the shabby chairs. "Ada?" he said softly.

"Yes. You did know her, then… Mr Price?"

He took a long while before answering, hanging his head. Then he looked up at her. "But how could you be so reckless? I'm dead for a reason, you know! Didn't it occur to you I might not want my name made famous all over Europe?"

It hadn't been Pierrette's intention to make his name famous. It had been her intention to make *herself* famous, and his name was along for the ride. She hadn't ever truly considered how he would feel about it.

"I suppose you're a deserter from the army, is that it? Yes, of course, I could see why it must frighten you, then, that someone knows you're alive."

"I'm not a coward."

"I didn't say you were. Just a frightened man in hiding, then." She frowned, suddenly annoyed at her own peevishness, and turned back to the boiling kettle to make them a pot of Assam tea. Simeon Price wasn't living up to her expectations, and somehow that made her grieve Ada all over again. But he was grieving too – that much was clear.

"Ada died two years ago," she said more softly, putting the teapot on the table.

"I read about it in a newspaper," he said with a nod, then paused. "She was always in poor health, her whole life. But all the same, it never seemed that she would actually… she had so much to do and discover. So much to give the world. You know what I mean, if you knew her."

"I do know, yes." Pierrette went over to the row of locked trunks at the end of the room, where the performers kept their street clothes and any valuables they didn't want to leave in their hotel or lodgings. From the back of her own jumbled trunk, she retrieved Ada's notebook, its pale blue covers only slightly more battered than they'd been when its creator had been alive. She cradled it in both hands, like a holy object, and held it out in front of him.

"This was hers?" he asked.

She nodded. "It's full of tables, numbers, notes, drawings. I can't make heads or tails of any of it." She pulled the book back, clasped it against her chest. "But you are Simeon Price, yes? How did you first meet Ada?"

His eyes flashed. "I was a child. I lived in her household, for a while – her mother had offered to educate me."

"And then you were sent away. Because?" She tested him.

"Because I wouldn't betray a confidence."

"Good." Pierrette put the notebook on the table. "Then I'll give you a new confidence to keep, Mr Price. Ada corresponded with men of science all over the world. You have heard of her notes on Charles Babbage's work?"

"I have."

"One of the men who wrote to her made a great impression on her, but never gave her his name. She knew him only as a nickname, 'the Magus'. She said he was a brilliant intellect, but she eventually realized that his heart was evil. By then, she'd already helped him with his work – work that she came to understand was the blueprint for a terrible weapon. She wouldn't burn this notebook, because she thought it might help you dismantle the weapon."

"Me!" Mr Price's eyebrows danced. "I'm no scientist."

"But she said you understood her mind."

He shook his head. "She thought too much of me." He picked up the notebook, turned some of the pages. "Do we know which of these is about the weapon? Or is it all…?"

"I don't know. I've read some of it, and it seems to refer to many different projects. A lot of it is in some sort of code. And I think the drawings on different pages may fit together in some way. It's a puzzle."

"The code, I can probably break. It's most likely the one we used together. But as for the rest, if it's a puzzle, it's a puzzle that I'm incapable of solving. I'm sorry." He let the closed notebook rest on his lap.

Pierrette pursed her lips and poured the tea. "She said you understood her mind, not her work. She didn't say that you'd be able to decipher the book, exactly. Instead, she said that you would know what to do."

"Well, I don't."

"Then she was wrong about you. She was wrong about a great many things, actually. Absolutely terrible at the racetrack. Picked the wrong horse every time."

Pierrette sipped her tea. It was hot, but not strong enough.

Mr Price took a deep breath. "I do know one person who might be able to shed some light on this. A philosopher and a man of science himself. I've often thought that he and Ada would have been great friends, had they known each other. And he keeps an eye on the sorts of people who develop terrible weapons. He might know who the Magus is."

"You trust this man?"

He paused. "I owe him everything. If you want me to do something about this book, that's the best course I can think of."

Pierrette nodded. The relief felt like landing on her feet. "Good. We're here for three more days, and then we leave. Off to Prague. How long do you need?"

"I'll ask him about it tomorrow. Tomorrow night, after the performance, can you meet me?"

"Why not come here?"

"I'd rather not associate myself with your act, and the name of Simeon Price, any more than I already have. Here, my name is Jack Straw. You have… ordinary clothing, don't you?"

She raised an eyebrow. "Yes. I have *ordinary* clothing. Why, do I need a ballgown to be admitted to your friend's presence?"

He smiled, just a little, for the first time since she'd met him. "A warm coat will do. It still gets chilly in the evenings. Let's see. If you walk down the Prater Strasse until you get to the Danube Canal, you'll see a boatman wearing a battered hat with a wide brim and a pink ribbon. That's Zoran: you can trust him. Tell him to take you to the new Elizabeth Bridge. It's on the Wien River, on the far side of the old city. I'll meet you on that bridge."

She laughed. "That all seems rather complicated. Who are we avoiding?"

"Just meet me on the bridge tomorrow night and I'll tell you what I've learned, Miss… um, Mademoiselle…"

"Pierrette Arnaud. Until tomorrow, then."

CHAPTER TEN

It was habit for Simeon now, moving through Vienna like a burrowing animal in a warren, hiding his activities from the Templars, corrupt officials and Kane's business rivals. She might well laugh, this little French woman, but in Vienna, where one had to register every use of post-horses or hotel rooms, where there were ledgers in the police office that recorded all your movements, there was plenty of cause for prudence – especially if Ada's story about this Magus figure had something to it.

Simeon hadn't seen Kane in over a week. The last time had been to return Kane's copy of an old Italian fighting manual, *De Arte Gladiatoria Dimicandi*, and receive his assignments for the coming days: a man to follow, a bribe to deliver, six buildings to climb. Simeon could sense that by doing the bare minimum Kane asked of him, he was slowing down his own training, and delaying the day that Kane would finally induct him into the Brotherhood. But he didn't care. He felt lately like he was fighting through water, every movement slow.

He knocked on his mentor's apartment door around ten

o'clock in the morning and felt an odd pang when Kane seemed genuinely pleased to see him. "I didn't know you were coming – here, sit down. This is a pleasant surprise."

"If you have a moment, I just came to talk." He'd brought Ada's notebook, tucked into his satchel. The mystery that had kept him up half the night and given him bad dreams the other half.

Kane had been growing out his mustache, or simply failing to trim it; it covered most of his mouth at its long ends. There was a bit of gray in it too – that was new. "Like the old days. I always have time for you, Straw. Shall I send for some coffee?"

The old days. They both knew what that meant: before Libenyi's execution. More than a year had passed, and although nothing had changed, everything had changed. Maybe it was Simeon's fault that he couldn't seem to trust his teacher. But then again, his teacher didn't tell him everything, either.

A few weeks after Libenyi's execution, his nemesis from the Hungarian war, the odious Baron Haynau, had died suddenly at home, in some sort of fit. Poison? Simeon had asked, casually. Kane said it seemed likely. Simeon didn't ask the next question, and Kane didn't answer it.

Now, Kane asked him to sit in the overstuffed chair by the fireplace, where he'd first sat on the day they had met.

"No coffee. Thanks. I wanted to ask you about the Templars. They're developing weapons. New weapons. Is that so?"

Kane cocked his head and studied him. "Where is this coming from?"

Simeon's satchel was resting on his lap. There was no reason not to open it, take out Ada's notebook, and ask his teacher to read it and analyze it. If there really was a Magus using Ada's

research to do something she found abhorrent, Simeon owed it
to her memory to make sure that didn't come to pass. For that,
he surely needed Kane's help. Simeon was no scientist. He was
a self-taught publican's son.

He knew all this, and yet, he couldn't make his hands perform
the simple action of revealing the book's existence. Maybe it
was the shock of his old life coming to meet him here, in the
form of a strange little circus performer who knew his name.
Maybe it was the grief for Ada he'd never been able to share,
a small private cupboard he didn't want to unlock. Maybe it
was the memory of Libenyi's sister, taking the money Simeon
brought her after her brother's death.

A year after his first – and so far only – assassination, it wasn't
the man he'd killed who haunted Simeon. It was the man he'd
failed to save. And here he was failing another friend.

Kane was waiting for an answer.

Simeon's hand on top of the satchel stretched, his finger
twitching. Finally, he forced himself to smile. "It's curiosity,
that's all. Two years we've been training together, and I feel I
ought to know my enemies better."

"Ah." Kane looked away, drumming his fingers on his knee.
Those hands of his, always stained with ink and who knows
what else, scorched and cut, but the fingernails neatly trimmed
so they wouldn't break, so that the man of burners and vials
could go to his dinners and be accepted. Hiding all the many
faces of Oscar Kane in plain sight.

At last, Kane looked at Simeon and smiled too, his mustache
lifting like the wings of a bird. "Good. I've been teaching
you to observe, to question, and here you are observing, and
questioning. And yet you took me by surprise." He paused.

"You've a quick mind. Use your powers of observation on yourself. Look back. Is there something new you've seen that reminded you of anyone, or anything, from your life before you knew me? Think back."

"I don't want a bloody lesson!" It burst out of Simeon. "I mean, I'm sorry, but I want you to tell me, please, to talk to me."

Kane stared at him for a moment. Then he rang for his valet and ordered coffee. Then, when the valet had gone, Kane spoke softly. "Forgive me. I'd like to talk to you, too, that's all. I've been patient, you know. For two years, I've waited for you to tell me what drove you to me. I've waited for you to tell me the name you were given at birth."

Simeon froze.

But Kane smiled like a father. "I'm an observer, too, my friend. I gather information. That's all. But I know that trust is earned. So let me earn yours. What would you like to know? Yes, of course the Templars are always developing new weapons, as are we. I am, however, not privy to every Templar plan and scheme. But I have made a study of them and found out everything I could. The thing about Templar science is – well, it isn't only discovery. It's rediscovery."

Simeon's brows knitted. "Rediscovery?"

"You will understand in a moment why I didn't tell you this the day we met," Kane said with a sardonic half-smile. "Humanity did not build the first civilization on Earth. Long, long ago, there were others. The Precursors. Great scientists, with abilities far beyond ours. They created humanity, engineered us in their image, and gave us the gifts they wanted us to have."

Simeon's eyebrows were trying to rejoin his hairline. "Is this your idea of a joke?"

"It must be evident to you, if you give it a little thought, that many of the stories we were taught as children, even the religions of humanity, have their origin in some common facts. We Assassins know, as the Templars know, that these stories lead us back to the Precursor era. The gods do exist, after a fashion. Once you know what to look for, you'll never see the world the same way again."

Shaking his head in amazement, Simeon asked, "Then what happened to these marvelous creators? Are they still among us now?"

It took a moment for Kane to answer. "Did you ever read Mary Shelley's first novel? *Frankenstein, or the Modern Prometheus*?"

Ada had lent it to him. They had talked about it together, one of the last times they went riding. The novel written in Byron's house, just after her father had left the infant Ada forever. But what had interested Ada were the possibilities. How little we understand life and death, even now, she'd exclaimed.

Simeon tamped down his memories of Ada. "I read it a few years ago, yes."

"Then you will recall how the creature rose up against its maker in resentment. A very human impulse. The evidence suggests that we did rise against the Precursors, to demand our freedom. We did not win. The battle was decided for us by a great disaster that wiped out the Precursors. We survived; they built us hardy, it seems."

"And what evidence do we have for this?"

"Now that is a question with a long answer," Kane said. "But

I'll tell you a part of it for now. The best evidence, if you ask me, is in the artifacts that the Precursors left behind. These objects can have effects that seem almost magical – which demonstrates how far advanced Precursor science was, even in comparison to our science today. Many of those artifacts were designed to have effects on the human mind, because the Precursors used their science to control us. But any weapon can be a tool." Kane looked into the dark, empty fireplace beside them. "I am financing an archaeological dig in Assyria right now, because I have heard rumors of artifacts that take the form of an eye. The Templars also speak of an eye, one that could see patterns and make predictions that no human device or mind ever could. This eye could see how the consequences of many events would play out. Imagine what the Assassins could do with that, eh? Imagine how precisely, how humanely, our blades could be guided."

Simeon's hand twitched on the satchel. What would Kane say, if he showed him the book? What if he saw Ada's plans for a weapon, and understood them? Ada's wishes had been very clear: she wanted the weapon destroyed, or its manufacture aborted. She didn't want to spread its knowledge to yet another scientist.

But Kane was his teacher, and a good man. Perhaps Ada had been frightened without cause.

"Are you going to tell me why you've come to me today with these questions?" Kane's request was quiet, but probing.

"Because I want to know what we're up against." Simeon swallowed. "Because I am a soldier. Was a soldier. But then you already knew that, or guessed it. Didn't you?"

Kane nodded, kindly. "I wanted you to tell me in your own

time. Another of the challenges of our side. We value choice. The right of the individual to rise to his potential in his own way. There should be no limits on what we choose to do."

"No limits other than consequences," Simeon said.

"Precisely."

"But how can you – can we – judge which consequences are best for thousands or millions of people?"

"We don't! That's just it. We are not our brothers' keepers. Unlike the Templars, we don't tell people they'll live in paradise if only we get our way. Every human has the freedom to make their own choices."

The valet came in, the same thin old man who had been working for Kane for two years yet never said a word to Simeon in all that time. He put the coffee service on a side table. The two men waited in silence, the silver coffeepot gleaming. The door clicked again and they were alone, looking at each other.

"You told me that Libenyi made his choice." Simeon's voice was thick, but he couldn't stop himself. He wanted to open the wound again. He needed to. "But he didn't make that choice in freedom, even if he wasn't compelled. Even if he hadn't lived under unjust laws and been harassed by corrupt lawyers, his poverty left him few options. He lived the consequences of actions and choices that were not his own. The price of cloth in bloody Berlin or Kiev being half the price as here, that gave him few choices. It's more complicated than just removing the Templars, surely."

"What is more complicated? What do you mean?"

Neither of them touched their coffee.

"The Creed!" he snapped. "I came here looking for something–"

"For a way to liberate the world from the incompetent parasites who run it. I well remember what you wanted. And I am showing you how we will achieve it."

"But it doesn't–" Simeon stopped, unable to find the words. "I'm sorry. I don't believe one scientist's greed is better or more responsible than another's, simply because the first scientist is wholly in it for himself and uninterested in ideology."

Kane was silent for a while. He crossed his arms. "Is that what you think I said?"

"I don't know. I'm not a philosopher."

"Aren't you? I see before me a man who can't stop thinking and *act*. A haunted man who wants to be haunted." Kane stopped, bit his lip under his great mustache, and exhaled hard through his nose. "If you truly want to be inducted into the Brotherhood, Jack Straw, there's a lesson I can't teach you. You have to come to it on your own. Learn to bury your dead. It's a necessary skill for an Assassin."

Simeon walked all afternoon, the book in the satchel banging lightly against his hip. The day was bright and warm, and the women out walking the green lawns of the glacis held parasols to do what their small, neat hats, pinned at an angle, could not. Gentlemen held their hands to the brims of their narrow silk hats. Simeon kept to the arched stone walkways beneath the bastions, until finally the afternoon cooled to evening, and he struck out for one of his favorite places to think.

The Karlskirche, a great domed eighteenth century church on the far side of the glacis, was flanked by two massive columns in front. Kane had set him the ascent of one as a climbing challenge, months ago. Carved stories from the life of a saint wound up each column like ribbons. Simeon had decided upon the righthand one, from the flip of a coin, and then something in him demanded that he return another day to do the left. The view of the city was slightly different from each. He kept out of view while climbing as much as possible, but he had found that most people simply didn't look up, or didn't see what they didn't expect to see. It was exhilarating, being out in the open and yet seemingly invisible. Simeon would sit cross-legged at the top of the column, a little cupola behind him and the spread wings of golden eagles in front of him, and gaze out at the landscape.

On this day, he chose the left column. He could have drawn the city from either view, now, in his sleep even. The way the angles of the streets connected, the slight differences in shadow and light. Kane had been right that Simeon would come to feel safer above the ground than on it, that he would come to think of the city in three dimensions. Kane was right about so many things. But he was also wrong sometimes. He had been wrong about his arc cutter, the day they failed to break Libenyi out. One of the smoke bombs he'd given Simeon had turned out to be a damp squib. He could make mistakes.

If Simeon truly had possession of the plans for a terrible weapon, could he trust Kane to do the right thing with it? What *was* the right thing?

Suddenly he wanted to be gone, to be away from this place. Kane had hinted that a great leap from a tall place would be necessary for Simeon to be accepted into the Brotherhood, whenever that might be. He had an urge to leap off the column, into the darkening sky – but there was nothing to catch him.

His whole life he'd been running toward something better.

When Lady Byron, Ada's mother, took him away to educate him, he thought he was escaping his bully of a father. Later, he told himself he'd escaped the ministrations of Lady Byron. A lucky break, Ada's affair. When he was a grown man and his working life stretched out before him, he'd joined the army. England had seemed stifling, so off he went to fight. He'd escaped shipwreck. He'd taken a new name. Wandered across Africa and then Europe to find something better.

Now, two years into his new education, he wanted to fly away.

Maybe the problem was him.

He watched the lamps being kindled all over the old city, like a mirror of the slower and fewer stars overhead. He knew the names of all of those, in several languages. He could draw a map of constellations, with all the sky's disputed territories, overlapping shapes and myriad names. When the sun's last light dimmed enough to show him Jupiter in the southern sky straight below Altair, where Capricorn and Aquila overlapped, he knew it was time to go and meet Pierrette Arnaud. He dropped over the golden eagles and started to make his descent, his body hugging the stone to prevent gravity from having its say, his fingers gripping the carvings in a way he would once have believed impossible.

The stone bridge was brand new, just opened that spring, and named after Emperor Franz Joseph's new bride. Although the people of Vienna were already calling her *Sisi* out of affection, the bridge bore her formal name, Elisabeth. It was a straight bridge, supported by stone arches. Lovely, dignified, and out of the way, at least at this time in the evening.

So why was there a crowd on the bank of the Wien, gazing toward the bridge and cheering?

Simeon stopped. There was a figure, little more than a silhouette, dancing on the stone railing. A small and trim silhouette, with a long skirt. She lifted one foot high, put it down again, leaned forward, and the back leg went up straight behind her. The little crowd cheered.

He pursed his lips, picked up his stride, walked right through the crowd and onto the bridge. In plain sight. Past the gamboling Pierrette Arnaud, who was in the middle of a handspring when he hissed, "Down, now."

He kept walking, and by the time he had made a loop of a few blocks and circled back, the crowd had thinned. Mademoiselle Arnaud had her feet on the ground and was leaning to gaze over the railing, as demure as anything, in a pale blue dress and matching hat.

"I thought you said you'd be inconspicuous," he grumbled, coming along beside her and looking out over the little river.

"Did I? I don't remember that. I said I would wear ordinary clothes, as you requested."

"I thought it was implied."

He was on his guard, here as everywhere. There were two men talking at the end of the bridge. An older man walking a dog down on the path by the river. Someone inside that boat. A rented fiacre rolled over the bridge; the driver's hat was pulled low.

Simeon spoke softly. "Thank you for bringing me the notebook. Even though I didn't appreciate your methods, I applaud your dedication. You didn't give me up for dead, and you might have."

"And now?"

"And now," he smiled ruefully, "I'd very much like you to give me up for dead."

"No, I meant, what are you going to do about the notebook? What did your friend say?"

It was jarring to hear Kane referred to as his "friend." His teacher, his employer, his mentor. The man who knew as much about Simeon – or at least about "Jack Straw" – as anyone alive. Of course, that wasn't saying much.

He said, "My friend hasn't been any help to me, I'm afraid."

"What? So you have no leads at all? Nothing to go on?"

"It's very likely this imaginary device of hers is nothing," he protested. "Ada was a genius, but I swear, sometimes she thought she was a god. She thought all the knowledge in the universe would unroll itself at her feet if she asked it. You have to understand what she was like."

"I know what she was like," Mademoiselle Arnaud said tightly. "I was with her when she died."

Simeon closed his eyes, just for a moment. Just long enough for a single breath, a moment of relief, of realization. Yes, this stranger had known Ada in a way he hadn't. She'd been there for her when Simeon was out running from himself.

"Forgive me," Simeon said at last. "But you must agree, then. You know as well as I do that she and Babbage had grandiose plans for a machine that no one will ever build. A machine that *thinks*? Wonderful in theory, but the parts list gave me a headache just to read. She had a great imagination, but she didn't always live in reality." He paused. "I might imagine that at the end, that was even more true."

Pierrette sighed. "She was taking a great deal of laudanum

and claret. And suffering from unimaginable pain, even so. Not
to mention arguing with her family all the while, and…" She
stopped. "I shouldn't say more. She is dead, and she was my
friend. I understand what you're saying, Mr Price, and I even
agree with you, but I made her a promise, you see. I would be
very happy to prove that Ada had made a mountain out of –
what's the English expression? We French say a mountain out
of nothing."

"Out of a molehill."

"I don't think I've ever seen a molehill," she said sadly. "Or a
mole for that matter. Plenty of rats in the circus, though."

"Plenty of rats everywhere." He grinned, despite everything.
He could see why Ada had liked this young woman, though she
must have been fifteen years her junior. She was impressive. But
impressive people often got themselves into trouble.

"Just so," she was saying. "And let us find this particular rat,
this Magus, and put Ada's fears to rest with evidence rather
than suppositions. She was utterly convinced that you were the
man to do it, Mr Price."

"Please don't say that name aloud."

"Arrrgh!" She lifted two small fists into the sky. "You're very
vexing! Fine, then, Mr… Hay, was it?"

"Straw," he said through clenched teeth.

"Mr Straw. Ada clung to a scrap of paper you sent her, saying
that you had discovered a Brotherhood that would protect
the common people from all those who would do them harm.
Something like that. Do you remember writing that?"

"Yes."

"And was it true?"

He hesitated, leaning over the stone railing, watching the

gaslight reflected in the ripples of the river. "I thought it was."

"Were you wrong?"

Was he? If the Brotherhood was what he'd imagined it to be, where was it? Why hadn't Kane introduced him to other Assassins? (Unless he had, and Simeon hadn't realized it.) There was so much he still didn't understand, after two years of training. He wasn't even inducted yet. And when it came down to it, he hadn't felt able to trust Kane with the knowledge that some Templar out there might be building a terrible weapon. The Creed demanded that he never compromise the Brotherhood, and Simeon wasn't sure he could promise that. Better not to make a promise than break it. Like the one that Mademoiselle Arnaud had made to Ada, a promise she couldn't keep.

"It's a dead end," he said at last. "Your search ends here. I don't have any ideas, no connections that might be able to help. I'm sorry. Ada's faith in me was misplaced."

"That much is obvious." She made a small, exasperated noise. "Give me the notebook, then, if you're not going to do anything with it."

"I didn't say I wouldn't do anything with it. I said your search ends here. Leave it with me, and I'll keep my eyes and ears open."

"Here in Vienna?"

He was about to answer in the negative, and the notion took him by surprise. Without realizing it, he had made up his mind to leave. To run again. "Wherever I go."

"And will you write to me, to tell me what you've learned? You can always find out where the troupe is, just check with the Renz circus people. They'll know."

He said nothing, watching a small covered, houseboat drift toward them. Then: "I don't think that would be a good idea. It would only endanger both of us."

"Very well then. I guess this is goodbye." She leaned toward him and kissed both his cheeks, then stepped back and looked at him. "You have been a thorough disappointment and the only reason that I didn't pluck that notebook back out of your satchel until now is that Ada wanted you to have it. But she was misinformed. The man she knew was dead indeed."

And with that, she stepped up onto the stone railing, two neat brown, heeled shoes showing as she lifted her skirt a little. She had something in her hand: the blue notebook.

Simeon put his hand on his satchel: empty.

Pierrette Arnaud stepped out into the air, dropping neatly to land in a crouch on the roof of the houseboat, then ducking down as it passed under the bridge.

He rushed to the other side of the bridge only to watch as the boat carried her away. She lifted her hat and waved it at him jauntily, already a silhouette in the gloom.

The next day, Simeon returned a pile of books to Kane, tied in a black strap. *A Historical and Moral View of the French Revolution* by Mary Wollstonecraft. *Paradoxes of Defense* by George Silver. *The Epistle of Forgiveness* by Abu al-'Ala' al-Ma'arri, in translation. Joachim Meyer's *Thorough Descriptions on the Art of Fencing*, in the original German. Arthur Schopenhauer's *On the Fourfold Root of the Principle of Sufficient Reason*, also in the original German. *The Tenant of Wildfell Hall* by Acton Bell. The three volumes of *London Labor and the London Poor* by Richard Mayhew.

The pile landed with a thud on the only available surface in the laboratory, a part of the table that until recently had an astrolabe sitting on it. Kane was, at that moment, wiping said astrolabe with brass polish as he sat in his worn red armchair.

"You've finished all those?"

"Not quite," said Simeon. "The Schopenhauer is unfinishable, if you ask me. But I'm returning them."

Kane was wearing his pince-nez, as he always did for close-up work. He looked at Simeon over the rims. "You're leaving, then."

That made it easy. But not exactly comfortable. "Yes. I need some time to think. On my own."

"I shan't ask where you're going."

"Good, because I don't know." Simeon was irritated now. Kane's total lack of surprise made him feel like a child. There was nothing for Simeon to be mad about, which was all the more irritating. "I've left the clothes you bought me with your valet."

"Those are yours to keep."

"I'm sure they'll fit another lanky fool with a skinny neck. Besides, I don't want them." He didn't want to feel as though he were being kept by Kane anymore. And he didn't want to wear the fine clothing that Janos had made for him.

"Sometimes," Kane said, thoughtfully, "we men of science see significance in everything. A connection may be only a connection, without a cause. The things in your past that you didn't want to talk about – they are private things, aren't they? Things that are no one's business but your own. Go and deal with them, and when you are ready, the Brotherhood will be here. We will always welcome you back, no matter how long it takes."

Simeon wanted to scream: who is "*we*"? He'd still never met another Assassin, to his knowledge. Only Kane. The room was stuffy; he'd told Kane before he should open a window when he used his brass polish, but Kane didn't like open windows. There was probably a story behind that. A story Simeon would never hear.

"You'll keep up the allowance to Miss Libenyi?"

Kane nodded. "I gave my word." He stopped, cocked his head. "She might make a good Assassin, come to think of it. I'll need a new student."

"No."

"You can't walk away from people and expect to control what happens to them after you leave, Simeon. That isn't how it works."

"I'm learning that."

It wasn't until his stagecoach reached Innsbruck that Simeon realized Kane had called him by his birth name. At some point, he must have figured it out.

CHAPTER ELEVEN

Pierrette found her trunk at the hippodrome in utter disarray. Scraps of her clothing were strewn around – even an old corset and stockings she'd been in the habit of keeping at the show, after an incident when Jovita had accidentally spilled paraffin on her. Corsets were nearly impossible to wash thoroughly, because of the cording inside, and she'd had to throw that one away.

Her private things, thrown on the floor. It filled her with fury. Then she looked up at the door to the tearoom and saw Tillie's white face.

"What happened here?" she asked the girl. "Who did this?"

"A man asked me who Simeon Price was," Tillie said.

"What sort of man? Not the one who came to see me yesterday?"

The girl shook her head. "A young man, but big, with a scar on his face. He wanted to know who Simeon Price was, and then he came in here and broke your lock. I ran for Hugh, but by the time he came, the man was gone. Did he take anything?"

Pierrette gripped the notebook in her hand. It couldn't be coincidence. But what did it all mean?

"I told him!" Tillie said stoutly. "I told him Simeon Price was your lover. I told him that's what everyone says. I didn't know he would get jealous, Pierrette."

"What? Oh, you silly goose. Go, and let me clean this up."

If she'd been here – if the notebook had been here… She needed a better hiding place, for when she was on stage, and some way to keep it on her person when she was traveling. If she was stopped by this man, if she was searched…

Her gaze landed on the corset, stiff with cord. Corsets were never washed, and didn't get very sweaty, since they were worn over the chemise. Sometimes, poor women covered them with newspaper, to keep out the cold and smooth out their shape. An extra layer.

Pierrette borrowed Nell's sewing basket, and spent the night pulling apart her corset, carefully tearing all of the pages out of Ada's book, and sewing them between the layers of cotton. When it was finished, it was no stiffer than many a corset she'd had, and it was, if she dared say it herself, the perfect hiding spot. When she was on the street, Ada's notes would be on her body, but not even a thorough body search would find them. And when she was performing in costume, well, let them ransack her room again. They'd throw the corset on the floor and think nothing of it.

But nobody did come back to ransack her room.

The circus performed three more nights in Vienna. At the end of every show, Pierrette half-expected the irksome Mr… Straw to turn up at the dressing room again, having come to his senses and made up plan. He had been right that Ada wasn't always grounded in reality, but how could Ada have been so wrong about him? How could Ada, Countess of Lovelace, who corresponded with the greatest philosophers of the age, who had friends in great households across Europe and America – how could she be so sure that this nincompoop was the best man to fix her mistake?

Oh, how she wished she could throw the thing into the fire! Corset disguise and all! But she couldn't bring herself to do it. Ada had believed it was the key to stopping this Magus – perhaps the very man who had ransacked her things. She might find a need for the book's secrets yet. And that notebook had more than just the plans for the weapon in it – of that, Pierrette was sure. It was crammed full of notes, plans, ideas, jottings, any one of which might have illuminated the age, if someone with the right sort of brain could only read it and recognize it. Part of Ada's disconnection with reality was never knowing which of her ideas was practical. She had a knack for betting on the wrong horse.

Pierrette packed up her things and prepared to leave, but not before giving a final performance that brought the house down. There were rumors that the emperor himself and his new bride had been in the audience, incognito.

The journey from Vienna to Prague seemed dull and gray. Pierrette nodded when Tillie pointed excitedly at statues and fountains and old buildings. She should have felt free of her obligation to Ada. She had done the one thing Ada asked of her, so now she was free to enjoy her life, to fly. Why, she could spell whatever words she wanted with her fire now! She had stopped spelling out "Simeon Price" after the night he appeared. It did seem unfair to keep doing it, given that the man was a deserter in hiding. On the other hand, she hadn't come up with a new final name with which to replace it.

In Prague, she decided she needed to add something else to the climax of her act, to replace the sense of finality she used to get from spelling the name whose significance no one else knew. She went to see Hugh Robinson and asked him to teach her knife-throwing.

"I'm not going to horn in on your act with Ariel, or anything like that," she assured him. "But I was thinking I might light the handles on fire and throw them into a board covered with black felt, and spell out my final word that way."

He nodded, thinking. "And what will your final word be? I notice you've dropped Simeon Price."

That she had. "I don't know. Any ideas?"

"Why not your own name? You're billed as the Flying Flame, I know, but I think you've cultivated enough mystery now. Reveal yourself as Pierrette, and the name will be on everyone's lips." He paused. "You'll need a lot of knives, made to order."

"And a lot of paraffin."

"Every act helps you build your own future. That's how I think of it. Always give them something new, something more."

"And what's your newest thing then, Hugh?"

He smiled. "I've found a way to convince Major Wallin to let me shoot a pistol in the circus. Not at anyone, no, never at anyone. At a candle flame, to snuff it out. I might try a deck of cards too."

"I had no idea you were that good a shot!"

"Yes, well, the whole world will know it soon. No money in being a man of hidden talents," he joked. "But the catch isn't how good a shot I am, you know. The catch is the gun itself.

Getting one that's reliable, won't chain-fire or misfire, that can hit a barn door at twenty paces – it's harder than you'd think. Before the show tomorrow, I'm going to visit the best gunsmith in Prague, in fact, to see if I can't get something better than the piece of garbage I've been practicing with."

Gunsmiths. A slow smile broke on Pierrette's face. Forget that coward Simeon Price. She didn't need him to find a weapons manufacturer. She'd been going about this all wrong for a year and a half, because of Ada's misguided faith in her old friend. Instead of searching for Simeon, she should have been searching for the Magus. And now she could. If there was a man ordering strange new weapons anywhere in Europe, he'd be working with a gunsmith or ironworks. And it was the most natural thing in the world that knife-throwing, wire-walking, fire-spinning, sharpshooting performers should want to visit exactly those sorts of people.

The Aurora Troupe made its haphazard way all around Europe, avoiding the cities where there were reports of cholera outbreaks. That included London, in the summer of 1854, and much of Spain in 1855. They also avoided theatres of war, or even the territories of the belligerents, although Major Wallin said he'd love to go to Constantinople one day, and far St Petersburg, too.

As they traveled, Pierrette toured ironworks, foundries and gun smithies in Copenhagen, Munich, Antwerp, and Kiel. After she had paid her money for new knives, new guns, new equipment for her fire act, she always asked about the latest designs. It was easy enough to couch it in chat about the war. She saw nothing that reminded her of anything in Ada's notes.

One night in Frankfurt, Tillie came to Pierrette shortly before the show was about to begin, clutching her stomach. "I don't think I can go on," she confided in a whisper.

Tillie was nearly twelve, so Pierrette put two and two together, and said, "It's that time for you, is it? Poor thing. Do you need anything? Don't worry about the show. I'll tell your father you're unwell."

"No, don't tell him. It isn't that, Pierrette. It's just an ordinary stomachache. But he always says we need to have some haute école in every performance, to remind people that we are artists of the grand tradition. He says that he promised my mother. Remember when I was little, he used to perform it too, beside me, or on the nights when I didn't. But lately it's just been me, and he's seemed so tired with all this travel. I'm afraid if I tell him, he'll do it himself, and he's fifty-five now and hasn't been on a horse… I wonder if you, or maybe Jovita–"

"Of course," said Pierrette, although she'd been looking forward to trying out her new two-headed chain, which ignited at either end. She thought that Major Wallin being all of fifty-five had little to do with anything, as ancient as it must seem to a twelve year-old. But Tillie was right that Major Wallin hadn't ridden much lately, and lack of practice could lead to injury. "I'll shorten my act down to just the letters of fire and the knives – that's what everyone likes best anyway. And I'll tell your father that it's all arranged, no arguments and no fuss. I have my black riding costume, and there's time for me to change when Jovita's on."

It all worked out perfectly, and Major Wallin didn't object. Indeed, he hardly seemed to be listening when Pierrette told him the plan, even though Pierrette was exhausted by the end of the night. She went into the tearoom, where Tillie was lying on a sofa with a cloth on her head.

"She has a fever," said Nell Robinson, who was tending to the girl. "Let's get her back to our rooms and call the doctor there."

"Why not let her rest, and call him here?"

"Because her father's very poorly, too, and I have the feeling this will be more than the matter of a night. The sooner we make them both comfortable, the better."

Nell was right, as usual. The doctor said it was typhoid. At Major Wallin's insistence, the show went on, every night, but they took turns skipping their act – or taking over for Nell in supervising ticket collection – so that someone could be with the Wallins all the time. Tillie had bad headaches, but she felt better after a few days. After a few more, her father did, too, and it seemed they were out of danger.

Then, a week later, Major Wallin collapsed during a rehearsal. By the time they got him into a hansom cab and back home into bed, he was raving about his dead son (he had no son, dead or alive), and demanding that the creatures with blue scales be kept out of his valise, please and thank you!

For several weeks, he alternated between delusions and a kind of half-sleep, when he lay barely breathing, his eyes half open. He got better so slowly that no one really understood that he was getting better at all, until the doctor met them in the parlor of their rented house and said, "The typhoid has exhausted his heart. He must have no exertion, and as little excitement as possible. I understand he has led a peripatetic life and I must advise against that continuing. He must stay in one place. Rest, and plenty of it, is what he needs now. It is very likely his heart will be weak for the rest of his life. We can thank God, at least, that his wits have returned."

Jovita's eyes were wide as she said what they were all thinking: "But he'll live? Are you sure?"

"As sure as any doctor can be, madame. He has a strong will."

And Tillie, who was fully recovered but convinced she was somehow totally to blame for her father's illness, turned to Pierrette, buried her face in her shawl and wept tears of relief.

Nell, Hugh, Jovita, Ariel and Pierrette stayed up drinking beer after Tillie had gone to bed. They talked over what to do next.

"He is a stubborn one, and no mistake," Nell said.

"A schtrong vill," Ariel said in a phony German accent, imitating the doctor, and got them all to smile.

"But that stubbornness means he won't retire," said Hugh. "I know the man. As long as there's an Aurora Troupe, he'll want to be involved."

"But we can't shut down the Aurora Troupe," Jovita protested. "That would hurt him even more. I know it would. He'd fade away."

Nell nodded. "Then let's make sure he has very little to do. I can take over booking the shows and dealing with the building managers and prop masters. I already handle the budget, and we can hire help if I need it. But what about rehearsals and training? And hiring new performers, if we need to?"

"Let's cross that bridge when we come to it," her husband said. "We have a full complement now, and we're all trained and can help each other practice. I've been teaching Pierrette knife throwing, and Ariel has been teaching Jovita some flips. We are already all teachers and all students. That part will be fine."

Ariel nodded. "It only leaves the question of where to go next. The doctor said to stay in one place, but we can't set up in Frankfurt permanently. There's far too much competition here. There isn't even building space available."

"No," said Nell sadly. "We can't stay here, but we'll have to find some place where we can settle for a few years at least. Become a permanent fixture somewhere. It won't be good for sales, I can tell you that."

Pierrette felt like a portcullis was closing on her plans. This was the end of it, then. The end of hoping that one day, she might put Ada's fears to rest once and for all. Without travel, there was no way to search. Unless… if she stayed in one place, but that place was one where all the latest techniques were tried, where news of metalwork from around the world would be sure to turn up. A city full of iron foundries and weapons makers.

She cleared her throat, giving herself one last moment to decide whether what she was about to propose was selfish. She convinced herself it wasn't. "What about Birmingham?"

They all looked at her.

"Birmingham?" asked Hugh, in the high tones of incredulity only a man from Manchester could summon.

"It's the second biggest city in England now," she said in a rush. "They've got all sorts of railways coming in, and new stations, new houses going in all the time. The heart of industrial England. Plenty of people there who need something to do on a Saturday night. And because it's *Birmingham*" – she said the city name in imitation of how Hugh had said it – "there won't be as much competition as if we were in London or here in Frankfurt. We can set up there and do nicely for ourselves."

Nell cocked her head. "No more moving about for the major. Of course we'd have to get him there in the first place, but we'd take our time. It'll be a money loser, until we get ourselves a good position. But it's not the worst idea. And close to home, too, for Hugh and me at least. What made you think of it, Pierrette?"

"Oh," she said, and laughed, and took refuge in truth. "The other day when I went to see that gunsmith about that trouble with the rifling we were having, you remember, Hugh, well, they were all talking about trade with Birmingham, and all that's happening there."

"Then it's settled, if we all agree," said Nell.

They all nodded, albeit some with more enthusiasm than others.

CHAPTER TWELVE

The scatter of new railway lines across Austria and Switzerland didn't connect to anywhere Simeon wanted to travel. Where *did* he want to go, exactly? He had no answer for that, but he found himself looking to the mountains. In that distant blue landscape, like another world sitting on top of this one, he thought maybe he could think clearly. And as each shabby stagecoach brought him higher, he felt his breath come free.

But he didn't want to stay anywhere. He walked through mountain passes, a walking stick in his hand, and came out the other side, regarded a landscape of impossible beauty, and thought only: *what now?* And then he did it again, and again. He slept in mountain villas and hostelries where the food all came in tins and the guests had to take out their own bedpans.

Southward he went, down from the peaks, toward Italy. Over to the east were Milan and Venice, but that side of Italy was a part of the Austrian Empire, and there was something he preferred about being outside those borders now, though why a line on a map should matter to the state of his mind, he couldn't say.

In the autumn of 1854, he made up his mind to visit Lake Como. He had a line of Mary Shelley in his head, from her novel *The Last Man*: "If some kind spirit had whispered forgetfulness to us, methinks we should have been happy here." As good a recommendation as anything in Baedeker.

Lake Como was exactly what he wanted. Long, slender and branching, more like a river in some places, it was full of quiet coves and outcrops where he could sit under a cypress and look out over the blue water, and just think. He liked the smell of sun-warmed rock. His room in a little salmon-colored villa was pleasant, and he could sing softly to himself up in the hills, where no one could hear. It wasn't quite wilderness – there were houses dotted all over the wooded hills by the lake – but it was a place where nobody bothered anyone else.

The villa was run by an Italian woman in her thirties named Laura. She had six rooms that she rented to travelers. Having picked up a little Italian in some of his dealings in Vienna, Simeon was eager to learn more, and she seemed to enjoy talking to him, smiling sometimes at his mistakes.

Simeon ran out of money after a week, and he offered to help in whatever way she needed, for room and board. Gratefully, Laura asked him if would repair the roof, with the winter coming on. He worked, and they ate trout or perch at the kitchen table together in the evenings. As the year grew colder, Simeon was usually the only guest at the villa, which was a little out of the way, a short walk from the shoreline. On the third week, he dared to lean over and kiss her, and it felt like they had been married for thirty years.

It became a very comfortable life. He became too busy to spend much time sitting up in the hills and thinking, but he took Laura's German Shepherd for walks, wrapping himself in a shawl as the wind got cold. Maybe the best life a man could lead is one that doesn't hurt anyone else, he thought. Sometimes, though, lying next to Laura at night and staring up at the darkness, he remembered the sensation of the razor sliding across Mayr's throat. The blood on his fingertips. He had kept the silver card case, and the visiting cards, including the bloody one. It seemed dishonorable to throw them away, although many times he daydreamed about what it would look like to see them all fluttering down over the water, hitting the surface of the lake, sinking down into oblivion.

He passed the winter there. In the early spring, another traveler came to the villa, and though they didn't know each other by name, they recognized each other's past right away.

"When did you scarper, Mr Straw?" whispered the man who called himself Oliver Fraser when the two of them were alone. They were out in the sandy courtyard behind the villa, checking all of the shutters. Indigo clouds were massing on the mountaintops, and Laura had said earlier that a storm was coming.

"I don't know what you mean," said Simeon, though he did.

"Oh, come off it. I know the look of a man who's worn a uniform. There's no one around but us."

Simeon said nothing. He was inclined to like Fraser; he was matter of fact, and everything he said, he said with good humor. But there was nothing to be gained by taking the risk.

"Have it your way," said Fraser. "If the army went looking for all of us, they'd have no time to do anything else."

"That would be a blessing for the world."

"That's the truth."

"Where were you stationed?" Simeon dared. "Were you in the Crimea?"

Fraser nodded, and they moved on to the next set of windows. "Have you heard about what happened at Balaclava?"

Simeon shook his head. "I don't read the newspaper, when it comes." This wasn't quite true; he collected them for using to light the fires or for spills to light lamps with, and as he tore them up, he checked them for news about a fearsome new weapon out in the world. Other than a new Enfield rifle, there hadn't been any.

"I was there, yes, with the 17th Lancers," said Fraser, in a dull slow voice. "The Russians had captured some Turkish guns on one side of the valley. They were just sitting there, those guns. Unguarded. Ready for the Russians to carry away if they wanted. So, the officer in charge of the whole show decides that we light cavalry should just nip over and make certain the Russians couldn't take them."

"Seems reasonable enough."

"More than reasonable," Fraser agreed. "So he sends a messenger over to our major general and tells him to send the light brigade over to take the guns. What guns? asks the major general. Because from where we were, lower in the valley, the only guns we could see were the Russian ones, with the Russian army all around them. The messenger points vaguely somewhere, says, those guns, and our major general decides that England expects every man to do his duty, and off we ride, straight down the valley at the artillery."

He paused, and Simeon whistled softly.

"Indeed," Fraser continued. "They were all shot or shelled, everyone around me. My horse was shot, reared, and I fell. The poor beast fell right on top of me. I was pinned, but it probably saved my life. Given up for dead. Might have been taken prisoner otherwise. Once the smoke had cleared, I stumbled to my feet and started walking. I don't know why nobody stopped me, on my side or theirs. I think everyone was stunned. My family will probably be told I've been taken prisoner, and that's the end of me, as far as anyone knows on Earth."

"Except for me."

"Except for you, Mr Straw. But I have faith that you won't tell."

Simeon raised his eyebrows. "I'm surprised you have faith in anything, after that."

"Ah," said Fraser. "I have faith in one thing, and I saw it in your eyes. I don't know what it is exactly. The shadow of doubt."

Simeon laughed. "You have faith in doubt?"

"Well, maybe I just have faith that you won't turn me in because that would put you in danger yourself. Don't worry, I won't ask again. You've heard my story. I don't need to know yours. I suspect we've both seen men's bodies and souls ripped apart for no reason at all, on the word of some officer who doesn't know his arse from a teakettle. And what's a man to do, faced with that? All we can do is see to ourselves, and our own bodies and souls. To be honest, I've been running for months, from one place to another. I expect I'll be running my whole life, but this seems as good a place as any to stop and catch my breath."

"It is," said Simeon, looking across the courtyard at Laura

closing up the chicken coop, as the first heavy raindrops hit the ground.

Laura had been right about the storm. It howled around the villa, rain drumming the roof. All the shutters were closed and locked, and the house was dark except for the warm dancing of the fire. The three of them sat in the parlor, close to the fire, with lamps and candles near if they needed them, and played cards: Trentuno, because it worked with three players.

There was a banging on the door, and it wasn't the wind.

Laura stood up and opened the door a crack, then wider, to admit a great deal of freezing rain and a very soggy man.

"Thank you," he said in Italian. "May God bless you. I don't have any money."

His clothes were all too big for him, and not warm enough for the weather.

"Never mind that," Laura said. "You're soaked through. Come over by the fire."

Fraser put a wool blanket around the stranger, as black as the man's full beard and mustache. He had no hat – it must have blown away – and a tall philosophical forehead.

"Ten days I've been walking, with only the help of patriots to keep me alive," he said, shivering. "My name is Felice Orsini. I've just escaped from the prison in the castle at Mantua. I'm a wanted man. You should know that. But I'm not a common criminal. I'm fighting for revolution."

Laura looked at Simeon, and said, "Let's get this man something hot from the kitchen."

Inside the villa's narrow kitchen, by the light of one lamp, they heated soup on the stove.

"What do you think of him?" Laura asked.

"If he's telling the truth, then it's your decision. Your villa at stake. Mantua – that would be the Austrian Empire, then."

"Does it matter who's pursuing him?"

"It matters because they won't give up. I have some experience with the soldiers of the Austrian Empire and their attitude toward revolutionaries."

It was the most he'd ever said to her about his past. She didn't press it. "Well, no matter who's after him, I can't imagine any policemen or even soldiers would be out on a night like this. We can't turn him out into that storm. Funny. He didn't have to tell us who he was."

Simeon thought of Fraser. "There's something about this place that seems to draw confessions out of people. Like church."

"Ha," she laughed, and pulled the front of his shirt to bring him closer to her. "And what do you have to confess?"

"That I've never been happier anywhere than I am here with you."

He kissed her, and they brought out the soup, broth with small noodles. Everyone had some, not only Orsini. But he ate it eagerly, slurping from his spoon. Laura put a bottle of brandy and some glasses on the sideboard.

"I thought you might come back with a rope to tie me up," he said, with a twinkle in his eye.

Laura shook her head. "We offered you our hospitality. Anyway, I don't answer to the Austrian Empire. How did you manage to escape?"

"Well, it wasn't easy! There were sentinels at every door, and far too many guards to bother trying bribery. And the castle has only one entrance. I couldn't see any way out of my predicament. For months, I was alone in my cell, and they wouldn't give me so much as a glass to drink out of – nothing I could use as a weapon or a tool. I spoke through the wall to another patriot, before they took him away to the execution grounds. After that, I was entirely alone and despaired of my fate. I came to believe the world must be a wasteland, in which there are no men willing to take action against their oppressors. It was a dark time."

There was something about the way this man talked that reminded Simeon of Libenyi. That passion, that deep integrity. It was a little discomfiting, but endearing all the same. Inspiring, even, if Simeon had anything left in him to be inspired.

"But you did get out," Simeon said, providing the encouragement Orsini seemed to be waiting for.

"Yes, because I obtained a few small metal files, very easy to conceal. I will not tell you where I obtained them, because I am a man who keeps his word once it is given. But that was my first glimmer of hope. All the same, it took me months to file through the bars of my window. It was so high off the ground that I had to stand on my chair, and it's a miracle the guards didn't catch me at it – I was always hopping on and off, exhausting myself from panic and getting very little done, some days. It took me twenty-four days to cut through eight bars. Then I made myself a rope out of bedsheets and I dropped down to the ditch outside the wall. A thirty-yard drop!"

The wind banged against the shutters. Orsini seemed warmer, either from the fire or the energy of his storytelling, and he'd even forgotten to finish the last of his soup.

"But then, I had a real obstacle. I'd hurt my foot in the fall and couldn't manage to scale the wall around the ditch. So, I lay there in the mud all night long, and when dawn came, I called to some of the townspeople to help me out, and they did. I said I'd been drunk and fallen in, but I'm sure they knew full well who I was and where I came from. That was my first sign that good people would help me, my reminder never to despair about humanity again. And I was right. I've been walking since, and everywhere I've gone, people have helped me. And I'm grateful, although some of the help I can't discuss, you know." He gave Laura a woebegone smile.

"You've been through an ordeal," said Fraser.

"That's the truth, but this wasn't the first time I was in prison," he said. "A few years ago, I was released when a new pope granted amnesty to political prisoners. Or, to some political prisoners, I should say. I knew when I went to Vienna, I'd be risking capture, but I wanted to see the emperor up close, and I had people to see. I made arrangements for my family in Zurich, in case anything should happen to me. Which it did! But not permanently."

He smiled, scratching his beard.

"You were in Vienna?" Simeon asked, keeping his voice even.

"Yes, that's where they grabbed me, and they brought me to Mantua. I'll take some of that brandy now, if you don't mind. My stomach doesn't take much to fill, these days. My bones are chilled."

Laura poured him a glass, and they talked for a little while longer, about the chances of a war for independence in Italy, about Orsini's dream of a free, united and republican Italy. But every great power in Europe would be able to put down such revolutions whenever they arose because Napoleon III in France had a large army and was willing to use it to prop up the old regimes. As France went, Europe would go, Orsini said.

"Do you know Lord Byron's great poem, 'Mazeppa'?" Orsini asked, his eyes shining. He quoted in English: "'There never yet was human power, which could evade, if unforgiven, the patient search, and vigil long, of him who treasures up a wrong.'"

Then Fraser poured more brandy, and Laura and Simeon, laughing and protesting they'd get a headache with any more political talk, went up to bed.

The soldiers came sooner than they'd expected. At dawn, there was a banging at the door. Laura was already up, putting on a loose dress over her stays. But Simeon had been up in the night, sharpening his knives. He'd acquired three of them on his journey from Vienna, and this time, he hadn't sold them for boots. Simeon took his Adams revolver out of the drawer beside the bed.

"I don't want Mr Orsini to go to jail, but I don't want any trouble either," said Laura, looking at the gun as he adjusted his holster.

"I promise you, I'll deal with them quickly and quietly. I know what I'm doing. The gun is just in case."

She looked skeptical.

"Laura, I've already seen one man go to the gallows because I failed to help him escape the Empire's jailors. I don't intend to let it happen again. Will you help me?"

"What do you want me to do?"

"Just don't tell them I'm here. Tell Orsini and Fraser to stay inside in their rooms and keep their heads down. If you have to tell anyone anything. it's you and Mr Fraser in the villa, and last night, a traveler came in from the storm. You don't know the traveler's name or anything about him. Keep them talking at the front door for as long as you can. Step out of the way at the first sign of trouble. And don't look up."

"Why would I look up?"

Simeon knew the roof of the villa intimately. He knew where it was slippery, and where he could squat behind a chimney without being seen from below. But these bloody soldiers knew their business. Two men at the front door, and two at the back. He'd have to be quick and quiet, or he'd lose the element of surprise.

When he heard Laura open the front door, he crawled forward, right onto the gable that overhung the porch. Hesitation was risky, but so was dropping before he was certain of his angles and his movements. One deep breath, and a knife in each hand. He talked himself through it, repeated Kane's lessons in his mind. A clean jump with the knees tucked in. Trust that you'll land on the point of your knife, and that is the surest foundation an Assassin can have.

He landed with his knife already sliding into the windpipe of the first soldier, knocking him against the column that flanked the villa door. Simeon didn't have time to get steady on his feet, but he didn't need to. He just needed to thrust his second knife upward and trust it would hit something vital. Whatever his knife hit, there was gurgling, and wordless wrestling before Simeon extricated himself from a soldier who was leaning on him like a drunk at a ball.

Laura had not stepped back. She had wrapped a scarf around

the mouth of the second man, which was probably the only reason he hadn't cried out. Simeon's second knife blow had been clumsy; it had done the job, but not silently. He thanked his stars for Laura, not for the first time. She pulled a silver pistol from her pocket. He smiled. She didn't want any trouble, she said, but she was certainly prepared for it.

"There are two men in the back," she whispered.

He nodded. "Keep talking, so they don't wonder what's going on."

She responded in a louder voice: "I don't know who you're talking about. There's no Mr Orsini here."

Bless her. He jumped up to grab the gable with his hands, and pulled himself up, stifling a groan. Then, breathless, onto the roof again. Crawling to the back. He could hear Laura talking still, pretending to get annoyed with the soldiers who were slumped at her feet.

As he made his way past the midpoint of the house, he heard a window shutter open, and a sash slide up. *Shit.*

Simeon crawled as fast as he could to the side of the house, and saw Felice Orsini trying to squeeze through the window, with his gaze down at the ground.

"Shh!" Simeon hissed but Orsini carried on. Simeon didn't dare say anything louder; he didn't want to draw the men from the back door.

Too late. They rounded the side of the house and shouted, pulling their guns. Orsini was half out of the window, unarmed. Simeon pushed himself to the edge of the roof, leaned out over it and shoved Orsini back in, then grabbed the top of the window frame, slid down so his feet touched the narrow lip at the sill, and dropped to his fingertips. He landed on the ground just as a bullet smashed into the frame of Orsini's window.

He pulled his revolver and fired twice. One of the men dropped, with a bullet in his leg. Simeon's hand was shaking, damn it. He was about to fire again when he saw Fraser running from behind the two men. As Fraser leapt onto the standing man from behind, Simeon tackled the one on the ground, who was waving his revolver from Simeon to Fraser and back again. A knife to the man's throat, and when he looked up, Fraser had his arm around the other one, easing him to the ground, the man's legs kicking.

When it was all over, he and Fraser looked at each other, breathing hard. Fraser's face looked as grim as Simeon felt.

"We have to get these bodies away from Laura, divert attention somewhere else," Fraser said.

Simeon nodded. He had already planned for that. "They would have come up a pass about three miles from here, and it would have been a good spot for an ambush. If we leave the bodies there, it'll look like that's where they ran into Orsini."

"And how are we going to get four bodies to a pass three miles from here, without being seen?"

"I'll drive them in Laura's fiacre. You go down and put a tree across the road or something, so we're not disturbed."

"And I?" Orsini appeared, red faced above his beard. "How can I help?"

"You can get yourself as far from here as quickly as possible, Mr Orsini," said Laura, coming around from the front. The pistol was still in her hand, but her arm hung at her side. She looked exhausted. "For your sake and ours."

• • •

By the time they'd arranged the scene in the mountain pass, it was late afternoon. Laura had scrubbed her porch and poured them all glasses of whiskey.

"Orsini left when we told him to, at least," Laura said. "He should be well away by the time they come looking for him, and their men."

"And so he lives another day," said Fraser. He raised his glass. "To Felice Orsini's continued life and freedom."

"To life and freedom for every man," Simeon replied, and raised his. Jameson's whiskey, the same kind Kane used to drink.

"I think he'll do fine for himself," Fraser said. "He seems to attract help wherever he goes."

"At least he doesn't talk about who helped him," Laura said. "Thank goodness for that."

"Well, you weren't there once he'd had a few belts of brandy last night," Fraser said. "We stayed up talking and drinking, and after a while, the stories became more detailed. But I wouldn't worry too much. He plainly loves to create an air of mystery, and to be frank, I wonder if half of the characters in his stories aren't his own invention. He started going on and on about the help he received from some mysterious character called the Sorcerer. No, wait, that wasn't it – the *Magus*, can you believe?"

Simeon nearly choked on his whiskey. "What?"

Fraser laughed. "I know, it's very dramatic. Maybe by the time he reaches Paris, the story will have evolved further, and this sorcerer will have built him wings, or smuggled a Pegasus into the prison for him to fly away on."

"No, in all seriousness, what did he say about this... Magus? Fraser, it's important. I've heard the name before."

The grin faded on Fraser's face. "Only that this character had encouraged Orsini to believe in himself, told him he would do great things. There was a hint of some more practical help too – I had the sense he was referring to those little metal files he talked about. Maybe it's a code name for a revolutionary."

Simeon shook his head. Could Ada's scientist have been a revolutionary? Simeon had thought a Templar more likely. But he wasn't sure what to think about anything anymore.

"You said Paris. Is that where he's heading for?"

Fraser thought for a minute. "I don't recall, now, exactly what he said about it. Just that Paris was mentioned. Maybe only that he'd like to see Paris one day, or that he admired the revolutions there – I don't recall. Sorry, old boy, I'd had a few myself."

He'd always known that this life couldn't last, that one day, he would leave. The look on Laura's face showed that she had always known it too.

CHAPTER THIRTEEN

For a few days, Simeon held out hope that he might be able to find Orsini well before either of them reached Paris. But he had to guess at the route: north to Zurich or west to Geneva?

Orsini had mentioned making arrangements for his family in Zurich. So, Simeon started there.

Whether he guessed wrong, or Orsini's good fortune kept him hidden, there was no sign of him in the passes through the mountains, and the coach drivers said they couldn't recall any particular skinny Italian with a black beard.

In Zurich, he stopped for two weeks, asking around at working men's bars, but found nothing. He found where Orsini's children were living and watched them from rooftops. Watched Orsini's brother and his wife with the children. Watched their governess. But there was never any sign of Orsini, or that they were hiding anyone. He nearly dropped to the ground to question them, several times, but always changed his mind. Simeon had made many mistakes in his life; he wasn't going to add frightening children to the mix. He had no idea what they knew about their father, or didn't know.

He'd failed to pick up Orsini's trail, but maybe he'd find him at his destination. There was a rail line from Basel to Strasbourg, and from Strasbourg to Paris.

Simeon had never traveled by rail before. He found it stifling, like being in the hold of a ship, with the steam and the noise and the rocking. He was glad when the journey ended. The Gare de l'Est in Paris reminded him of a cathedral, with its long nave rising to a curved glass ceiling, its stone arcades, and its half-rose window and statues over the entrance.

He walked out into a wide, bustling courtyard full of carriages, horses stamping, people walking in all directions. The sky was a deep blue, punctuated by clouds that looked like their paint was still wet. All in all, he felt exposed, and the impossibility of his task made him reel. He'd been failing Ada for a long time – not to mention the dogged Mademoiselle Arnaud – and he'd made some kind of peace with that, convinced himself it was all a dying woman's imaginings. And maybe some of it was, but all of a sudden the Magus seemed to be all too real.

He had to get his bearings. The Gare de l'Est was only a few stories high, but it would be enough to get him up and out of his bustle. A place to think and get the lie of the land. He slipped around to the side of the building, waited for a moment when there was no one near and looking his way, then pulled himself up by the masonry around the windows. Up to the very top of the roof, from where he stood looking out over a stone railing at the sea of buildings, all the walls the color of cream, topped with silver roofs, and dotted here and there with flower boxes. There was scaffolding on every block, and digging in

every second street. The whole city was under construction, or
at least, the parts of it he could see. Up here, the air was fresher,
and he could smell the hint of rain on the breeze.

He'd been standing there for ten minutes, maybe a little
more, when he felt a hand on his shoulder.

Simeon whirled, his knife in his hand by the time he saw the
woman's face. She was wearing a hood very much like Kane's,
with a point coming low over her brow. A woman in her forties
or fifties, with dark eyes that didn't seem at all surprised by
him or his knife. Probably because she had a blade attached to
her own wrist, on the inside of the hand that had grabbed his
shoulder and that was now pointed at his throat.

"Explain yourself," she said.

"To whom?" Simeon was always a bit abrupt in French, a
long habit that came from mistrusting his accent. When knives
were involved, he was even more inclined to be brief.

"Come on. I recognize the marks in the way you move.
And yet – you didn't hear me coming, and I don't know your
face. Are you Templar or Assassin? And if you say 'neither', I'll
have to assume common criminal, and then I will have more
questions."

"Is there anything I can say that won't result in more
questions?"

"No."

He decided her cloak said Assassin more than it said Templar,
so took a gamble. "I was trained by an Assassin, in Vienna. But
I have not been inducted into the Brotherhood."

"Ah, that explains a lot. Did a council send you here? We've
had no word."

"No, I'm not in contact with any Assassins nowadays."

"You've lost your faith."

"I didn't think Assassins had faith."

"Clearly, you still have a lot to learn. Come on down, then. It's going to rain."

She was right about the rain. By the time she had taken him in through a window and onto a set of gantries high up inside the station, it was beating on the glass roof, even trickling down between the joins here and there. He followed her along the beams, wondering whether she was turning her back to him because she'd decided he posed no threat – and trying to work out whether that was a compliment or an insult.

At the edge of the roof, she dropped to her hands, and then to the floor inside a room stacked with baggage. She pulled a cart filled with suitcases to one side, revealing a plain door, which they went through. Then down three flights of narrow stairs, into darkness. He had just decided that this was probably where he died, when the woman pressed something, a door opened, and they stepped through into the light.

He wasn't sure what he'd expected to see, but this wasn't it. A vast room, with a high ceiling. Mosaic tiled floors, sofas and low tables, and small gas lamps. The whole effect was rather like the lobby of a grand hotel. A map of Paris was painted along one wall, and a map of the world along the other. At the far end was another door.

"I've caught a stray," said the woman to the two men sitting on either side of a low table, consulting some sort of document. They looked up when she and Simeon came in.

She took off her cloak, a little damp from the rain. Her curly silver hair, loosely tied, came to a widow's peak in the center of her forehead, like an echo of the shape of her hood. She shook out the rain from her cloak and hung it on a carved hat rack next to an umbrella stand. Under the cloak, she was wearing trousers and a jacket.

"I'm Amira Benyamina," she said. "And these two are Michel Moulin and Henri Escoffier."

The two men approached, one very young and pale, and the other older, with deep golden skin.

"This is where you give us your name," she prompted Simeon.

"Simeon Price," he said.

Maybe he gave his real name out of instinct, or some desire to put Vienna, Kane and Lake Como behind him. Or maybe he was simply distracted, because as he looked into Henri Escoffier's face, he recognized the man who had been on the *HMS Birkenhead* three years before, the man who had first told Simeon that there was such a thing as a brotherhood of conscience.

Henri Escoffier was a middle-aged Mauritian, clean-shaven, in a dark blue waistcoat and crisp white cravat. He remembered Simeon, and recognized him immediately, clasping his hand.

"I always hoped that you would find your way to us," he said. "Come and have a drink."

The younger man, Michel Moulin, brought a tray with fresh brioche, camembert, honey, and jars of cherry preserve. There was Burgundy wine and apple cider; Simeon chose the latter. He realized that he hadn't eaten since he boarded the train at Strasbourg.

"You seem quite comfortable down here," he said, feeling oddly warm and sleepy for the first time in months.

"Too comfortable, Amira says," Escoffier admitted with a small smile. "She is always on the lookout."

"If I weren't, I wouldn't have spotted this one, and he'd be in a dingy hotel."

"I liked the look of you, on the *Birkenhead*," Escoffier said, ignoring Madame Benyamina. "You seemed appropriately disgusted, which is more than I can say for any of the officers on board. If I'd done my other job, it might have turned out differently."

"Your other job?" Simeon asked.

"I was there to carry out an assassination, and we had a plan. From the moment I stepped on board, I felt I should act, but I told myself to wait and follow the plan. Instead of listening to my gut, I hesitated. If the ship had been under different leadership, if it hadn't sailed so close to the rocks… well, it's in the past now. I was younger then, and faster in some ways, slower in others."

"Pish," said Benyamina, coming to sit with them. "You can still beat me in a footrace across the roof of Notre Dame, Escoffier."

Simeon put up a hand. "I don't understand – forgive me. Monsieur Escoffier, you said the assassination was your other job. Were you looking for me?"

"Of course! Kane sent me. That's why I told you to go to Vienna. And it seems you found him."

Simeon stood up, abruptly, on guard. "*Kane*… sent you to *find me*? I don't understand."

Escoffier's brows lowered. "He said he had met a young man in Ireland, an English soldier who got very drunk one night in a pub, but said things that suggested he would be useful to the Brotherhood. He said he'd been thinking about that conversation for years, regretting that he hadn't recruited you. I was living in Vienna then, and when the council sent me to assassinate an officer on the *Birkenhead*, Kane asked me to recruit you while I was there. Alas that we didn't have the chance for a longer conversation."

It must have been in Tipperary, that night after the crowd of hungry people came to the storehouse Simeon was helping to guard. That was the only night he'd been drunk enough, in Ireland, not to remember meeting a man like Oscar Kane. What in the devil's name had Simeon said, in that state, that would have made Kane think he'd make a good Assassin? Maybe he'd simply been railing against the army.

And why hadn't Kane told him that they knew each other? Simeon thought back to the day he'd walked into the hallway, with Kane at the apartment door, waiting for him. *Your own mother wouldn't recognize you.*

Simeon had held back too. Given a false name. Maybe that explained it – Kane had been waiting for Simeon to be honest with him. And he hadn't been ready. Maybe he hadn't been ready to be an Assassin; maybe Kane had sensed that his pupil needed more time.

And now? The army hadn't found him, had probably given up on him, and Simeon was ready to be himself again. Jack Straw was a being born out of the bloody waves, out of the memory of a boy at sea, clinging to a last jape and a bundle of straw, a boy who was probably drowned. But then again, maybe he wasn't. Escoffier had survived. Simeon had survived.

"Well, you've come to us now," said Madame Benyamina. "You're most welcome here. We'll continue your training, if you choose."

Simeon stared at her for a moment, thinking. "I don't know how long I'll remain in Paris. I'm looking for someone. A man named Felice Orsini, who might be planning violence. A revolutionary. And he may be making contact with another man, a dangerous man, whose name I don't know. Some people call him the Magus. I fear he may be a Templar, but I can't be sure."

Michel Moulin scratched his freckled nose. "Well, I've never heard of the Magus, but I have certainly heard the name Felice Orsini. I was in England for a few days, and have just returned. He's in all the newspapers there. About to give a lecture in Liverpool, I think it was, all about the unification of Italy and the plight of the common man, that kind of thing. He escaped from prison, or something, I think? Has some story of derring-do." He said this last part in very good English.

"Yes!" Simeon could hardly believe it. Then his heart dropped. England: the one place to which he had no desire to return. All it would take would be someone from his old life to recognize him and report him to the police, and he'd be court-martialed, whipped, jailed, put on a transportation ship.

"But you thought he'd be in Paris?" Madame Benyamina leaned forward, her chin in her hand.

"He mentioned Paris, but maybe we misunderstood." Simeon frowned. "I don't know what he has planned. Lectures… I didn't expect that. Maybe he's raising money for something. Or recruiting."

"I'll tell you what," said Moulin. "We'll send a telegram to the British Assassins and ask them to keep an eye on him. They'll report on all his activities. Will that do?"

Simeon sighed, relieved. "That'll be smashing."

A Brotherhood. After all.

The Assassins of Paris had been scattered by revolution after revolution, for more than half a century. They used to meet in a sanctuary at Sainte-Chapelle, but Madame Benyamina told him that place wasn't safe for them anymore. They had several bases now, all over the city.

Madame Benyamina wrote articles for a radical newspaper, and wore trousers and waistcoats like her idol, the novelist Aurore Dupin, aka George Sand. She offered to continue Simeon's training, and he gratefully agreed. She set him frequent challenges, such as getting from the Pantheon to the Arc de Triomphe without touching the ground.

There was no Kane trying to educate him in philosophy, but he made regular visits to the Conservatoire des Arts et Métiers, to watch Foucault's Pendulum, and to think. In the evenings, he went to the bars where working men drank. He grew out his beard, to show his sympathy with republicanism. It seemed likely that if he was going to hear about the Magus again, it would be from one of these men, like Libenyi or Orsini, men who were so eager to know that there were men of action in the world. What kind of action, though? Simeon wondered.

In the summer, Madame Benyamina asked him to drive out to Versailles with her. The old palace was mostly empty, with some talk of museum exhibits, but the gardens were still lovely. Out beyond the sculpture of Apollo, half-submerged in water to look as though his horses were rising out of it, was a long, deep canal, starting from nowhere and going to nowhere, one of the most arrogant gestures of Louis XIV.

Madame Benyamina had Simeon take the oars in a rowboat.

It seemed to take forever to get anywhere, and facing backward, he watched the palace become smaller, smaller.

"The day has come for your leap of faith, Simeon," said Madame Benyamina softly.

He stopped rowing, looked up into the empty sky. "I don't see anything to leap off, madame."

She raised her eyebrows and looked over the side. "Sometimes it's a leap *off*. Sometimes it's a leap *into*. This is different for each of us. But I'll tell you what every Assassin realizes on that day. The leap is only a symbol and a celebration of the decisions one has already learned how to make, every day. You left the army when you realized you couldn't serve with integrity. You left Oscar Kane when you realized he was the wrong teacher for you. You have never shied away from leaving, from leaping. But you do fear the deep water, and I can't say that I blame you. There's nowhere to hide, in the water, is there? Hiding means death, down there."

He swallowed. "Do I swim to shore?"

"If you like. But that's not the leap. The leap is the dive. You have to go down, Simeon, down to the bottom. You'll see it. You'll know where to go. Bring me back what you find at the bottom."

"The bottom! Madame Benyamina, I–"

"As of today, please call me Amira. We are soon to be Brothers. I have faith."

The water was cold. He pushed downward as hard as his legs could manage, but could feel the water rejecting him. Soon he'd bob back to the surface, ridiculous, but safe. Alive. His throat closed and he pushed the last bubbles out of his nose, let the pressure squeeze his temples. He opened his eyes. Somehow, he was still moving downward, kicking hard, his arms straight in front of him.

And down below, at some distance he couldn't judge, was a light. What was it? Some sort of Templar artifact?

A few more pushes, and his eyes were going dark. He wouldn't have enough air to make it back to the surface. He would drown at last, consigned to fish and rot. A burial at sea without the salutes or flags, without any words from the chaplain. Here in the most ridiculous of bodies of water, where he wasn't doing anyone any good, where there were no lives to save. Maybe he'd see them down here, before the end: all the men he didn't save on the *Birkenhead*. When he had swum for his life in that terrible ocean, could he have found the strength to get pieces of flotsam under dying men, or pull them along a little closer to the shore? Maybe. There was probably something he could have done.

He could have stopped it all. Like Escoffier, he had known from the start what needed to be done, though he hadn't put it into words. Hadn't dared, back then. The only creed they had ever taught in the pub in Ealing was look out for yourself. And that was the creed they taught in the drawing rooms of people like Lady Byron, too, although they twisted it up with privilege and made it "do well for yourself." In the army, it was "do as you're told."

And now? He was living his new creed, and he was ready to swear to it, in these last moments of consciousness. He would do as Madame Benyamina asked him, because she was ready to be his Sister. He would not let another innocent die, never again. And he was at home wherever he was, never leaving and never arriving. He was where he needed to be.

His fingers closed around cold stony dirt, then his lungs rebelled, pushing him back up, back up to life. By the time he surfaced, he was gasping deeply, and lacked the strength to get back in the boat or even to tread water. Madame Benyamina – Amira – calmly pushed the oar out a little more so he could hang on it, suspended in the water until he caught his breath.

"Take your time," she said.

"I saw it, but I didn't get it, whatever it was," he said, and showed her his fingers, dark with mud.

"Ah, but you did. Sometimes our eyes play tricks on us, when we're hoping to see something. If you saw something, that meant you hoped. That's faith, Simeon. Faith shouldn't cause us to stop looking. It should make us more curious. It should make us seek the very bottom. Welcome to the Brotherhood."

CHAPTER FOURTEEN

The ironworks on the edge of Birmingham smelled like Hell, but Pierrette had come to appreciate it. Unlike the muddy, tepid, organic smells of the circus, this place was hot metal and steam and acid. And unlike the circus, where everyone's gaze was directed at a central point, the ironworks was a sprawling, nonsensical city all to itself. The first building had gone up on the street front, not far from the canal, but as other parts of the operation were added, they built more and more buildings, and connected them by rickety passages – sometimes walkways, two or three stories up.

The gun shop was in the middle of the complex. Pierrette preferred it to the self-contained shops in the Gun Quarter, because here, she could keep an eye on other things being manufactured: ordnance, parts for artillery. Anything that this Magus might potentially have his hand in. She'd found a way to inspect all manner of new developments in weapons, under cover of her curiosity. At one point, she had mused about adding a cannon to the act. This was not something she would have actually contemplated, especially not at the Jennings Theatre, which was very small and not in very good repair. It had gone out of business as the Aurora Troupe moved to Birmingham, and Pierrette had persuaded Nell it was a bargain. It was also not in the fashionable part of town, but it was close enough to the new workers' neighborhoods that they were able to do a steady business, with cut-rate tickets and toffee for the kids. Here, the traveling Aurora Troupe could establish itself as the permanent Aurora Circus. It even had several rooms in the top levels, so the troupe could live right above the theatre.

Fortuitously, it was also close to an ironworks.

Pierrette waited for Isaac to finish stamping something, and then called out to him.

"Ah, mademoiselle," he said. Isaac, who couldn't have been more than thirty himself, always called her that, though it came out something like "mamzel." He shifted his clay pipe to another part of his mouth, where the teeth were arranged in a way that made talking through a pipe easier. "Don't tell me you're unhappy with that little revolver. I tell you it'll beat any Colt on the market. And didn't I tell you there's no recoil with that rimfire cartridge? You can shoot it while you're walking on the tightrope and never fall off."

"I don't walk on the tightrope, Isaac, that's Ariel. Which you would know, if you ever bothered to come and see one of our shows."

He shrugged. "One of these days. Did you bring the revolver? I'll have a look, if it's giving you grief."

She shook her head. "It's fine. I just thought I'd see if there was anything new in the works."

"New? No, nothing new. The war with Russia has ended, the boys have come home."

"Well, not all of them."

"No, not all of them, that's the truth. But those who haven't come home don't need new guns. The bottom's gone out of the military business."

"But there's war in the east, and rebellion in India."

"Try to cheer me up all you like, but I've made my peace with it. I've been making shotguns for the toffs to shoot partridges with, but that wouldn't interest you, unless you've taken it into your head to pick off your audience members."

"No, God forbid. I'll do my best to keep business up, but I don't want a shotgun."

"I don't blame you. It's all right. I've had to let half my men go, but they've found work in the other buildings." He gestured to indicate the rest of the complex. "That's where all the new designs are these days. Gas containers and pipes and machines and I don't know what. Workings for the railroads. But that doesn't interest you, mamzel."

He was right: only weapons interested her. Weapons that might once have been designed by Ada Lovelace, in collaboration with her mysterious Magus. But it was 1857; five years, now, since Ada had died. Five years seemed long enough. Maybe Simeon Price had been right, and there was nothing to find. Maybe it had been easier for him to judge Ada's real flaws, since he hadn't been at her side in those terrible last months. The inventor had thought herself evil, but she had also talked about shadowy men trying to get into her room, and all the light of the universe entering her body and refracting there. Pierrette had heard gossip about a lawsuit after Ada's death, in which one of her betting ring co-conspirators had walked out of her room with a six hundred pound life insurance policy made out in his name, and all he'd given Ada in return was ten shillings. Yes, the Countess of Lovelace had been desperate for money in her last years – a problem Pierrette hadn't known rich people could have, and still couldn't quite fathom. But all the same, Ada surely wouldn't have done such a thing if she hadn't been addled by pain and laudanum.

Pierrette thanked Isaac, then slowly climbed the metal stairs up to one of the walkways that would take her over to the way out. She was so deep in thought about Ada that she didn't realize for a while that she had taken completely the wrong one, and was heading deeper into the complex, not back toward the street. As she tried to get her bearings, she ended up on a kind of catwalk over a small factory space where half a dozen workers were toiling over round metal casings. But wait… Pierrette leaned over the railing and peered down at them. The shape of them, those weird little nubs on the ends – they looked just like a drawing in Ada's notebook.

This was it. She knew, just knew. She knew by the look of the things, so familiar even now, though she hadn't read the notes in years. She absentmindedly patted her corset below her dress, where it was safe.

And she knew, too, because the men were working on them in such a careful, deliberate way. These were new things, untested, machines that they didn't understand. They had no instincts for them. And that made every instinct of Pierrette's *clang*. One thing you learned in the circus was to recognize the whiff of danger when you smelled it.

Three of the men were on the far side of a separating wall,

talking rather than working on the round devices. Two were wearing peaked caps like the other workers in the room, and one of them held a clipboard. They were talking to a man in a brown top hat, who was smoking a cigar – clearly an outsider to the factory. She tried to make out what they were saying.

"They leak," said the man with the clipboard. "One of our men got a nasty shock the other day."

"They're *supposed* to leak," said his colleague. "That's how it works. They're meant to give people shocks. It's in the design. I bloody *told* him," he explained to the man with the cigar, in a long-suffering voice.

"Well, you're both right," said the man with the cigar. "The original design was unpredictable. That's why I've brought a new design from the client. Completely safe for your men, and if you ask me, you want something with a bang anyway. Here's a parts list and new prints."

Cigar-smoker pulled an envelope out of his breast pocket and handed it to the man with the clipboard, who said, "But this is a big shift. And where are we to get …"

Pierrette could hardly hear what came next, over the banging of the workmen in the other part of the room. It sounded like "fumigated mercury," but that couldn't be right.

"Any chemist," said the long-suffering colleague. "Here, give it to me, you get on with telling the boys to down tools while we take this one. It'll add a bloody week to the time, I hope you know."

"The client is well aware this will require changes, and is also well aware that once those changes are in place, the construction will be faster and simpler. They are to be at Bousquet-Lang by the twenty-eighth."

"If they need to be in Paris by the twenty-eighth, we'll have to work through bloody Christmas," grumbled the man with the clipboard.

His colleague spoke to him privately, softer, causing Pierrette to lean over the railing to hear.

She leaned so far over that the catwalk started to swing and creak on its chains. One of the men looked up and yelled, "Oi, you! You're not meant to be in here!"

Pierrette considered trying to pretend she was, in fact, meant to be there. A client? No good. She wasn't exactly dressed the part, in her dowdy brown dress and old straw hat. (Every member of the Aurora Troupe had been making economies in recent years.) She didn't know what she was talking about or even where she was. A messenger? But from whom? A silly woman who'd lost her way? That at least had the virtue of being true, by one way of looking at things, but it meant she'd have to turn and leave now, and she would never again get a chance to take one of those casings.

And that would simply not do.

She'd lifted Ada Lovelace out of a crowd when she was nineteen. Surely, she could grab an inanimate object away from a startled worker. But in the circus, she'd had ropes and hoops to work with. In the factory, there was just this metal catwalk.

It creaked alarmingly as it swung.

Pierrette ran to the other side, then back again, and repeated the move, rocking it like a boat. The supervisor was yelling more now, but what could he do? Someone blew a whistle – damn, that would bring guards, proper trouble. The catwalk was swinging more and more, nearly over the heads of the workers now, the chains complaining mightily. It wasn't meant to take this kind of movement. But just a few inches more, and then she could hang down by her knees, grab the casing, flip back up, step onto the walkway that led out of here, and run.

It would have been a perfect plan – if the catwalk hadn't come off its chain while Pierrette was dangling by her knees.

Luckily, the workers were spooked enough by the creaking catwalk suddenly falling toward them at an angle that they all stepped out of her way. She grabbed the casing, which was slippery, and heavy too, damn it, and flipped to land on her feet. It wasn't easy to judge the distance or angle, so she landed too hard on one ankle, and cringed as she ran toward the closed door. As she tried to lift the latch with her free hand, a guard was on her, out of nowhere.

And out of nowhere, she swung the heavy iron casing at him. It made sickening contact, and he went down. She yanked the latch up with her left hand, kicked the door open, and ran out into a foggy Birmingham autumn day. She could hardly believe what she'd just done.

By the time Pierrette arrived back at the theatre, with the strange iron dome in her hand, she'd made up her mind. She had to leave England, that very night. She could be out of Birmingham within the hour, and over the Channel by this time tomorrow.

The sooner the better, because the police wouldn't take long to find her name. She was already known to some people in the ironworks, and she'd been seen there yesterday. And she wasn't sure how far the excuse of her small stature and sex would go, given that her circus act was known throughout the city.

The troupe would lie for her in an instant, say she had been

with them the whole time, but it might not work, and she
wouldn't ask it of them in any case.

Besides, she now knew where the weapons were headed: to
Paris. To something called Bousquet-Lang.

Tillie Wallin was upset. She was practically a woman now,
and had grown up so much over the last year and a half, with
her father still ill and the troupe living its relatively quiet new
life. Ariel had said, when they settled in Birmingham, that it
might be good for Tillie to finally be in one place for a while,
to make some friends. But Jovita had said that staying in one
place was prison if you weren't used to it, and she was proven
right. Tillie didn't make friends outside the troupe. She spent
her time helping Nell with the accounts, taking care of her
father, and practicing her riding. She was the most precise and
talented rider Pierrette had seen, in any troupe, in any city. But
she didn't seem happy.

So, when Pierrette announced that she had to leave them for
a little while, to travel to southern France, Tillie took it badly.

"It's my aunt," Pierrette pleaded, hating the lie. She had no
aunt that she knew of. There was no letter from France, asking
Pierrette to come for the dying old lady's final moments.

Meanwhile, a very real old man was sorry to see her go.
Pierrette knew that Major Wallin would worry, that she was
leaving the troupe without its final act. Birmingham in the
winter of 1857 was not London in the summer of 1851; there
were no other performers who could fill in. And when Major
Wallin worried, his daughter's face showed it.

"Listen, Tillie, you can do the pyramid with Hugh and
Jovita. Move Hugh to the end, make that his final trick, and
it will close out the show nicely. It's good to change things

up every so often. I'll bring you back something pretty from
France, will I?"

"I don't want anything from France."

"For Adolphus, then. Some pretty bows for his hair."

"Adolphus doesn't want anything either. And what will
Sabine do, with you away?"

"You can ride her and brush her for me. I won't be away for
long, Tillie. Believe me, I have to do this."

She had to hope that when the police came around, as they
surely eventually would, the troupe would tell them the truth:
that she had left England. But she wasn't going to southern
France. She was going to Paris.

Pierrette took a twelve-car locomotive from Birmingham to
Euston Station in London, and the stagecoach to Dover from
there. The coach was crowded, and at one point, a man tried
to help her with her hatbox, though she hadn't asked for help,
and the look on his face when he felt its weight made her smile
every time she thought of it afterwards. At the time, she did a
very good job of keeping a straight face, and acting as though
there was nothing strange in her hatbox at all, certainly not a
cast iron dome that she suspected was a weapon.

At every stage, she very deliberately did not look at any
policemen.

After a smooth ferry crossing, she took a train from Calais
to Paris, on a line that had been under construction when
the troupe left France. Almost ten years ago. She walked out
of the Gare du Nord into a vast new boulevard, lined with
cream-colored buildings, where before there had been a
medieval jumble. Napoleon III, as he called himself now,

had been remaking Paris, cutting new streets through the old neighborhoods, to make sure that his troops would have access, as rumors had it. Streets she had known as a child were gone. Everything was familiar and yet unfamiliar. It was a relief to speak French in the streets and hear it spoken back, after all this time. But she felt as gutted and altered as Paris was.

The streets where her parents had fought and died had been erased from the map.

A map. That's what she needed. She needed to find something or somewhere called Bousquet-Lang.

But first, a place to put down her things, including the blasted heavy hat box. A place to stay. The practical consequence of the tearing down of poor neighborhoods to build fancy boulevards was that lodgings were hard to find. Pierrette eventually took a room in a small, poorly decorated hotel. It was cold in Paris the week before Christmas, and the room had no fire and the wind whistled through the window. But what could she do? Paris was expensive.

CHAPTER FIFTEEN

Simeon stood on the top of the opera house, looking down at the Rue le Peletier like a man watching a show on stage, with the statues beside him his fellow audience members. It was eight-thirty in the evening, and he was in darkness, while the street below glowed with gaslight. The night was just cold enough to make Paris more beautiful. The rays of light caught white steam billowing from the horses' noses, and they stamped their marks on the sparkling gray flagstones. The streetlamps caught the frost on the bare trees. The narrow street was filled with people stepping out of carriages, dressed in furs and felt.

As for Simeon, he was dressed in a tailcoat and top hat like the rest, although in truth he would have been more comfortable on the rooftops in his hooded cloak, darkness or not. But he didn't know where the attack would come from, outside the opera or inside it. He patted his jacket pocket, where there was one ticket, for his usual box. The performance tonight was a mix of songs from various operas, including "Bal Masqué", which was about the assassination of the Swedish king in an opera house, and from "William Tell," an opera about a Swiss folk hero who had become an icon of the revolutionaries of 1848. All in all, an odd selection – or perhaps not.

The English Assassins had lost all track of Orsini and so Simeon had been watching for him in every working men's bar in Paris. He'd even grown his beard, to fit in better. But he'd seen no sign of him. He had seen other signs, though. Letters in Amira's favorite newspapers about the need for nations to rise through republicanism. Sidelong glances in the darkest corners of the bars when someone mentioned the upcoming performance of the opera, at which the emperor and his wife were planning to appear.

The emperor knew well enough that he was always at risk of assassination – every ruler was. A few years before, the tyrannical Duke of Parma had died in agony, twenty-three hours after being stabbed in the abdomen with a poignard by two hooded figures. The queen of Spain had recently been saved from a gunman while she was riding in her carriage. The savage King of Naples had died not long after getting the business end of an assassin's bayonet.

Simeon felt no sympathy for any of them. That King of Naples had bombarded the city of Messina for hours after it had already surrendered, to punish it for rising against him. His men had raped and killed old people and children. He deserved that bayonet. But Simeon was looking for patterns, from as high up as he could get. Ultimately, he was looking for the Magus.

Why a bayonet? Why a poignard? If these had been actual Assassins, they would have done a better job, as Amira said drily. The Brotherhood was careful with its blades; it wasn't interested in starting wars, or replacing one tyrant with another.

Where was this terrible weapon of Ada's? When would it appear?

Out of the corner of his eye, Simeon caught sight of the imperial carriages arriving. Over on the Boulevard des Italiens, he could see the glint of military helmets and lances, the occasional flutter of pennants. This emperor, who had survived three assassination attempts himself, rode in a carriage that had steel plates built into it. So the attack would likely come when the emperor was out of the carriage, walking into the opera house.

Simeon scanned the crowd, looking for the gleam of a gun, a knife, or whatever monstrosity the Magus might have designed. From this angle, in the darkness, and with everyone wearing a hat, it would be hard to spot Orsini's face. But he kept his eye out for a person with their hand in their pocket who might be Orsini. That made it harder; there were all kinds of fur wraps, cloaks, greatcoats. It would be the matter of a moment to draw a weapon and fire when the moment came. He paused to peer at the buildings around him, where someone might be waiting with a rifle. Nothing.

His fellow Assassins found his focus on political leaders strange, he knew. They had enough to occupy them with the Templars; Escoffier was convinced their numbers were converging on Paris to look for an artifact. But Simeon felt he could see patterns shaping, that he could half-understand them, even without the benefit of any Precursor Eye. He could smell a storm coming in on the January winds. If it happened today, Simeon would be ready, unlike that winter's day in Vienna when Libenyi had lunged at another emperor.

And if it really was Orsini, he'd surely be caught and hanged, just as Libenyi had been. He'd very likely fail – imagine trying to get a shot off in the darkness, in a crowd, at a moving target. Or trying to get close enough to the emperor to slip a knife into something vital. Unlikely, on the whole. And if the weapon was some type of explosive, a grenade maybe, surely Orsini wouldn't use it in a crowd like this. No, the most likely outcome was another quixotic failure that would accomplish nothing but Orsini's arrest and capture. If the Magus was behind this, he was not the scientific wizard Ada had imagined.

Simeon glanced north, where he could just see the roof of the neoclassical Notre-Dame-de-Lorette. It looked like a Roman temple, as did the home of the stock exchange, the Palais Brongniart, over to the south. In between, the new boulevard with its apartment blocks was still fronted with scaffolding.

The imperial cortege had turned the corner now, into the street, and the crowd had noticed. Everyone was turned to see them. The lancers in front, and the imperial guards. Three carriages. The emperor would be in the final one. It would be a few minutes, once they'd stopped, time for the guards–

A sharp bang, and a white light from below. The blast wave slammed into Simeon, and he slipped, grabbing on to one of the statues. A bomb, after all. The carriages hadn't even come to a halt before the device went off. There was screaming – a horse, and then a human.

With his hands still on the statue's head, Simeon swung down onto the balcony and perched on the railing, ready to leap down at Orsini. The street had been transformed into a battlefield after hours of carnage. Bodies on the ground, soldiers trying to get to their feet. Blood and broken glass catching the light. Horses rearing in their traces.

All three carriages had stopped now. There was at least one carriage window blown out – not enough to account for all the glass; some must be from the building. Where was Orsini? Had he planted it somehow? Thrown a grenade? Simeon had never seen a grenade with that kind of light, that kind of sound.

Oh, Ada, he thought.

He heard a clattering of hoofbeats over to his left and swung his attention to see what it was – probably just a horse desperate to get away, but it might have been Orsini. Had he been on horseback?

The horse was as dark as the night, dressed in military regalia, and the rider on it wasn't Orsini – but it wasn't a soldier either. A small figure in a smart hat – a woman? But riding astride, her skirts pulled up to her thighs. She was galloping straight up a builder's ramp, toward a tower of scaffolding. Maybe the horse really was a runaway; it must have had a soldier on its back not long ago. It clattered onto the wooden ramp – good God, the woman was controlling it, but why was she leading it up into that rickety–

He realized who it was. The circus performer, Pierrette Arnaud.

As she urged the horse up the ramp he spotted a second figure halfway up the scaffolding, silhouetted against the sunset, holding something like a football.

No, not a football.

Simeon jumped to the cobbles, ignored the shock from the hard stones, and ran for the scaffold.

Pierrette's horse slammed into the figure, and the bomb flew into the air. Simeon reached for it and dove, landing so hard he lost all his breath, but he was alive, with a cold metal sphere in his hands, so heavy he could barely grasp it. He scrambled to his feet, groaning from the pain, and screamed something incoherent but unmistakable at the man who had now pulled Pierrette off the frightened horse.

By the time Simeon reached her, she was lying motionless on the ground, with blood at her temple, and the man was gone.

Chapter Sixteen

Pierrette woke up in semi-darkness, lying on a sofa that was slightly too narrow even for her small frame. There was a paraffin lamp on a table by her feet, and a thin wool blanket keeping her body relatively warm, but her nose and fingertips were freezing. Her head ached and she felt as though she might vomit.

She turned her head and saw Simeon Price, sitting on a wooden chair, his arms crossed, glaring at her.

"I like the beard," she croaked.

He said nothing. Behind him, a cavernous room stretched. There were more lamps, and they caught a brightly tiled floor. No daylight.

"What time is it?" she asked.

"Noon, Friday. You slept right through the night, until now. How's the head?"

She moved her finger up to touch the spot that hurt the most, felt dried blood and pain, and cringed. "Not good."

"I had a doctor in to see it last night, when you were out. I don't know how much you remember. He gave you laudanum and you've been sleeping since."

"And where exactly am I?"

"Somewhere away from prying eyes. Anywhere with a doorman or a nun or a nurse, they'd have called the police, and given your behavior last night, it seemed very likely they'd hang you as a participant, along with Orsini and his accomplices. Except, of course, for the one you knocked off the scaffolding."

She remembered that well enough. The bomb in his hand, the same shape as the device hidden in her hat box. And she remembered Simeon catching it – good God, that had been close. They might both have been killed. She shivered.

"After that – when I fell – the horse. Is it–"

"That particular horse is all right, and deserves a medal. Those spikes on one side of the bomb: I think they're pins that trigger the detonation, so me catching it in the way I did saved our skins. I can't say the same for some of the other horses on the road last night. Several people are dead. I don't know how many are wounded – dozens, I'd guess. Four men were arrested, one of whom I know. One of whom I was trying to save. To stop. But I couldn't get to them in time, after your little stunt. The emperor was all right tucked up in his iron carriage, and his wife just has a scratch."

"Little *stunt*!" She did sit up this time, ignoring the nausea. "You just said I knocked one of them off the roof, and that bomb in his hands – who knows where it would have landed. How many more it might have killed. The horse deserves a medal, but I am treated as a fool?"

"The horse had little choice," he said through gritted teeth.

She lay back down. "Well, that's simply untrue. Horses

always have a choice. He knew what he was doing, and did it bravely. I couldn't have forced him up there, especially a horse with no circus training and no idea who I was. I agree about the medal. I disagree about everything else."

"It's down to luck that you didn't die, kill me, and let the bomb fall into the crowd anyway. It was a ridiculous risk to take, and drew attention. I'm not the only one who saw you riding up there."

"I had to make a decision," she reasoned. "I made it. It wasn't a very good one, but there weren't any good decisions to make."

If she'd only figured it out sooner. She'd never imagined anything like that weapon. To think that Ada had had a hand in creating that. But perhaps she hadn't. Perhaps whatever this weapon was, six years after her death, bore no resemblance to her imaginings.

"So, you did find a friend to tell you about the Magus?" She tried to proper herself on her elbow, but the room swam and she slumped back down.

He paused. "I did not. I followed Felice Orsini here from Italy. He went to England for a while. Is that where you became aware of him?"

"I don't know the name. Who's Felice Orsini?"

"One of the bombers. I thought he'd be the only one; I didn't know he had co-conspirators. Some of them came from England, I think."

"How do you know that?"

He stared at her, saying nothing. As her eyes adjusted, she realized there were other figures, standing at the far end of the room. Cloaked. Giving them their privacy, or standing guard, or both.

"Well, I didn't find any conspirators," Pierrette said, irritated. "I did find the place where they were making the bombs. I overheard them talking about them. There was an argument – the client said they weren't built to the original design. I gathered there was something… I believe that in Ada's design, they were supposed to do something odd to people, not merely explode. But they couldn't get that design to work. They'd figured out a simpler approach, one that would do a lot of damage."

She paused, thinking of the broken bodies strewn across the flagstones.

"Wait," Simeon said. "So Ada's original design was something different? Not – just a bomb?"

"I think it was a bomb of a kind. But I couldn't say. There was talk of a leak, of a shock – some sort of electricity? I don't know. The new design had something else in it. I thought they said it was fumigated."

"Fumigated?" Simeon's forehead wrinkled. "That doesn't – wait, could it have been 'fulminated'?"

Pierrette hadn't heard it well at the time and couldn't really say now. She shrugged, which just made her head hurt more. "They mentioned the name Bousquet-Lang, which, it turned out, was a warehouse. I went there and waited, every day, until I saw the crates come in from England, and then waited some more until I saw the buyer come and take them away. Listened to his conversation. I tried to follow him, but I was spotted and had to hide. It was several days before I found him again. He had a square sort of suitcase that seemed heavier than it ought to be. So, I followed him to the opera house, and you know the rest."

She lay back, exhausted.

"Well, we both failed," Simeon said. "A moment too late, yet again. And now Orsini will hang for it."

"Whoever this Orsini is, he killed and wounded innocent people."

"That he did. And I am damned curious about who talked him into it. I don't think the slaughter of innocents was in his character or in his plan. But then, I barely knew him. Maybe I'm wrong. I would like to know what his connection was to this Magus."

"Well, he'll be hard to talk to, in prison, even if he wanted to tell all."

"That's certain. He'll be silent, and then he'll be dead. Conveniently for someone, I suspect."

"So what happens now?"

Simeon sighed. "I suppose that's it, then. We've lost the thread. And we know what the weapons do. Whether that was what Ada originally designed or not, we know what they do now. Or maybe the Magus was one of the conspirators who was arrested. Maybe that's the end of it."

Pierrette shook her aching head, and immediately regretted that decision. "In Birmingham, the men said there were a dozen bombs. We know of four, isn't that right? The one that I – that you caught, yes, thank you very much – you said there were three explosions on the ground. That leaves eight."

"Maybe they were duds. Damp squibs." He looked unhappy. "Strange that they attacked so near the reinforced carriage, which probably shielded the emperor and saved his life. This whole thing makes no sense. I don't like it. A poorly planned, bloody assassination attempt out in public that seems designed to make sure the target survives and the assassins are hanged.

Bombers with a powerful new weapon, but no intelligence to speak of."

"They knew where the emperor would be."

"*Everyone* knew where the emperor would be. He made a point of it. He's afraid of looking afraid – he and his wife even carried on with their plans last night and went to the performance in the theatre, to show how unbothered they were."

"Good God," Pierrette said. "With those poor people lying dead outside on the street? With all the blood?"

He shrugged. "Neither you nor I think like an emperor, I suppose. And neither did our bombers. They only knew what the public knew. And they didn't even think about the best place to put them, or they would have known about the reinforced carriage. They would have waited until the emperor was out in the crowd. A minute more, and they would have had their man – and probably dozens more dead."

She shivered.

"This place is chilly, I know." Simeon did sound apologetic, at least. "Under a rail station. It's a place for hiding out."

Despite his worry over the bombing, Simeon seemed more at ease than he'd been in Vienna. No, ease wasn't the word – more at home. She looked again at the quiet figures at the back of the big room.

"A place for hiding out. For your Brotherhood?"

He hesitated. "Yes."

"Will they help us?"

"Help us do what?"

"Find the rest of the bombs. Find the Magus, and make sure he can do no more damage."

"They will help me do that, yes. Not you."

"Why not me?" Pierrette demanded.

"Because you nearly got yourself killed. Not only that, you made a spectacle. I have asked a friend to make sure the newspapers print no word about you and your horse, or the fourth bomb. Luckily for you. Otherwise, you'd be in jail, or worse. No, you are going to recover and then you are going home."

It probably wasn't the right time for Pierrette to bring up that the English police were looking for her at home. It made her ill to think of the troupe. Of Tillie and her ailing father, and Jovita, Ariel, Hugh and Nell. Oh, they'd be all right. But they would miss her. By now they'd have had a visit from the police; by now they'd have known she'd been less than truthful with them. She'd sent them one letter from Paris, saying she had stopped there briefly on her way to southern France, but not telling them much more other than that she was fine, and that she was sorry. She hadn't insulted them by making up any more lies.

What kind of life would she have now, outside the circus? She had almost no money, no friends in Paris, and no leads. But she did have promises to keep.

"I won't stop, Mr Price. At home or here. I am going to find the rest of these bombs, and all the blueprints, and this damned Magus, even if it costs the rest of my life to do it." She had fistfuls of blanket in her clenched fists.

"Bloody hell. I believe you." Simeon grimaced, then ran his hands through his hair. "If you're going to keep searching, you're going to put yourself in danger, which means putting me and my Brothers in danger, and I can't compromise them, and I can't let you get yourself killed, and I can't let you expose me."

"Then what? You'll have to kill me?"

"Worse," he said. "I'm going to have to teach you. That is, if you're willing to be taught. I can show you how to chase someone without being spotted, as you seem to have issues with that. And I can show you how to eliminate your enemies without alerting the whole of Paris to it."

She made a face. There were many things she knew, many things she'd learned, that he didn't even know about. She could throw a knife and kill a man if she wanted to. Her being spotted hadn't been her fault – had it? Well, maybe a little. Simeon was utterly wrong about several things, but he also had contacts and weapons – and an uncanny ability to go unseen. She hadn't even known he was there last night, until a second before he caught the bomb.

"Offer accepted," she said.

Pierrette was particularly interested in Simeon's knives: the black-handled folding one, and the big Bowie knife he kept in his belt, beneath his jacket. She'd picked up a Laguiole folding knife in a street market in Calais, to supplement the penknife she had always carried. Buying knives was a habit now, and her newest was lovely, with a wicked curve to the blade and a deer-horn handle.

On a cold afternoon a week after the bombing, she sat throwing it at an old wooden door, long off its hinges, on which she'd painted a bullseye. It leaned against a wall on the roof of her hotel. Simeon sat leaning against the chimney, a notebook on his knees, drawing something intently. She was sick of waiting for him to finish. He was certainly taking his damn time over it, whatever it was.

"You said you were going to teach me," she said, and threw the knife again. *Thwack.*

"I have been teaching you."

She stood up, retrieved the knife, idly whistling the three notes that Simeon had taught her to practice: a distress signal, he had said. "You gave me books to read. And a very odd doll."

"Anatomy model. You want to be an assassin, you have to learn how the body works."

Pierrette knew well enough how the body worked. It carried you up into glory, until the day came when it betrayed you. It worked until it didn't. Until you were Major Wallin, the greatest horseman in Europe, sitting with a blanket over your knees.

"I think you've just been keeping me out of your way, while you hunt down the Magus without me."

"There, you see? You're so clever, you don't need me to teach you anything."

She stuck out her tongue at him, and without looking, threw the knife at the door. *Thwack.* She looked, and laughed. It was right in the middle of the target.

He put his pencil between his teeth long enough to clap, then took it out of his mouth again. "I don't know any other way to teach. I'm sorry. I haven't had many teachers myself. Or none for very long, anyway."

She shielded her eyes from the winter sun's glare to look at him better. "Bad student, eh?"

"You could say that. Who taught you to throw knives?"

"A friend. I could teach you, if you want."

He made a face of his own. "Who's to say I need teaching?"

From her rooftop, she could just see the dome of the Pantheon. All of Paris was laid out before her. The streets where she'd grown up. But those streets had changed, and so had she.

Pierrette walked over to the target, pulled out the knife and presented it to him, with her hand on her hip.

He put his pencil back in his mouth and lined up his shot. It landed on the edge of the circle.

She raised her eyebrow at him, but he just shrugged.

"It doesn't matter," he said.

"Why, because I'm good at it and you're not?"

"No, because my aim from one inch away is perfect. You don't need to throw a knife if you can move unseen through a crowd quickly. You appear, you do the job, you disappear. No need for theatrics. Less chance of something going wrong."

She looked at the gauntlet on his right wrist. He'd shown her the spring mechanism that released the hidden blade, a tool he'd been given by Henri Escoffier after Simeon had been inducted into the Brotherhood. He was twirling the pencil around the fingers of his left hand.

"I never noticed that you were lefthanded before," she said.

"Learning to notice details is one of the lessons I'm apparently failing to teach you. The schoolmaster tried to beat it out of me, but I was a stubborn son of a bitch even then. Slow to get my work done." He picked up the paper he'd been working on and held it out to her. "But I get there eventually."

She took the paper. It was covered in gray pencil, a web of short, straight lines connecting little circles, each of which had two letters inside.

"Names of people connected to the men who were arrested in the bombing. I don't know how much any of them might know. We're trying to find out as much as we can about who else might have been involved."

"You don't think the Magus is one of the arrested men?"

Simeon shrugged. "Maybe he is. Maybe he's Orsini himself, and he planted misinformation to throw me off track."

He didn't sound convinced. He also didn't sound curious. He sounded despairing, but not defeated. Like a man facing something inevitable.

Pierrette's breath fogged in the cold air as she looked at the paper in her hand. She was suddenly certain of something that scared her, and she wanted to bring it out into the open, to look it in the eye. "But you already know who he is. Don't you?"

He shook his head. "I don't know anything. Yes, I have fears. Suspicions. Nightmares forming at the edges of my thoughts. None of that is very helpful."

CHAPTER SEVENTEEN

Simeon wrote a letter to Oscar Kane. In it, he asked for his help in finding the Magus, or, failing that, in understanding this pattern of assassinations. Between every word he wrote were other words, whispered words. He tore it up. Then he wrote another one, and tore that letter up too.

He was halfway into a fresh attempt when Pierrette came into the room beneath the Gare de l'Est and reported that her mission to watch one of the people on Simeon's chart the day before had ended badly. This was something that Simeon already knew, because Amira had brought him a newspaper that morning.

"I would have thought that by now you could be trusted to watch an octogenarian without being so bloody reckless."

Pierrette shifted from one foot to another. "Nothing happened."

"Is that so? Then how do you explain the report in the newspaper of the girl who saw an apparition in precisely the same little out of the way cemetery that sits around the corner from the cafe where I told you to go? Just like Our Lady of Lourdes, she said. Only younger, and wearing a gray cloak."

Pierrette failed to suppress a smile. That spring, people were flocking to the south of France to see for themselves the girl who claimed to see a lady in a grotto.

"You may think it's a lark to mock people's beliefs, but I don't," Simeon said.

Pierrette's smile vanished. "What about 'nothing is true, everything is permitted'? But *nothing* is permitted to me. If I had a smoke bomb, or even a proper Assassin's cloak, it would be easier. You permit me nothing, so I made my own choices, and found my own disguise."

Amira and Michel pushed open the door from the stairwell. Simeon kept his attention on Pierrette. "Just because something is permitted, doesn't mean it's wise. Now they know they're being watched. We've lost the element of secrecy."

"Oh, leave her be, Simeon," Amira said, removing her bowler hat. "Keeping out of sight can take years to learn."

Pierrette blushed, and Simeon felt badly for her – and then he was angry that he felt badly for her. He stayed perfectly still, as he always did when he was trying not to feel anything and failing miserably.

"Kane says you were a natural at it," Michel said, flopping into a chair and lighting a cigarette. "He has nothing but good things to say about you, Simeon."

Simeon turned to stare at him. "You've heard from Oscar Kane?"

The cigarette drooped in Michel's mouth. "He was here in Paris, until yesterday. Helping us with that business with the artifact the Templars have been so excited about. They didn't find it, but we only know that because Kane told us where they were going to search for it, and when. He's been a great help. I thought since he was here, you would have seen him."

"No." Simeon shook his head, thinking. "He didn't tell me."

Amira said gently, "You asked for time, when you left Vienna. He's probably giving you your space to think, letting you be the one to approach him. After all, you haven't written to him in all these years, have you?"

"I've thought about it many times, but I've never known what to say." Simeon paused a moment. "Michel, don't you think it's a coincidence that he was here in Paris when Orsini was? Orsini went to Vienna before he was arrested. He spoke about the Magus. So did Libenyi. And Kane sent Henri looking for me after we met in Ireland. What did I say to Kane that night, when I was drunk? Did I talk about Ada? I probably did, you know. And he didn't think much of it, because she was still working with him, then. But by '52, she'd cut off correspondence with him. He was desperate for her notes, for anything that could help him build his infernal weapon – something that would use electricity to manipulate people, their bodies, maybe even their thoughts."

"Your teacher is the Magus?" Pierrette demanded, her cheeks even redder now.

It seemed impossible, but Simeon suddenly wondered. He was sick with the knowledge of it. And he'd nearly handed over Ada's notes to him – but he hadn't, had he? Because he had had a suspicion, even then. He just hadn't wanted to admit it. But…
Kane?

"No, no, come on, Simeon, this makes no sense!" said

Michel. "Kane is an Assassin, one of great reputation. He'd tell us if he were working on something like this. And anyway, as you've said many times yourself, both Libenyi and Orsini seem to have been set up to fail. Why would an Assassin send an amateur out to be killed in such a clumsy and public way? Why would an Assassin attempt to eliminate a sovereign, for Christ's sake, without so much as telling the rest of us?"

Simeon shook his head again, violently. "I don't know. I don't know. Maybe to test something – to test the weapons? Or maybe he didn't mean for it to happen. I don't understand it, but there are too many connections to ignore. You said he'd left Paris. Yesterday? Where did he go? Back to Vienna?"

Michel shrugged. "Probably. I didn't ask. He said he was taking a train."

"From here?"

"I don't think so, or he would have stopped by." Michel corrected himself. "Or perhaps not. Anyway, this was yesterday. Wherever he's gone, he'll be there by now. But whether Vienna, Ireland, or somewhere else, we'll ask the Assassins everywhere to let us know."

"The old woman said something about an Irishman," Pierrette said suddenly.

Simeon turned to her. "The woman you were watching? What did she say? Did she say anything about Oscar Kane?"

"No, she used another name. It might have been a nickname, come to think of it. Monsieur Gilet." She looked at him, her face shining, glad that she was getting something right. He knew that look. He'd had it himself, every time he'd been a student.

"Monsieur Gilet," Amira repeated slowly, realization dawning across her face.

Pierrette translated, for Simeon's benefit. "Mr Waistcoat."

Simeon sank into a chair as though she had hit him.

CHAPTER EIGHTEEN

Pierrette couldn't help wondering, on many occasions across the next two years, whether they could have identified the Magus back in Vienna in 1853 if Simeon had only been less... Simeon. If he'd talked more, listened more. But if there was any blame to be put at his feet, she wasn't going to lay it there. She watched him follow every trail, spending weeks tracing every one of Orsini's accomplices until they led nowhere. He told her once that he'd had some conversations with a few of them. She'd half-seriously asked whether they were still alive, to which he'd responded, "I don't torture people."

But he could not ignore the facts: the bombs had come from England. The bombers had been in contact with someone named the Magus. Their associates had mentioned an Irishman they called "Mr Waistcoat." Oscar Kane always wore striking waistcoats. Janos Libenyi had known Oscar Kane. Oscar Kane had come through Paris at the time of the Orsini bombing. Orsini had been in contact with someone named the Magus. So had Ada Lovelace.

After months of investigating and pondering, Simeon traveled to Vienna and returned a month later, to report that Kane's rooms were rented to someone else now, and all his businesses had been sold.

Somehow, knowing the identity of the Magus made the man no less elusive.

At least Simeon hadn't given him Ada's notebook, Pierrette thought with some satisfaction. That was still sewn inside her corset – albeit a new one that fit her better. Simeon wasn't happy about this hiding place, saying it put her in danger, but she countered with a joke that there was nothing safer than a corset thick enough to stop a bullet, and he'd let the matter rest. She'd given Michel the bomb casing she'd brought from Birmingham, so that he could keep it with other objects the Assassins didn't want anyone else to find. But the notebook was hers, her constant duty. She wanted it with her all the time.

Concealing weapons was a more difficult matter. Simeon had smiled, watching her slip her new Apache revolver – a gun that was also a knife or a set of knuckle dusters, depending on how it was folded – into a reticule.

"It's this or under my skirt, and one can't get at them quickly enough there," Pierrette had sighed, speaking from experience.

She did like wearing her cage crinoline, though. It had a lovely silhouette, slimmer in the front than her old horsehair, and it made her new mauve dress drape beautifully. Simeon had only shaken his head at the color.

"It's mauve," Pierrette had said defensively. "A brand new dye. The latest fashion."

"Well, you won't be hard to spot in a crowd," he grumbled.

"On the contrary. This, my dear teacher, is what hiding in

plain sight looks like, when one is a twenty-eight year-old woman in Paris. I told you years ago that I'd find my own disguises, and I have. Believe me, I'd stand out more if I skulked in a cloak and hood all the time."

So Pierrette wore her new dress when she went out on her own on a Thursday evening in late May, riding on the top deck of the omnibus as she always did, in all weathers. Easier to watch for attacks from there, and more companionable with the horses, especially when she got a seat up front above the driver. She liked to see the world around her, and for the world to see her too. This dress had cost her a week of posing for an artist, hanging from her knees for hours on end. She would damn well show it off!

None of the Assassins of Paris particularly liked mixing with society to gather gossip on what the Templars were up to. Simeon hated it, and Amira only traveled in very particular circles. So Pierrette gladly took it on herself to go to parties and find out what she could. She didn't have any smoke bombs, but she had a lovely perfume.

She stepped lightly down at seven o'clock outside the home of an artist in Montmartre who was exhibiting works rejected by that year's Paris Salon. Up the stairs to a dark and smoky room, where a woman took her cloak and gloves.

There were other flashes of color in the room – sapphire and emerald green – although no one else in mauve. The people were brighter than the paintings, which stared down at them as if the people trapped in them were watching them from another world. Out of the corner of her eye, Pierrette could see a painting of a woman on a trapeze. It wasn't her, but it was very similar to the paintings she'd been the model for back in London. Nearly a decade ago now, and Pierrette hadn't performed in several years. She barely wrote to the Aurora Troupe anymore, though she had the occasional letter from Nell. None of them had come to any harm from the police after Pierrette's escapade, thank goodness, but life in Birmingham was hard, and ticket sales were low.

She looked away from the trapeze painting. Her gaze was drawn to another painting in the middle of the wall: a black piano, a somber woman playing it, a girl in a white dress leaning on it and watching her.

Pierrette stepped closer, examining it. The little sign beside it said it was by Whistler. It astonished her, how the people in it were reduced to shapes and colors, somehow – as though they were as artificial an arrangement as a bowl of fruit. But that was an illusion, because the closer she got, the more human they were. A trick of the eye.

"Mademoiselle Arnaud, isn't it?" She turned to see a red-haired woman. "It is Pierrette Arnaud?"

The woman spoke in English. She was about Pierrette's age, but thin, with dark hollows in her cheeks.

It took a moment for Pierrette to recognize her, from an evening at Ada's home, ten years before.

"Miss Siddall?"

"Yes, but I'm Mrs Rossetti now. I'm here on my honeymoon, in fact." She indicated a figure with dark curly hair, engaged in animated discussion with other men in a corner of the room. Pierrette thought she recognized him: one of Ruskin's protégés.

"My very best wishes. I'm so glad you recognized me, and after all this time!"

"Oh, I never forget a face," said Lizzie Siddall with a smile.

"I suppose you wouldn't, being a painter."

"More often a painter's model these days, although not much of that either. My health has been poor. I do still draw a little. I see you're still inspiring." She pointed at the trapeze picture.

"It isn't me," Pierrette said. "Just someone who looks like I used to look."

"It's very odd that I should run into you here," said Lizzie, looking off into the distance. "Just as we were leaving England, I met another friend of Countless Lovelace. I hadn't thought of her in so, so long, even though for the longest time I couldn't see Ruskin without thinking of her. And then it seemed that no one ever spoke of her except to voice some opinion about her mother, or her father, or both. I'd locked away my memories of her in a little box, so that none of that could get to her. And so, when this friend of hers asked me about her, I found I had nothing to say. I hope he didn't find me rude. I was unwell."

"Which friend was it? Someone who used to come to her house when I knew her?"

"Oh, I don't think so. He had a Biblical name."

"What, like Ezekiel or Jeremiah?"

"I think it was his surname." Lizzie turned her bright eyes back on Pierrette, and said, "Cain. That was it. A Mr Cain. Do you know him at all?"

Life's chances didn't last. Pierrette knew that. You could be stretching your arms to the heavens, your foot planted on the back of a broad, strong horse, with perfect form on a perfect day, and in the blink of an eye everything could go wrong for any reason, or none, and you could be on the ground, breathless from pain, twisted, trampled. You could be talented young parents with a stubborn streak, just standing their ground against an unjust government, and you could fall at the first shots fired, the dream of revolution evaporated. For that matter, you could be going about your business and a wave of typhoid or cholera would pass through your city and you would find yourself among the unlucky. Risk didn't come into it. A hoof could turn just as easily in a rutted country road as it could in the raked sand of the circus, and the most careful passenger could be thrown into a twisted bloody heap.

There was no point in hesitating. Even as she was telling Simeon what Lizzie Siddall had told her about Oscar Kane, she was packing her suitcase, the hatbox now holding only hats.

But Simeon stayed very still and said nothing.

"We have to go, tonight if possible," Pierrette said. "We've finally got him."

"If he was in London two months ago, he could be anywhere in the world now."

"But the longer we hesitate, the colder the trail will get."

"If we run off at every report, we'll always be following. We have to think about where he's going next, not where he just was. We have to consider the possibility of traps and feints. He's eluded us this long for a reason, Pierrette."

Pierrette couldn't believe what she was hearing. Simeon had never for a moment lost his obsession with the Magus, with Kane, even though there had been no further hints of activity after the Orsini bombings. Governments throughout Europe rounded up dissidents and hardened their laws. The emperor lived. But if Kane had been willing to build and disseminate a bomb as terrible as the one that had caked a Parisian street in gore, how much more terrible must the original design be? Not having Ada – or her notes – had slowed Kane down, but there was no reason to think it had stopped him.

"Yes, he could be anywhere," Pierrette said. "But given that he was in London two months ago, he's more likely to be there than anywhere else. And he has no idea that we know he was there. He had no way of knowing that Lizzie and I would run into each other. Luck is on our side, for once, and it doesn't happen often, and it won't last long."

But Simeon was stubborn. He sent wires to the few Assassins left in England. He glowered at the responses, worrying the edges of the telegram paper in his fingers until it curled. None of the English Assassins had heard from Oscar Kane recently – and they all said that surely he wasn't in England, or they would know about it. This thought brought Pierrette no comfort, and she could tell it brought Simeon none either. Pierrette knew Kane had been in England – Lizzie Siddall had said so, and she had no reason to lie. So the fact that Kane had been avoiding the Assassins there suggested he really was working on his own now, even hiding his activities from them.

Finally, she said, "You'll never have peace until you confront him. You know he's there. Why are you so unwilling to go?"

"I swore I'd never go back to England."

"The weather's not that bad."

He glowered at her. "Pierrette, I was a soldier. In the British Army. My troop ship struck a rock and sank, back in 1852, and I took the opportunity to leave His Majesty's Service. Without saying goodbye."

Several things clicked into place: the way he kept himself to himself, as Nell would say. The way he would never talk about his past. The way he looked warily at soldiers in the street.

"So, if you go back to England, what would happen?"

"To me? Likely nothing if I'm lucky. If the army finds me, however, they could court martial me, and throw me in prison for desertion, and they'd be well within the law to do it. Brand me with a 'D' on my arm. Maybe lashes too."

"Then send me. I know London well enough. I'll find him."

Simeon shook his head. "No, I'm not sending a student who hasn't even been inducted into the Brotherhood yet – and don't even ask; you're not ready. I won't ask Amira, Henri or Michel to go either. None of them know Kane the way I do. Besides, you were right. I need to talk to him. To understand."

"Are you willing to kill him?" Pierrette asked.

Simeon took a long time answering. "If he really is the Magus, if he created those bombs, I don't think the British courts would show him much mercy. A hidden blade would be kinder, and more certain."

The Orsini Affair, as it was called in the newspapers, had brought down the British prime minister. The French accused England of sheltering assassins, since Orsini had recruited in England, where the granting of asylum for political exiles made it easy for radicals to find each other. Diplomatic relations cooled, and there was even talk of war between England and France. To calm things down, Lord Palmerston introduced a bill increasing the punishment for conspiracy, but many saw this as giving in to French bullying, and his government fell. The next government was just as eager to prove that England took assassination seriously. It rounded up radicals and put them on trial for conspiracy, libel… anything it could. As had happened in Vienna, the failed assassination attempt had had only one effect: less freedom and worse laws. And those laws would deal harshly with a man who worked with the bombers, especially if he really had helped in the design of what the newspapers called "infernal devices."

"But it doesn't have to be *your* hidden blade," Pierrette protested. "He was your teacher."

"All the more reason he should have been honest with me."

"Then you must always be honest with me, because I'm your student," Pierrette said.

"Haven't I been?"

She shrugged. "I wouldn't know, would I? But promise me at least that you'll tell me when you need help."

"The best help you can give me, is to stay safely away. Don't come looking for me, no matter what."

Her eyes went wide. "What? You're dropping me like luggage again?"

"Not like luggage. It's just that... Pierrette, I need to have this conversation with him alone."

"And if it turns out to be more than a conversation?"

He paused. "If that happens, then there is all the more reason for you to be well away." He shifted in his chair, crossing one leg over the other, then smoothing his hand over a twisted seam in his trousers, as though his thoughts were five hundred miles away. "The man who sewed my clothes took pride in his work. Well, so do I. I swore to protect the innocent, and not to compromise the Brotherhood. And if our suspicions are right, and Oscar Kane was secretly behind the attack that night – well, he has to answer for it. To me."

She leaned back and crossed her arms. "Great. Then I'll stay in Paris by myself, with no one to tell me to stop walking on the rails of bridges on the Seine, and no one to tell me not to sit in the front row at the opera with my back to the audience. I'm looking forward to it."

They stared at each other for a few minutes, until at last Simeon said, "Oh, bloody hell. Pack your bag, then."

Chapter Nineteen

Either London smelled worse than when he left it, or Simeon had forgotten how bad it was. The city was putting in sewers everywhere to try to make the river less foul, but whenever the wind blew from the direction of the Thames, there was a whiff of the chamber pot.

And there was always a wind off the Thames in the rented rooms where Lizzie Siddall and Dante Gabriel Rossetti lived, at the north end of where the recently demolished Blackfriars Bridge had been. They had the second floor of a rowhouse, with a landlady downstairs who brought them meals.

The Rossettis had traveled back to England at the same time as Pierrette and Simeon, and told them there were empty rooms next door. Simeon took the rooms; Pierrette was a more difficult question. With their different accents, they couldn't pass for brother and sister, and they both cringed whenever anyone assumed romance. Beyond the assumptions of other people, it was important to Simeon that Pierrette feel safe and comfortable.

When Pierrette explained that Simeon was her teacher, and

that she would try to find a lodging close by, Gabriel and Lizzie both insisted that Pierrette should stay with them for the time being instead.

"Lizzie could use the company," Gabriel said. "I got her a little bullfinch for just that purpose. You'll do even better!"

As far as Pierrette and Simeon were concerned, the location couldn't have been better, despite the stink. Right in the middle of the city, with windows facing several directions – they could see any enemies coming. There was some noise from the early stages of construction of the new bridge, but they didn't mind that.

The summer stretched on, and turned to autumn, then winter, but they found no sign of Kane. They continued Pierrette's training on a different set of rooftops and learned all they could about radicals and political exiles. They found plenty of connections to Orsini, but the trail to the Magus always went cold.

They needed allies, but London was lacking in Assassins. Michel had advised Simeon to talk to a man named Ethan Frye. It took Simeon a year, but he finally tracked him down: a man in his thirties, who seemed very tired. Frye knew Kane but hadn't seen the man in years. If he was in London, Frye knew nothing about it – but he had been travelling recently and might have missed Kane's arrival. He sent Simeon to an alleyway to see someone called the Ghost, who turned out to be a skillful young man from India, with connections throughout London. The Ghost hadn't seen or heard anything about Kane either, but promised to ask around.

As Simeon was walking out of the shadows, the Ghost called out, "How discreet would you like me to be?"

Simeon turned back. "Discreet?"

"This man you're looking for. He's an Assassin, but I have the sense – well, I'll put it this way. Do you want me to make sure he doesn't hear that someone is looking for him?"

Simeon thought for a moment. If Kane was still in London, he didn't want to give him a reason to leave. Then again, it might flush him out. He might make a mistake. And at this point, Simeon had very few tricks left to try.

"Discretion is not required," he had said.

Weeks passed with no word from the Ghost, no new leads to follow. Simeon settled into a pattern: in the evenings he went with Rossetti to the Working Men's College or a pub nearby, and talked to people about science and art, hoping to hear someone say something about an inventor, about Ada... something.

In the daytime, he sat with Pierrette and went through the newspapers. If the Magus was in London, maybe he was here to encourage violence among doomed radicals, just as he had in Paris and Vienna. So Simeon read the crime stories, looking for any mention of Orsini, of bombs, of any advertisements for meetings of people interested in the unification of Italy, in nationalism, in republicanism.

On a Saturday in early October, Gabriel stood in his little studio overlooking the Thames and painting in the light, while Lizzie sat dozing with a blanket over her knees in the sitting room. Pierrette and Simeon were going over the newspapers at a little table. He had the *Police Gazette* and she had the *Times*, laid out flat on the table. She sighed, flipped a page, and then sat straight up as though startled.

"What is it?"

"I just... let me read a moment."

She picked up the newspaper so he couldn't see what was in it, and furrowed her brows, then cocked her head to look at him around the edge of the paper, then frowned even deeper.

"For Christ's sake, Pierrette."

She let the paper drop and turned it around so he could read it. Across the top was written: "DESERTERS FROM HER MAJESTY'S SERVICE." Then, on the lines beneath: *"Until further notice, the Reward given by the War Office for the Apprehension of a Deserter will be TWENTY SHILLINGS, the object being to prevent the crime of Desertion, and to hold out a greater inducement for the recovery of Deserters into Her Majesty's Service."*

Under that was a table listing names, regiment, place of birth, physical appearance, place of desertion, identifying marks. He stared at it for a moment, not focusing on the names. He was presumed dead. His name was a fairly common one. There was no reason for his eyes not to focus.

Pierrette grabbed it again and read aloud: "Simeon Price. Regiment: 74th. Where born: Ealing, London. Trade: laborer. Age: 35. Size: 5-10. Eyes: Blue. Face: Fair. Hair: Light brown. Coat and trousers: regimental." She paused for long enough to look at Simeon, who was in his shirtsleeves, with a waistcoat that had once been bottle green and a neckerchief of very unregimental yellow. "Date of desertion: 26 February, 1852. Place of desertion: Cape Colony. Marks and remarks: Shipwrecked and presumed dead until intelligence received to the contrary."

She shoved the paper back down onto the table.

"That could be anyone," Simeon joked, keeping it light,

keeping her from worrying. He needed time to think. "Intelligence received." Someone had turned him in. How recently? He hadn't been checking the deserters columns carefully, but he thought he would have noticed it, if it were there before today.

Lizzie's little red and blue bullfinch started cheeping in its wicker cage, but Lizzie herself was still sleeping, and Gabriel was painting in the next room.

He picked up the newspaper and looked at it in the way Kane had taught him to observe, letting his subconscious absorb the shapes, the patterns. Letting his instincts take the reins. Through the thin paper as it slackened in his hands, he could see the long dark columns of text. He turned the page.

There in the middle, exactly on the reverse side of where his name was printed, was a short news item:

ASSYRIAN ARTIFACT

Mr George Smith, who is engaged in cleaning stored artifacts at the British Museum, has uncovered an unusual clay object in the shape of an eye, buried among the many tablets, tiles and statues gathered at the recent excavations at Nimrud, in Mesopotamia. Precisely what this eye may have represented is as yet unknown, but a number of learned gentlemen, including Mr Henry Rawlinson and Mr Hormuzd Rassam, have been invited to examine the object in the afternoon of Monday the 7th of October, when the museum will open the storage area to those gentlemen for the purpose.

Simeon closed the newspaper. He didn't focus on Pierrette's

face – he didn't focus on anything – but he knew she was watching him, concerned. An eye from Assyria! Just what Kane had been obsessed with, years ago. It couldn't be a coincidence that it was printed on the reverse of the list of deserters that bore his name. But if it wasn't a coincidence, that meant it was a deliberate provocation. Which meant, very likely, an invitation. Or a trap.

All the same, he couldn't ignore it. If Kane was baiting him, that was Kane's mistake. It was a chance, finally. But one he would take alone.

"Pierrette, there's nothing to worry about. I expect someone saw me in Paris or Vienna years ago, and mentioned it to my father, who probably went straight away to the police to tell them everything he knew for the reward. For twenty shillings, my father would hold the whip himself."

She frowned at him. "We're not safe here."

"We're as safe here as we are anywhere. None of them know where I am, clearly, or they'd have burst down my door by now. It's nothing. Oh, but look at this." He grabbed the newspaper again, casually. "*'Charles Blondin, the tightrope walker who crossed Niagara Falls, is giving an exhibition of his most famous feats at the Crystal Palace on Monday.'* One of your countrymen, and you haven't had a chance to see any performances. You've been stuck in here with me, poring over newspapers. Why don't you go?"

On Monday afternoon, the October chill in the air brought on a classic London fog. There was something rich and tangy in it, like the aftertaste of a pint of stout. It hung sulfurous around the streets, so thick that the classical columns of the British

Museum seemed like the borders of an island by the time he walked up the great stone steps. He couldn't see the city that surrounded it at all. Just gas flames in the mirk, like marsh lights. And rising out of it all, the carved frieze, like a great Greek temple.

As he paused at the threshold, a porter in a smart blue uniform with gilt buttons tipped his top hat.

"Your first visit to the museum, is it, sir?"

It was. In his London years, the new museum building had been under construction, and closed to the public. There had been some sections open, to scholars and other people who could say they had a reason to be there. Ada might have taken him, if he'd asked. He hadn't asked.

But now there were children playing around the drinking fountain near the door, and two old women in shawls arguing and waving what seemed to be a map of the museum. Ordinary people. Simeon had worn his top hat and frock coat, to hide in plain sight, but he had his cloak under his coat – for warmth, and in case he needed it.

Simeon nodded politely to the porter.

"Ah, well, I warn you the museum is likely to close early. I wouldn't give it more than an hour."

"Close early? But why?"

Talking made him realize he could taste the fog, acrid and thick as a pint of stout.

"The fog, sir." The porter made a gesture that took in the general miasma. "They don't like to have any candles or lamps inside, for fear of starting a fire, you see. The only light comes from the windows, and today it's getting darker by the second. I don't know if you'll have time to see many exhibits."

"That's all right, thank you. I have some very particular business to take care of."

"Ah – if it's the new Reading Room you're after, you'll need to apply for a reading ticket."

"Not the Reading Room, no." Simeon took a step past the doorman, then stopped. "Where would I find Assyrian artifacts? The storage rooms?"

"Ah, yes, not the first inquiry I've had about that today. Just through the Roman Gallery, to your left, sir, you'll find the Assyrian Transept. And then if you pass through the Transept, take the first right, you'll go through a long gallery in the Egyptian section, then to your left you'll see a circular staircase. Take that down a flight and there's all the Assyrian artifacts you could wish for, if the Keeper's about to show you what you want to find."

"I think I'll find it without help. Thank you, sir." Simeon paused, uncertain, then handed the man a shilling.

"Thank you, sir! Very generous."

He stepped inside. A vast entry hall opened in front of him, and in the center, a great stone vase as tall as a horse presided over it all. He veered left, into a long hall dimly lit by skylights, with deep shadows playing around the statues and objects on columns. A few small knots of people were looking at the exhibits and took no notice of him.

He followed the porter's directions, past massive sculptures of winged beasts with human heads, and a tall black obelisk around which a number of fashionably dressed ladies were listening to another woman give a lecture. No sign of Kane.

At the end of a long gallery, he saw the small, curving staircase. It was dim, and he slowed down with every step.

The dark, vast hall at the bottom of the stairs was as quiet as a tomb and nearly as dark. It was crowded with glass cases, and low columns holding objects in stone and clay. Shadows played along the great stone reliefs that lined one wall, so he could almost imagine the figures carved on it were moving. He couldn't see anyone, but he could sense someone there. The whole room was holding its breath.

"I have always hoped you'd find your way back to me eventually," said Kane from the shadows, and then stepped out from behind an obelisk.

"Have you? You could have made it easier, and simply come to see me when we were both in Paris."

"I had business there."

"I know," Simeon said, remembering the blood on the cobblestones.

It was even darker down here than on the floor above. A few distant windows cast what could hardly even be characterized as light. It was gloom and deeper gloom. But Kane looked as he always had, imposing in a brilliant blue waistcoat with a bit of a shine that managed to catch what little light there was. His top hat was low over his eyes, his shillelagh was in his hand, and his gaze was steady on Simeon. Beneath the brim, his eyes had the same bright, wide glare, the curl of his lip the same detached fascination.

"My business in Paris was in aid of the Brotherhood. We feared the Templars would find an artifact. I made sure that didn't happen, by the simple expedient of finding it first." He smiled a bit at Simeon's surprise. He'd found something, and kept it from Michel, from everyone. "At long last, we are matching the Templars, pace by pace."

"It doesn't seem that way to me. London seems to have hardly any Assassins left."

"We are building up our resources. Artifacts. Weapons." He took a step closer. "And it's weapons you want to talk to me about, isn't it, Simeon? I know you've been greatly troubled by what you've learned about Orsini and his comrades." Another step forward. "I'm sorry I didn't take you into my confidence from the beginning, in Vienna, when it came to the affair with the tailor."

"Janos Libenyi."

"Yes. An early experiment. I had hoped to use him to test a prototype, but he was, I fear, overly susceptible to the idea of assassinating the emperor. I don't know where he got the notion to go after him with a kitchen knife. That had nothing to do with me."

"But you *were* preparing to use him as an assassin, the way you used Orsini. Why? Why send untrained, incompetent men after the best-guarded men in Europe?"

"Because any good scientist knows the value of experimentation," Oscar snapped. "And any good Assassin knows not to trust a key assassination to an experimental weapon. I needed to know whether the bombs worked, and I needed the experiments to happen without any connection to us. I was protecting the Brotherhood. And yes, I admit, I was proving a point."

"Proving a point? To whom?"

Oscar paused. "Vision is a peculiar thing. I have never been able to cultivate the ability to see the world the way some Assassins can: they can spot an enemy or a friend at a glance. Oh, I like to think I've made up for it by honing my powers of observation – ordinary human skills, but disciplined, and put to use. And I believe I have a different kind of vision. I can see the way the world is tending. We can't free humanity from the Templars by hiding around corners with knives in our hands. There are members of the Brotherhood who cannot see what I see, and naturally, they don't understand my work."

Simeon had known that of Kane for some time, and had suspected for longer, but it still made him feel slightly sick to hear it confirmed.

"Is it your work? Or is it Ada's?"

"Ah yes, beloved Ada." Kane walked toward Simeon, turning toward a bas-relief and tracing the ancient writing on it. "A true genius. Someday, the world will learn just what a remarkable mind she had. Not a very practical one, perhaps, but an imagination that could hold galaxies within it. Her original design for the bombs was, well, a disappointment, to be frank. So much promise, but I couldn't get it to work reliably, and then she turned against me. So, I had to make a simpler version. It took me years, even so. And I kept hoping there was something she had left behind, some clue."

Simeon stood very still. "It was never a coincidence, then, that I became your student."

"It was not. When you spilled your heart out to me in Ireland, I couldn't see how you'd be any use. Ada was still writing to me back then. But after she turned against me, I thought of you a great deal. I found out where you'd been posted. I suggested an assassination on the *Birkenhead*, and asked my old friend Henri to add another job while he was at it. And then I made sure you found your way to Vienna."

Oscar Kane, the Magus, high in his tower with his books and

devices, sending his pigeons out over Europe, a spider in a vast web. And Simeon had been caught.

"Then you only ever wanted to use me, in case I knew something about Ada."

"Not at all. I did want to find out what you knew, but as soon as I met you, I wanted to teach you for your own sake, for my sake. I wanted to stand beside you as we walked into the future. And I still do, Simeon. You've had time now to do your research on me, just as I once did my research on you. You're no longer a student. In fact, I hear you have a protégé of your own."

Pierrette. Safely away at the Crystal Palace, watching a tightrope walker. Pierrette who had risked so much, given up so much, to carry out Ada's final commission. And she had succeeded, better than Simeon ever had. Kane didn't know that she had Ada's notes. She'd kept them safe for a decade.

"You have to stop this, Kane. You've made your experiments. Now–"

A commotion, voices in an adjoining room. It was hard to tell where they were coming from, down here. The only passages Simeon could see were on either side, near the staircase where he stood. He thought the voices were coming from his right, but he wasn't sure.

One of the echoing voices said the name "Price", and every sinew in Simeon's body thrummed.

"I don't have to do anything," Kane said, spreading his hands out, the shillelagh in one. "You are the one who has to make a choice. And I believe you have approximately ten seconds in which to do it, before the police come and take you to prison for desertion."

Of course. All this time, as they'd been talking, Kane had

known the police were on their way – because he had told them. He'd turned Simeon in. And while the British police would no doubt be happy to put Orsini's bomb-maker on trial, Simeon had not a shred of evidence against Kane.

There had to be various staircases down to the basement. They'd come down another, leaving the one behind Simeon free – he hoped. He resisted taking a step backward, closer to escape.

"It would be easy to tell them their tipster was mistaken," Kane said. "I'll vouch for your identity, Mr Straw. Are you with me or not?"

There was no hope of a trial. Kane would keep making his terrible weapons, keep up his bloody experiments. The only way to save lives was to take one.

A gunshot was risky; he'd only get one chance, and that would bring the police even faster. Kane knew about the hidden blade attached to Simeon's right wrist, but he didn't know that his old ivory-handled razor was in his left. A few big steps forward, a flick of the thumb, a slash across the throat, a silent death. Leaving Simeon little time to get away before the police came, but he'd think about that when it happened. It was worth the risk.

"I'm with you," he said confidently, stepping toward Kane. "You leave me little choice. But we have to be true partners. You want me to stand beside you? Here I am."

Kane eyed him curiously. Footsteps, shouts nearby. Simeon didn't know whether Kane would let him get close, and he wasn't a good enough actor to try to convince him for long. Keep it short and keep it fast.

His left thumb snicked the razor open as he approached, and

it flashed as he swung it at Kane's neck. He didn't expect it to make contact. The natural response would be to either move to the right, away from the blade, or grab for Simeon's left hand. The hidden blade was ready in Simeon's right, to plunge into Kane's neck from that direction. He focused on the skin right above the stiff collar, to the right of the Adam's apple. A collar would be no match for a hidden blade – this wasn't Libenyi's kitchen knife – but Simeon was taking no chances.

But Kane didn't do the natural thing. He knew well enough what was waiting in Simeon's right hand. He puffed his chest, pushed Simeon's right elbow down toward the floor.

Simeon slashed with the razor, across Kane's shoulder blade, parting the wool jacket and drawing blood. But Kane's weight on Simeon's right side sent Simeon stumbling backward, into a column.

The clay tablet wobbled on top, and Kane's eyes darted up at it. He reached his left hand over to stabilize it – he couldn't help himself – and Simeon was on the ground but still had the razor in his hand, and Kane's shoulder was bleeding. Simeon slashed again, this time aiming for the ligaments behind Kane's knee, but out of the corner of his eye he could see Kane's own hidden blade coming down from above.

Simeon rolled away. When he found his bearings, he saw Kane running up the round staircase. Simeon clambered to his feet and ran after him, ignoring the loud shouts from behind him.

The stairs let him out between the Assyrian and Egyptian rooms. He stepped forward cautiously into an empty hall, the razor still in his hand. There was one comforting thought:

Kane wouldn't risk gunfire in here. Simeon kept his distance from every artifact big enough to conceal a man, but didn't turn his back on any of them until he'd had a chance to see behind them.

He came to a threshold, beyond which was a bigger hall, lined with massive statues, with deep shadows behind them. He felt exposed in his top hat and constricted in his coat. An easy solution to that, at least. The hat came off, and he perched it on top of a bust of a pharaoh. The coat went around the pharaoh's shoulders. Simeon slipped forward, feeling much more comfortable in just his stone-colored cloak, the hood pulled over his head.

Kane's voice came from somewhere off to the right. Simeon froze.

"The most important part of the Rosetta Stone is missing, of course."

Lecturing as always. His voice sounded faint and muffled, as though he were concealed in or behind something. Simeon walked slowly toward the voice, looking for a sarcophagus or something similar, but there was nothing like that in this part of the hall. Only some thin statues, and a massive black slab with writing on it.

"But you won't find the missing text in any museum," Kane's voice continued. "There was so much I still had to teach you, Simeon. So much about our history that you don't yet know."

"I never thanked you properly for what you did teach me," Simeon said, stepping forward. "A bitter lesson, but I'm better for it."

The razor was back in his pocket, and his Italian knife was in his hand. Better for stabbing, or, God help him, throwing.

Pierrette would never let him hear the end of it if he chose that, here, in public. He could hear a group of scholars talking in the next hall, the murmurs of their voices like the incantation of monks. But he would do whatever was necessary to stop Kane, the moment he appeared. His voice had seemed to come from here, but there was no one behind the black stone slab, no one near the statues of lions with human bodies.

Wait – there *was* something. In the corner, on the floor. A wooden box, with its lid slightly open. Some copper coils peeked out, and a thin wire ran along the wall. An explosive? Surely Kane wouldn't blow up the British Museum, not even with Simeon inside it.

"So many things I have discovered, and invented," said the voice, and Simeon froze. It was coming from the box. "You think me vain, for calling myself the Magus, but it's the nickname Ada gave me herself. Did she tell you that?"

Simeon stood well back, but followed the wire with his eyes in the gloom. He ran the length of it, through the hall, around a corner, and smack into a man with a monocle. With the man protesting after him, Simeon ran into the room that held the great staircase leading to the upper floor. There was the end of the wire, leading into what looked like a display case, and some odd device with a conical top. No sign of Kane.

Had he gone up the stairs? He had to have. What other reason would there be for the speaking device to end here? But the halls leading to the other side of the ground floor opened in front of him. And to his right, the main entrance to the museum, and beyond that, London.

Simeon dashed to the front door, and nearly collided with the porter he'd spoken to before.

"Has a man come this way – mustache a blue waistcoat, carrying a blackthorn stick? Maybe in something of a hurry? Just in the last minute?"

The porter swore that nobody had come out, and Simeon believed him. He'd never been so glad to have given a man a shilling.

Kane had clearly had that speaking device ready. He'd wanted Simeon to think he'd gone outside. Wanted to send Simeon running into the fog. To give him a chance to escape the police? Maybe. Or maybe it was a double bluff, and Kane wanted Simeon to do precisely what he was about to do – and run back into the trap.

The fog outside was a wall; he'd never find anyone out there. And Kane would never be found.

He had to make a decision. He made it.

Back inside, he ran up the stairs, and startled a young couple who looked as though they were grateful for the museum's dark corners. Up ahead, he could see large skeletons of beasts and taxidermy, and he could hear Kane's voice again, lecturing about the museum: "…so overstuffed with bones and books, they'll have to open more museums…"

Simeon didn't take the bait. He ran back down the stairs, slipping a little on the stone. Ahead of him, another hall opened up, filled with bookcases. And to the left, a set of double doors, with Reading Room painted over the top.

Another decision, but this time, the coppers made it for him. They came barreling around a corner up ahead. Three of them, not in uniform, but Simeon knew by the way they walked, fast and abrupt, their gaze slipping off everything into the corners.

One of them broke off and headed for the main entrance, where Simeon had just been.

So Simeon opened the door on his left instead, and slipped into a warm wood-paneled corridor. There were doors leading off it, and he pushed them open as he passed. Cloakroom. Cloakroom. A passage into a maze of metal scaffolding. His gaze raked every corner, searching for Kane. But with the police behind him, he kept walking.

At the end of the corridor there was another set of doors, and a man in the same blue, red and gold uniform as the porter at the entrance. He smiled nastily at Simeon and said, "Your ticket, sir?"

"For the museum? I thought–"

"For the Reading Room. Reader tickets must be obtained in advance."

Of course Kane had gone in here. It made sense. Out in the fog of London, he couldn't have been sure Simeon wasn't following him. Here, in the center of the museum, where Simeon would be barred entry, he was safe. Cheese in a trap, while the police closed off the exits.

Well, they were behind him now, and Kane was ahead. And if Kane thought Simeon would put his own safety ahead of his goal, he was very wrong.

And here was an officious tit demanding a reading ticket from a man in a hurry who was wearing a hood.

Simeon drew his Italian knife and put it to the doorkeeper's throat. "I don't have a fucking ticket. But I am going in."

The man didn't flinch. Simeon wouldn't harm him, but the man had no way of knowing that. All the same, he just stared back at Simeon. "If you insist, sir."

"I do."

The man said nothing more, so Simeon slowly took his knife away a few inches, and gestured that the man should open the door.

"You'll have to sign the book," the doorkeeper said implacably.

Simeon's eyebrow went up. "The book?"

The doorkeeper's eyes indicated a plain brown visitors' book on a little stand in the corner next to the door, with an inkstand and pens at the top of it.

"It'll be my job if there are more people in the reading room than have signed the book. The book is compulsory."

"Bloody hell," Simeon muttered. "Very well. Step this way."

With his right hand still holding the knife, and the man obligingly accompanying him, Simeon went to the bookstand and flipped it open to the first unfilled page. Under the typewritten line, "I have read the directions respecting the Reading Room and I declare that I am not under twenty-one years of age", he signed the name *Ezio Auditore*.

The doorkeeper read it, nodded, and opened the doors for him.

The Reading Room took Simeon's breath away. It was perfectly round, with churchlike windows breaking the blue and gold walls at regular intervals. On days when the sun shone, it would shine like a miracle in this room. On this day, it was almost too dark to read, and the only occupants might as well have been ghosts: dark figures, the silhouettes of men in frock coats.

The walls were lined with two stories of bookshelves, accessible from railed walkways. Desks and shelves radiated from a concentric pattern of desks in the center.

Simeon had to get a better view. He jumped up onto the nearest desk, and from there to a shelf, ignoring the shouts of protest from all around. Then he swung up to a railing, and then to another, so that he was on the highest walkway. There, at last, off to one side, was the familiar silhouette of Kane, surrounded by a few other dark figures. He was talking to them, gesturing, as though he were the only person in the room who hadn't heard the clang of iron as a man without a ticket clambered up where he had no reason to be.

Footsteps on the walkway behind him, and he saw the shapes of others on the far wall, coming in the other direction. Policemen, plainly. He'd be surrounded in a moment.

Simeon's hand was in his pocket, and his Adams revolver was in his hand. If he shot at Kane from this distance, the bullet could easily hit one of the other men. Damn him. He ran along the curving walkway, to get closer.

"Come and face me, coward," Simeon yelled.

The low hubbub in the room stilled to silence. He could see the dark figures like the shadows of crumbled statues, their faces turned up to him.

Kane said, after a moment, "Are you addressing me, sir?"

"You know I won't take the blood of an innocent. I can't say the same for you, but I never thought I'd see you use them as shields."

At that, there was a small perceptible shuffling of men away from Kane. Not enough – they were all trying to put distance between them without actually losing their dignity.

"You must define your terms, Mr Price!" Kane barked. "Who are the innocent? And what are they innocent of? Are they innocent of maintaining the very tyrants who would starve them at the earliest opportunity? Are they innocent of scrabbling for their own comfort at the expense of their neighbors' lives? This museum is full of specimens from thousands of years of human history, but I defy you to find me a display case or a pedestal to which you can point and say, there, there is an innocent man."

At this, the toffs around him forgot about dignity and spread wide. This was the moment. Kane could move quickly, and even mid-lecture he was sharp.

As Simeon's finger found the trigger, a firm hand closed around his left forearm and pulled the gun up. The shot went wide and smashed one of the pretty windows. In a moment, Simeon's arm was twisted behind him, and two other men were on him. One was dressed in police uniform. The other was holding a revolver, a foot from Simeon's chest.

"Simeon Price, I am a police officer, and I am arresting you on a charge of desertion."

Simeon swung his right hand around and released the hidden blade, judging the distance so that he wouldn't take blood, but would startle the uniformed man into letting him go. In the split second between that and the man with the revolver taking his shot, he could leap–

Instead, though, the grip loosened on his arm, and the startled man pushed him from behind. Simeon toppled over the railing, scrambled for purchase, and fell hard, first onto a shelf and then onto the floor. Pain radiated all through one side of his body, and when he tried to get to his feet, he found that he couldn't.

CHAPTER TWENTY

There was something unnerving about seeing the Crystal Palace rising in front of her, but in a totally different place than the last time Pierrette had seen it, at Hyde Park as part of the Great Exhibition. Its new location near Sydenham was a half-hour's train ride south of the city, on a slope that probably had a wide vista on days when the palace wasn't hemmed in by fog. As it was, it rose in seeming solitude, as people hurried off the trains to the main entrance.

Ten years ago, Pierrette had been performing just outside this building, in another place, in another world. That same great glass building had been off to her right, the evening when she and Ada had run from her captors. Men that Ada had gone to her grave believing were after her for her debts, her bad gambles on horses. Now Pierrette reconsidered. Maybe even then, the Magus had been trying to get Ada's notebook. She shivered inside the corset that hid its secrets.

The interior of the Crystal Palace felt like a world unto itself, the tropical plants and statues lining the glass walls, with the gray fog beyond them. It was stuffy, and packed with people, many of whom smelled as though they'd stopped at Rimmel's Toilet Vinegar Fountain for a two-penny dab of the astringent perfume on their handkerchief or the back of their necks. Pierrette gently elbowed her way through then stopped short in a knot of people with penknives in their hands, before she realized that they were all trying to cut a sliver of thick rope off a massive coil. The rope that Charles Blondin had used to walk across Niagara Falls, according to the whispers around her. They wanted souvenirs.

And there was the man himself, greeted with gasps and the tilting of a thousand heads. He'd stretched another rope across the transept of the Crystal Palace, high in the air. He ran nimbly along it, then paused as though he had forgotten something, and the crowd roared.

Back he came on short stilts, an umbrella in his hand.

Pierrette watched, feeling a pang of remembrance for Ariel Fine and the other members of the Aurora Troupe. It had been more than a year since she'd had a letter from them. The last one had come from Nell Robinson, telling her that their beloved Major Wallin had finally passed away, and that they were selling the Aurora Theatre. Perhaps, if she had stayed in Birmingham, she could have kept the troupe in business. But she had promises to keep.

Blondin pushed a wheelbarrow onto the tightrope, and the gasps changed character. Pierrette jostled to get a better view, and spied a pudgy arm waving from the barrow, and a head of curls. A child.

"It's his own daughter," said a woman beside her, with a

pinched mouth. "I've seen her photograph in the papers. What is he thinking, putting her in such danger?"

Pierrette's stomach sank. No one in the Aurora Troupe would have risked such a thing. Not that children couldn't be trusted in high places; she had crawled around ropes herself when she was only a few years older than Blondin's girl. But in a wheelbarrow, there was nothing she could do to save herself if the wheel slipped. There was no backup plan.

When the cheers turned to boos, Blondin wheeled her back safely, then came back out and did a somersault on the rope.

Pierrette didn't want to watch anymore. She'd really only come because Simeon had insisted. He seemed to feel that she was languishing, all these tedious months spent scouring the newspapers and asking for information from newsboys and flower sellers. It was true that the Rossetti residence had the feel of a sickroom much of the time, but Pierrette was well used to that. Lizzie reminded her of Ada in some ways, though her mind was not as terrifyingly prone to wander. And there was one major difference: Lizzie was getting stronger.

Still, Lizzie would be all alone this afternoon, with Gabriel at his paints and Simeon most likely out making the rounds of his mysterious contacts. And Pierrette didn't like this business in the newspaper, advertising for Simeon as a deserter. Pierrette would be of better use in the city, and, truth be told, she'd had enough of Blondin. Watching his performance only made her sad for the life she might have led. It was time to go. Besides, this way, the train back wouldn't be too crowded.

However, she wasn't the only one with that idea. As she was leaving, she was nearly barreled into by a young woman with a vacant expression – and it was only "nearly" because Simeon's training in observation hadn't fallen entirely on barren ground. Pierrette noticed her coming, saw she wasn't looking and stepped aside. But it was only after she registered the pink patchwork dress, the threadbare shawl, the honey-colored hair, that she recognized the face: Tillie Wallin.

They walked outside to get clear of the crowd, and embraced on the path near a holly bush, with the damp mist clinging to their skin.

"You came back to England," Tillie said, in a tone somewhere between question and accusation.

"Just recently," Pierrette said, though it had been months now. "I thought you were still in Birmingham."

Tillie shook her head. She looked very grown-up, with her hair tucked into a snood at the nape of her neck, and a braid encircling her head from ear to ear. Pierrette did some quick calculating in her head: Tillie must have turned eighteen that summer.

"The audiences were getting tired of us in Birmingham," Tillie said. "When Father died, we came to London. Ariel is doing well, but as for me, well, nobody wants to watch a girl prance around on a horse anymore. My tricks are going out of style."

They both glanced at the Crystal Palace, where shouts and cheers suggested that Blondin's performance was still in full swing, and that nobody had died, at least not yet.

"That's because they aren't tricks," Pierrette smiled, squeezing her arm affectionately. "They're *art*, and don't you forget it. Have you got work in London, then?"

Tillie shrugged and looked away. "In the summer, I was able to ride a little in some agricultural shows here and there. I've been staying in a boarding house, for as long as the money lasts. My father put a little away for me, but we spent most of it on doctors for him." She focused on Pierrette again. "We can't all find great adventures the way you seem to, Pierrette. It's funny – I'd been thinking lately about spending my last shillings on passage to France, to seek you out in Paris. I'm glad now that I didn't!"

"So am I, you goose. Well, come on back with me for supper at least. I have a room with some friends near Blackfriars Bridge. We have so much to talk about."

On the train, Tillie told her that Ariel was performing as an acrobat at Astley's Amphitheatre, but Jovita had fallen in love with a musician and sailed for New York! Nell and Hugh Robinson had gone into business together, after Hugh's latest back injury made it impossible for him to continue in the circus. They had opened a small theatrical costume and fancy dress shop, and were making a go of it. They had Tillie over for Sunday dinner every week.

By the time they emerged from London Bridge station, the sun was setting, and the fog had thickened. Their fellow pedestrians were silhouettes against the weird halos cast by the gas lamps. It was a London in which anyone might be a friend, or an enemy. And though Pierrette had chosen to wear one of her bright dresses – "it's chartreuse," she had haughtily informed Simeon that morning – the yellow green was much the same as the sickly cast of the gas lamps, and she felt as though the fog were painting her out of existence. It stank of sulfur and sewer. It was impossible to see people properly until they were nearly upon them. Pierrette held tight to her reticule, which contained her Apache revolver.

At London Bridge, they crossed the Stygian Thames, where the boats were hulking shadows cast by their own struggling lamps. Pierrette could see the lighted windows of the building where the Rossettis lived. There, on the second floor, a lace curtain with a lamp behind it, and the shadow of movement.

Simeon's window, next door, was dark. He was probably over talking to Gabriel, waiting for Pierrette.

"It looks like Gabriel and Lizzie are home," Pierrette said cheerfully. "They were out looking at a house today. They look at houses quite frequently. They have a notion that they must have a house now that they are married, even though these rooms suit them perfectly, and the price is good."

"You're sure they won't mind me coming for supper?"

"They won't mind at all, my dear. Gabriel's quite chatty, and Lizzie likes to have people around – it's good for her spirits."

Pierrette turned her key in the door. They were halfway up the stairs when they became aware of someone talking loudly, very upset, with the few pauses punctuated by the steady *cheep, cheep, cheep* of a distressed bullfinch.

The bird flew at them when Pierrette opened the door into the Rossetti sitting room. Inside, it was bedlam. Piles of books pulled off the shelves, clothes strewn everywhere, drawers lying on the floor with their contents scattered. Lizzie was standing stiffly up against her new green wallpaper, her stricken face like a sheet.

Gabriel was sitting among a heap of books, his back to the door, railing against no one and everyone. "What in the devil were they looking for? Do they think I keep money in a family Bible, like an old lady? I tell you, Lizzie, if this was someone trying to sabotage my work–"

Pierrette took Tillie by the arm and walked into the room. Gabriel looked up at her, and at Tillie.

"This is my old friend, Tillie Wallin," Pierrette explained. "I'd brought her to meet you. What's happened?"

He nodded the merest acknowledgment of Tillie; it was as much politeness as he could muster. His expression was defeated. "Someone broke in while Lizzie and I were out today."

"Broke in! Did they take anything?"

"Not that I have found yet, but it's such a mess, who's to say?"

"There was nothing worth taking," Lizzie said mournfully.

"There are all my paintings, and my notebooks," Gabriel snapped. Then, more softly, "Not to mention your own drawings."

"But everything seems to be accounted for?" Pierrette asked.

Gabriel shrugged, picking up a notebook lying splayed on the floor and flipping through it as though checking to see whether the burglars had taken any of the words.

Looking uncomfortable, Tillie sat on the sofa where Pierrette indicated.

Pierrette went to the window and pulled back the lace curtain. This window didn't face the river the way the one in Rossetti's painting room did. Instead, it looked over a low roof that jutted out of the house next door where Simeon lodged. The window showed signs of being forced, some splintered wood near the bent latch. It would have been a minor matter for a competent burglar to climb up, get in and out again without being seen, especially in this fog. A competent burglar, or a trained Assassin, or a Templar.

She shivered.

"Isn't Simeon home? He didn't hear anything?"

Gabriel shook his head. "We banged on his door as soon as we saw this. He's out. Mrs Burrell downstairs said she heard nothing, but of course she's half deaf. She's sent a boy to get a policeman."

"We might ask her to bring a cup of tea for Lizzie's nerves," said Pierrette.

Lizzie edged toward them, leaving the safety of the wall as though approaching a wild animal. She shook her head. "I don't need tea. But look, they broke my laudanum bottle."

"There's one in the washstand in my room, I noticed," Pierrette said, and saw from the gratitude on Lizzie's face that she was very aware of that and had been hoping someone else would mention it. "Let me fetch it for you – I don't use it."

Pierrette went into her own little room, and gasped. If anything, it was worse in here. The bedclothes on the little brass bed looked as though they'd been slept in by a troop of monkeys. Her half-dozen books, most of them borrowed from Simeon, were flung around the floor, and some of the pages were torn out. The rag rug was scrunched over in the corner, and it took Pierrette a moment to register why: someone had pried up all the floorboards, though they were settled back in place. Little nails lay scattered here and there like dead ants.

Whoever it was, they were plainly looking for something. She put her hands to her ribs, to the corset stuffed with Ada's careful handwriting. Thank goodness it had been a cold day.

Too late, Pierrette heard Gabriel's voice from the sitting room, toward the door. "Lives downstairs but half deaf, you know. Our guest was out too. Pierrette Arnaud. France. Yes. And our neighbor's name? Well, he wasn't here. Yes, all right, his name is Simeon Price. I'm sure he won't mind you looking, when he comes–"

Pierrette raced out, her heart in her throat. She and Simeon had never told Gabriel and Lizzie that he was wanted for desertion, and they must be discreet with his name. They hadn't seen a reason to.

Maybe it wouldn't come to anything, she thought, looking at the constables standing at the door. After all, it's not as though every policeman would have the names of every deserter memorized. But then the one without a notebook said, "Simeon Price? We just arrested an army deserter by that name, at the British Museum, not two hours ago."

"Well, then I suppose he has an alibi," said the other, his expression hard to read under a ferocious mustache. He looked up at Pierrette and his eyes softened. "Ah, the French guest, is it?"

Her hands became clenched fists, the fingernails nearly breaking the skin. She was afraid to breathe. Simeon had been arrested.

Chapter Twenty-One

His leg was broken. There was no doubt of that. He could put no weight on it, and the shape of it was wrong. After they'd stripped his weapons, two policemen grabbed him under his arms and hauled him into a police wagon, and then hauled him out again half an hour later.

Millbank Prison was on the same side of the Thames as the Rossetti home, but two bends over, down below Westminster. Although Simeon wasn't able to catch much of the journey through the tiny window in the police wagon, with the pain from his leg clouding his thoughts, he knew precisely where they were heading.

Kane had once lent him a book of essays by the late philosopher and social reformer Jeremy Bentham, which had included his plans to build a prison in a "panopticon" model, where a central security post could watch from all directions. In the end, Millbank Prison had not followed Bentham's proposed design, but something of his vision lingered.

The prison was shaped like a flower, with five pentagons surrounding a central chapel: God's panopticon. The walls and turrets that Simeon glimpsed from the courtyard gave him the impression of a medieval fortress, though the place was only half a century old.

Inside, it was a dark and drafty maze. Simeon was carried into a cell by himself, but he heard the voices of other prisoners all day and night: their prayers, their complaints, their conversations with ghosts. It was hard to tell how far away anyone was from the strange way the sound carried. The whole place had a faint stench of decay, dysentery and scurvy.

The first night, they brought in an army bonesetter, who wrenched and realigned his leg, then bandaged it with leather splints. Simeon refused laudanum; he needed all his wits. But the pain wasn't very good for his wits either.

On the third day, they let him out into the yard in a wheeled chair – they wouldn't let him have access to crutches. It was a clear day, so he could see the newly built Houses of Parliament, emerging from their scaffolding.

Prison reminded him of being in the army, and he could feel himself slipping into its drumbeat. Meals came at regular intervals. When he asked for a book, they gave him *The Pilgrim's Progress*, and he read it, then read it again. They had taken his hidden blade and the cloak Pierrette had made him. They had taken his Italian knife and his Adams revolver. They had taken his choices. He could forget about the world outside, could give in. Everything hurt less that way. Simeon could feel that pull within himself. It had always been there, and he hated it and resisted it. That resistance, too, had always been there.

Bentham had described his ideal prison as a "mill for grinding rogues honest", but "honest" wasn't the word for the men he saw out in the yard. Some of them had been fairly ground into powder.

What bolstered his resistance this time – as it had on that ship nearly a decade before – was knowing that giving in would harm people other than himself. Kane was still out there, free and able to test his weapons, to twist young men of ideals into testing them for him. Pierrette was out there too, no doubt worried, and angry, her face scrunched and her eyes blazing, wearing Ada's notes like armor. Pierrette would not hesitate to put herself in danger.

So he thought about ways to escape, as soon as his leg was strong enough. On Sunday, after they wheeled him to the chapel, where the prisoners stood in stalls to be preached at, he drew a little map in his head. He noticed which parts of the corridors were darkest. He noticed which guards seemed melancholy or indifferent. He gathered information, and he thought.

He hoped that Pierrette wouldn't do anything foolish, like try to break him out – the way he'd once tried and failed to break out Janos Libenyi. No, he hadn't failed. He'd been sabotaged, by the man he thought he could trust.

A week into his imprisonment, Simeon was attempting a set of pushups on the floor with the foot of his injured leg over the other foot, wincing with each one. A shadow fell from the iron grate that served as his cell door. He turned his head and saw a ghost.

"Good afternoon, Mr Price," said Private Halford.

• • •

Private Halford was, in fact, Corporal Halford now. No longer the skinny freckled lad. He was fuller in the jacket, carried a cane, and walked with a limp. His eyes were dull, but Simeon remembered them staring. He remembered blood on the boards.

"I thought you were dead," Simeon said, pulling his leg into a more comfortable position, with his backside on the cold floor.

"Likewise."

The iron door closed behind Halford, the guard turning the key. Halford was carrying a leather case. They looked awkwardly at each other; there was nowhere for Halford to sit except the bedframe with the blanket folded on top of it.

"'For God's sake, let us sit upon the ground, and tell sad stories of the death of kings,'" Simeon quoted from *Richard II*, with a smile.

Halford barked a laugh, then took the blanket and sat on it on the floor, opposite Simeon.

"I came to my senses in a lifeboat," Halford explained. "How I got there, I still don't know. I have a benefactor to thank, somewhere. I wondered whether it was you."

"I wish I could say it was. Christ, Halford, I thought you were done for! I dove into the water, and then..." Simeon stopped, and then said, "So if you've come to thank me, you've wasted your hansom money, I'm afraid."

A gentle smile broke on Halford's face. "No, that's not why I'm here. A man facing a court martial may have a fellow soldier stand as a friend and counsel in the proceedings. When I heard you'd been nabbed, I decided to come and ask whether you'd be willing to let me be that friend."

Simeon had no words. "That would be great. Truly excellent.

It would be wonderful to have a friend there." He hadn't thought that far ahead. His court martial proceeding might be a good moment to escape. "How long until that happens?"

"A month or so, probably."

A month might as well be a year. By then, Kane could be anywhere, have done anything. He could have already. But there wasn't much Simeon could do with his leg the way it was. Even if he managed to pinch a key from the guards, or make something into a weapon, he wouldn't get far. He made a little noise of frustration.

"What's the worst they can do to me?"

"It'll be a district court martial, so they can't pronounce death or transportation. Lashes, possibly, up to one hundred and fifty. Imprisonment, no limit under the law but probably no more than six months, with or without hard labor, with or without solitary confinement. Also, almost certainly, they'll brand your arm with a D. It's more of a tattoo than a brand, the way they do it these days. No burning."

"Well, that's a comfort."

"But it doesn't matter, because I intend you to walk free." Halford seemed most earnest.

Simeon laughed. "Why the devil would they let me off?"

"Because you enlisted in 1847, and under the Act of Parliament passed in that year, your term of service was for ten years. Which means that your time was up in 1857. Four years ago."

"Oh, come off it, Halford. Surely time spent after desertion doesn't count as years of service."

"Ordinarily not, no. But in the case of a man who was shipwrecked, and hit his head, and lost his memory, well, there might be an exception to be made."

Simeon said, very quietly, "That is not what happened."

"It is the God's honest truth," Halford said, wagging his finger, his face serious. "Just as it's the God's honest truth that every man who went down in the Birkenhead Drill showed extraordinary courage in the face of tragic and unavoidable disaster, that the officers led their men in what had to be done, that the reasons those men drowned were to protect women and children. The *truth* is that a British soldier is not a miserable drudge protecting the wealth of the rich for pennies a day. If he stands stock still and does what he's told until he dies or someone else does, it's not because he carries all the value of a wet rag – no, it's because he is stoic. If he walks off a cliff like a lemming, it is because he is chivalrous. If he does bugger-all to save his ship, his comrades, or himself from preventable harms, it's because he is unflappable. Oh, everyone at your proceeding will know exactly what sort of men went down on the *Birkenhead*, Mr Price. You'll just have to tell them how the story ends, every bit as true as all the rest of it."

By this time, Halford's eyes had grown too big, stretching his plain friendly face into something that told Simeon, very clearly, that in the years since they'd last spoken, Halford had killed his first man, and many others. And that was something Simeon knew a little about himself. But looking at Halford, he thought of everything he'd been spared in these last ten years since he and the British Army had gone their separate ways.

"I heard the regiment went to India, after the Cape Colony," Simeon said, quietly.

Halford's face recomposed itself, not to the frank good

humor of the old days, but at least back to world-weary patience. "We did indeed. It was up to us to pay back every act of rebellion against the East India Company, with interest. If the man was a sepoy in service to the Company, charged with mutiny or desertion, he was strapped in front of the muzzle of a cannon or some other big gun, and when it went off, his head would fly thirty, forty feet in the air, and maybe his arms too, up to the waiting vultures, and down below, we'd have to make sure people stood well back so they wouldn't get a bit of bone flying at them. Sometimes their crime was just looking the wrong way, or looking at someone the wrong way. We slaughtered whole towns and villages. Left farmers hanging by the roadside."

"You got out."

"I got injured." Halford scratched his chin, where he had grown a small, neatly trimmed beard. "I'm on a pension now, with a wife and a baby. Emily and Susan."

"And yet you want to stick your neck out for me?"

"I'll stand up for you and deliver your statement. Just say the word and I'll write something up that you can put your name to."

Simeon's leg ached. He shifted on the floor. He didn't want to think about it – he didn't want to think about the army, or its rules, or what it gloried in. He had personal business, and the army was keeping him from it.

"Halford, can I have visitors? Other than you, I mean."

"What, ain't I pretty enough?" Halford's mouth twitched. "I'm sorry, Mr Price, but you're not allowed visitors."

"Balls," Simeon swore. Then he thought for a moment. "Can you take a message to someone for me?"

Halford opened his little leather case, taking out a pencil and paper. "You can write it yourself, and I'll deliver, by hand if need be."

CHAPTER TWENTY-TWO

Simeon had never told Pierrette where she might find the Assassins of London; he had only grumbled that they were few. She'd send a telegram to Paris in the morning, but she knew that Paris had its own problems with the Templars at the moment. She had nowhere to turn, and no way to make contact with Simeon himself. From the bemused constable, Pierrette learned that Simeon would likely end up in Millbank Prison for the time being. And that it was very unlikely he'd be accorded the privilege of having visitors there. Then the policemen had left them to their ransacked rooms and thoughts.

Simeon was prudent – to a fault, she often thought – but he wouldn't take well to being locked up while Kane laughed. And if he got wind of the break-in, he'd be all the more furious. That Simeon could get himself out of prison, Pierrette had no doubt. But Kane would expect that. And Kane, it seemed, had allies in high places. Perhaps they hoped Simeon *would* break out, to give them a chance to shoot him. Or perhaps they'd shoot him before he tried.

She rifled through the mess in the Rossetti sitting room, looking for the newspaper that had listed his name, for some clue as to what they might do to him. She succeeded only in exhausting herself and making the mess worse.

"You aren't going to find him in here, you know," said Lizzie at last, in her dry way. She looked exhausted, worn out and see-through like an old apron. And Pierrette wasn't helping.

Tillie, though, was the daughter of a military man, and had already succeeded in restoring order to one of the bookshelves. She seemed to be getting on with Lizzie already.

Pierrette left Tillie with Lizzie and Gabriel for an hour, taking her flushed face and clenched fists down to the Working Men's College and the pubs nearby, to see if she could catch sight of anyone who might have been friendly to Simeon. She looked up at the rooftops, and into the shadows, but only succeeded in spending a tedious evening in the company of men.

When she got home, smelling of stout, the rooms were tidier. Lizzie lay on the sofa with an Afghan blanket over her legs, laughing with her hand over her mouth at Tillie's antics. Tillie was wearing a linen sheet over her head like a wedding veil, held by a ring of silk flowers, and on top of that she had a stack of books, and was walking on her tiptoes.

In the other room, Gabriel was standing at the dark window, and for once, he didn't have a pencil or a brush in his hand. Through the open door, he was just a shadow against the gloom, illuminated only by a thousand distant gas lamps.

"He's standing on guard," Lizzie whispered, with a small grin that changed to something else as she added, "He would go to his death rather than let anyone hurt me, and yet he has hurt me more than anyone. Well, except myself." Lizzie looked at Pierrette, and said, "I'm sorry about Simeon. No sign of him?"

"No sign of him." Pierrette caught Lizzie's train of thought, and said, "It isn't like that, you know. I'm not in love with him. He's far too old, for one thing. He's thirty-five."

"Not so old," said Lizzie wryly.

"But six years older than me. He's like – I won't say a father or a brother, because neither of those is right either. But he's family. That's all, and that is enough."

"So you have no one to make you miserable," Lizzie said.

"Ha, no. And never will have."

"You seem quite certain. What if someone comes and sweeps you off your feet?"

There had been a man in Brussels, and a woman in Paris, and another man in Birmingham. Three experiments, which Pierrette felt was enough. "I've been swept a few times, thank you, and to be honest, I don't see what the fuss is about. I can sweep myself off my own feet well enough."

Tillie laughed and took her hand, and said proudly to Lizzie, "Watching Pierrette perform always makes me believe anything is possible."

"I feel that way about watching her do anything," Lizzie said.

Pierrette took Lizzie's hand with her left, and Tillie held her right. She might not have the access she wanted to the Brotherhood, but maybe she had something just as useful.

London was like a theatre, Pierrette thought, as she and Tillie stepped out of the waterman's boat at the coal wharf. To their right were the Houses of Parliament, so unreal, like painted sets in a theatre. But here, tucked in behind it, were the backstage works: the ropes and grease that made the city run. They dodged horse dung as they walked behind carts piled high with coal, headed for the gasworks. And what an edifice that was! A round tower higher than any amphitheater, to hold the coal gas that powered the lights of the city.

The whole place stank. Thin people stooped over their shovels, and whenever the horses and shovels stopped, there was a steady rattle of coughing and retching. The faces were as blank as the walls of the gasworks.

But this neighborhood was close to busy Westminster, an easy walk to Astley's Amphitheatre, and affordable, all of which had recommended it to the Robinsons as a good place to set up a shop and live above it. In a ramshackle building in a narrow lane, Tillie showed Pierrette a gaily painted sign: *Robinson & Co: Purveyors of Theatrical Apparatus, Costumes & Stage Properties.*

Inside the dim shop, the outlines of familiar costumes greeted her like ghosts. A Harlequin that Ariel had worn. The stuffed head of a real lion. Jovita's feathered headdress. Thick golden ropes hung from the ceiling in various lengths as though one could ring for a servant or climb to the flies above a stage, but they were only attached to hooks. Scimitars glistened on the walls. And in a glass-topped cabinet in the corner, a collection of real guns that would once have caught Simeon's eye.

"Tillie? Is that you?" Nell came around a screen with an armful of velvet and stopped in her tracks. "Pierrette."

Tillie pushed her way past a table piled high with raffia torches and ropes. "I'm here too. Pierrette is visiting from Paris."

"Visiting." About six different expressions passed over Nell's face. "Well, that is a nice surprise."

"I'm here as a customer," Pierrette said.

Nobody said anything for a few moments. Then Nell nodded with her head and said, "Come into the back."

The back room of the shop was even more jumbled than out front. One wall was dominated by a massive cabinet with three wardrobe-length doors. There were paper lanterns hanging from the ceiling, and tea caddies stacked high – probably full of papers, given the overflowing state of the pigeonholes in the little writing desk in the corner. Bowls and baskets were filled with miscellanies. Another wall hung with more costumes in need of repair, and several bows, torches and targets lay on the floor against one wall.

In the midst of all this was a small dark table, and Nell poured the tea from her red and white Aesop's Fables tea set. Good, strong tea, milk first. Pierrette took a lump of sugar with the tongs and smiled as she dropped it into the familiar fox and grapes teacup.

Hugh was sitting across from her, with Nell and Tillie on either side. He looked at Pierrette appraisingly.

"You look tired," he said.

"I didn't get much sleep."

She took a sip. There was a chip out of the fox and grapes teacup; she couldn't remember there being a chip out of any of the cups before. She looked around the little room, with its pigeonholes stuffed with scraps, its careful boxes of string and accounts noted on the backs of whatever paper lay to hand. Lizzie had said she had decided to be a poet, as a girl, when she saw a poem printed on a butter wrapper.

"Pierrette," Nell said gently, "I don't know what you have been doing these last years, what friends you made in Paris–"

"I know life hasn't been easy for you since I left," Pierrette dared to interrupt. "I know that. And it's my fault. I left you high and dry."

It hurt to admit that, just as it hurt to see the small changes in their familiar faces and realize how much time had passed. She hadn't realized how much she missed them.

"You were under no obligation," Nell said.

"But I *was*." Pierrette looked at Tillie, who was sitting quietly, with a stunned look on her face. Four years was a long time in the life of an eighteen year-old. It must have been odd for her to have Pierrette and the Robinsons back in the same room, arguing again. "I was under the obligation of friendship, and I was thinking only of myself. I had a job to do – I still have a job to do – and I needed to learn things in order to do it. And I have learned things," Pierrette said, putting the teacup down on the table, silently.

"I'm glad you could learn those things," Hugh said softly. "I'm only sorry you had to leave us to do it."

"I didn't want to put you in any more danger," she protested. "The police were looking for me. It was safest for me to stay away. I wouldn't be here now if I had anywhere else to turn."

Nell reached over and put a warm hand on Pierrette's. "We face danger together. Whatever you need, we will give you, and I hope you know you don't have to stay away from us, no matter what."

Pierrette left the shop with a large carpet bag filled with several sturdy yet thin ropes, grappling hooks, and a clutch of throwing knives. Hugh had also given her a mourning pendant that had come in secondhand. It was made of heavy gold, with a crisscross pattern of brown human hair on the front.

"Why in God's name are you giving this to me?" she asked with a grimace.

"It came in as a trade, and I filled it with clubmoss powder. Do you know it? It's a favorite of stage magicians."

She shook her head. "I haven't been around performers these last years, I'm sorry to say."

"When it's blown into the air, it catches fire a treat, with just a match or a spark nearby. I put some in the necklace, thinking it would be lovely for an act: put this to your lips and breathe fire!" Hugh's eyes shone. "But nobody's bought it yet. I suppose that is because it's so ugly. Nell said I should sell it for the gold and save my powder for something else."

"It's perfect," Pierrette said. She could wear this even somewhere where she would be searched for weapons. Somewhere like a prison.

With her heavy bag in hand, Pierrette walked south to Millbank and stared at the walls for a while, then turned and walked back alone to Blackfriars, her hat pinned firmly on again, her head in the clouds.

Simeon was in prison. She would get him out. Perhaps before that, she could get a message to him. Was it worth the risk to climb up and see if she could get something in through a window? What she wouldn't give for one of Kane's legendary trained pigeons now. She looked up, automatically, but saw only the pediments of buildings along the Strand. The birds were probably here, in London, or wherever the man himself had gone to roost. Something told her it wouldn't be far. He'd want to make sure of his slow victory over Simeon. And he still wanted information about Ada's inventions. She wriggled inside her corset.

A few streets along, two white pillars and a golden lion announced the narrow entrance of the Twinings shop, and on a lark, she went in to buy some tea for Nell. The least she could do. Ten minutes later, a man in a white swallow-tail coat had talked her into a bespoke blend of souchong and bohea that smelled like smoke when she crushed it in her hand. Nell, who liked what she liked, would probably hate it. But it was wrapped up in stamped paper nevertheless. And she had a second package, because at the last moment, she'd turned back to get some gunpowder tea for herself. She had some hard thinking to do tonight.

And then, as she passed through the arched gateway at Temple Bar, she became suddenly aware that a man was following her.

How long had he been behind her? God in heaven, but Simeon's face if he could see her now. Forgetting all her training. Failing to observe. And here, of all places – near the Temple Church, an ancient stronghold of their enemies. The worst place to let her guard down.

The Temple was on the right. To her left, the church of St Dunstan in the West stood, with its inviting old tower. A place to get high up and get some perspective. Never easy in a full skirt and heeled shoes, but she'd done it before.

She ducked into the churchyard, already looking for a handhold, but the man behind her called out, "Is it Pierrette Arnaud?"

She froze. A Templar calling her name in the street?

Her hand in the pocket that held her knife, she turned and smiled brilliantly. "You have the advantage of me, sir." She took in the leather case in his right hand that could contain weapons or an incendiary, the soldier's uniform, the neat beard, the face full of freckles. If this was a trick, it was one she had never encountered before.

He stepped closer, and she moved carefully back into the street, nearer to a cart that two men were loading with crates.

"I'm sorry to startle you, mademoiselle. I was on my way to your lodgings, and you see, he described you and your favorite dress to a tee."

Pierrette was wearing her mauve dress. Well, right now she needed all the luck she could get. Her stomach flipped. Did they know her that well, then? She'd never even met Oscar Kane, and yet he'd been in her room. And in her mind, it seemed. And would slip a knife between her ribs on the way to slicing open her corset.

"Where do you want to do this?" she asked, softly. This one was clearly a trap, with his curious, open expression and leather case. There must be others. She noted the charwoman on the corner. The men loading the cart! She edged backwards, away from them.

"I thought in your rooms – if you have a chaperone – or if you prefer, a coffeehouse? I saw you come out of Twinings – we could have a cup back there. Or if you like, it won't take long, here–"

Her grip on the knife relaxed a fraction. "Perhaps you'd better tell me what this is about."

"My name is Corporal Halford. I've come with a message from Simeon Price."

The message was written in code, and Pierrette almost smiled at the idea that Simeon finally had a chance to make her use all those tedious lessons. She asked for a minute to work it out, standing in the light from Gabriel's window and scribbling in the margins with a pencil, while Gabriel and Lizzie entertained Halford. Gabriel was always eager to talk to men, especially those whose life experience he might mine, somehow, for his poetry and paintings.

But it didn't take long. The message was short. Simeon's leg was broken; he could not attempt an escape. But he didn't ask Pierrette to sit quietly and wait. He asked her to find and stop the Magus, because they finally had him within their grasp, because he clearly had reason to be in London and Simeon didn't think it was the Assyrian artifact; that had all been a mere trap for Simeon. No, Kane was up to something big, something he didn't want Simeon interfering with, and their cause couldn't wait for Simeon to get well and get free. It was up to Pierrette now.

The last lines did make her smile, with tears in her eyes: "And yes, you can use smoke bombs. There's a half-dozen in the trunk under my bed."

She would gladly use the smoke bombs, but she had to find the Magus again first. Simeon was right: he wouldn't have gone far. Pierrette went over to the fire and fed Simeon's message to it. Gabriel, Lizzie and Halford all looked at her expectantly.

"Corporal Halford, will you take a message to Simeon from me?"

"Certainly."

"Are you all right, Pierrette?" Lizzie asked. "You look very much as if you want to do something rash."

Pierrette focused on her, smiling her most winning smile. "If it's all right, I'd very much like to throw a party."

Chapter Twenty-Three

The party took some time to plan. When Pierrette asked Gabriel to invite all the artists and writers and scientists he knew, she was expecting an atmosphere something like the salons Ada used to have in her house near Hyde Park. In her memory, at least, those evenings were populated by women with bare arms and round skirts, men who might as well have been in uniform, everyone standing as though a conversation were a dance.

The party at the Rossettis' was a different picture. The men slouched in chairs, their legs crossed, their suits as slapdash as their postures. Thin women wore simple, straight dresses, and did their best to look ethereal. If there was a dance happening, it was one with complex moves. Rossetti went from arguing with William Morris to flirting with Morris's wife, while Lizzie kept her eyes firmly fixed on a young man reading her a poem.

Near to Lizzie sat a beautiful woman with serious eyes and a small half-smile, one of only two Black women in the room. She looked quite bored by the young man's ode.

"Are the parties here always like this?" Pierrette asked her conspiratorially, sliding onto the sofa beside her.

"I wouldn't know. My first one." She had an East End accent. "I'm only a model."

Half the women in the room had been models for the men here – including Lizzie.

"Ah, well, we have that in common," Pierrette said. "Well, except they only paint me when I perform my acrobatics. I can't imagine having to sit stock still for hours on end. It sounds like torture."

"It's a little extra money, which is the main thing. My husband drives a cab, and he's been robbed three times in the last month." She put out her hand. "Fanny Eaton."

"Pierrette Arnaud."

"From France, is it?"

"Yes. I'm sorry to hear about your husband. That must be frightening, as well as a nuisance. We had a break-in here a few days ago."

Fanny's mouth went taut. "London's proper lawless these days, and the police do nothing about it. Nothing at all. Anything taken? Anyone hurt?"

"Not this time." Pierrette took a chance. "I'm afraid there's a man behind the break-in. A man who's looking for something that he thinks I have. Oscar Kane. Do you know him? He has an Irish accent and is very given to wearing fancy waistcoats."

Fanny raised an eyebrow. "Unless he's a painter, I wouldn't know him."

"He's a scholar and a businessman."

"Sounds like a real scoundrel, all right."

Pierrette laughed. She was comfortable here, talking to

Fanny, but the room was full of people who would be less pleasant to talk to and more likely to give her what she needed. She excused herself to get a drink and took stock of the crowded room. There were people sitting on the arms of chairs and slipping into laps. The air smelled of tobacco and whiskey, and the fire under the mantel smoked, though it didn't seem to bother the people knotted around it.

But what mattered was that it was a room full of people who would surely know where to find a visiting scholar.

And there by the fire was the man who knew everyone and everything: John Ruskin, ten years older than he'd been the last time Pierrette had seen him, at Ada's. She had been a teenager then, and he didn't seem to recognize her now. So she explained only that she was a guest of the Rossettis. She flattered him about his reputation in art, botany, architecture, literature, and history. She asked him what he thought of the theories of Oscar Kane, who had lately been studying artifacts at the British Museum.

"Kane, you say?" He looked down at her, his muttonchops a yard long. "Can't say I know the fellow. Someone you know from the continent, mademoiselle?"

She could read his assumptions in his face: this little Frenchwoman in front of him, pretty, but inconsequential, asking about a man. Pierrette made her excuses and turned to find someone else to talk to – and nearly bumped into a serious-faced young woman with big eyes, a sharp nose, a thin unsmiling mouth, and a head of wavy brown hair.

"Good evening, Mademoiselle Arnaud," she said. "You may not remember me. I'm Ada's daughter. I was so young–"

"Annabella! Oh, of course I remember." Pierrette took her hand warmly. "Lady Annabella, I should say."

"Just Anne, now. I was named after my grandmother, and I never felt it was my name."

"I heard of her death last year," Pierrette said. "I'm so sorry for yet another loss for your family."

Anne nodded curtly. "That's the reason I'm here – we don't respond to many invitations these days, but I had heard you were staying with the Rossettis. Truthfully, I hoped to have a chance to ask you about my mother. After my grandmother died, we learned she had destroyed many of my mother's papers. I thought perhaps… if there was anything you remember, or letters you might have."

Pierrette froze. Anne was a few years younger than her, but from birth deeply ingrained in high society. It was hard to imagine she would be in league with Kane, or the Templars, or that she would be working to undo her mother's wishes. But how could Pierrette be sure?

"We?" she asked, stalling while she thought. "I didn't realize you'd married."

"Oh no, I meant my younger brother, Byron. Viscount Ockham, I should say." She gestured next to her, to a young man with a beard and big dark eyes much like his sister's. He was wearing a plain suit with a neckerchief, very much not looking like a lord – but then again, in this room of artists, most of the men were dressed like workers. He'd been a boy sailor when he came home from sea to be with his mother as she died, and Pierrette had not been paying attention to much beyond Ada and her pain and sorrow in those dark days.

She shook his hand. "Are you not in the Navy anymore, then, Lord Ockham?"

His mouth twisted into a weird smile. "It didn't agree with

me, I fear. So I left. I'd have been hauled up for a court martial if I weren't Lord Ockham. I prefer to go by plain Byron Ockham, these days."

"Byron's been working down at an ironworks, building steamships," said Anne with defiant pride.

"I have a friend who's been taken for desertion," Pierrette said quietly but with a sudden urgency. "Another friend of your mother's, though she hadn't seen him since you were very young." She stopped, reminded herself that the plan was to get information, not give it. She wasn't cut out for this sort of thing; she had never been subtle. Now, looking into the faces of Anne and Byron, she realized how much she missed their mother still. Ada's mind had been away in the stars, but her heart had always been with her friends. And how she made friends! With immediate and fierce devotion.

But one of the consequences of that openness had been her correspondence with Kane. Ada had been too trusting. And now Pierrette owed it to her, and to Simeon, not to make the same mistake. Her children were not her. And besides, this room really was very crowded. Just beyond Anne's elbow, a beautiful dark-haired woman was hovering, apparently listening to a gray-bearded man, but within earshot of Pierrette. She was not wearing artistic dress, like many of the other women here; she had a full red skirt and a beautifully tailored golden bodice.

Pierrette had asked for this party so she could sound out London's intelligentsia. Time to take the leap.

"Your mother made friends so easily," Pierrette said, a little louder and more cheerfully. "I encountered another of them in Paris. An Oscar Kane. Someone said he was in London. Do you know him?"

The beautiful woman turned slightly. Just a little change of course, but Pierrette had her wits about her now, and she was trained to notice things. A dinner party was not so different from a street battle, after all. Not so different from a circus show, either.

"I don't know the name, but I'm interested to know any friend of my mother's," said Anne. "Anyone who might have a letter or know something of her work. She had so many ideas and what she actually published was a mere fraction of it. I'm rather afraid that my grandmother's overdeveloped sense of propriety will have destroyed most of it."

The beautiful woman turned to fix Pierrette in her sights. It was casual, as though her conversation with the gray-bearded man had naturally met its end, and she was moving on. She looked Pierrette up and down, smiling slightly. "Forgive me," she said in a German accent. "I couldn't help but overhear another accent from the Continent. It's good to know I am not the only foreigner here. I am Countess von Visler. Konstanze."

Pierrette took her hand. "Pierrette Arnaud. Delighted."

"I believe we have a mutual friend. But you have not heard of me, it seems."

Pierrette kept her face even. "Ah, then you know Mr Kane?"

She said nothing for a moment, cocked her eyebrow. "I was referring to Mr Rossetti. Why don't you and I have coffee sometime soon? We non-Londoners have to stick together. I'm staying at Brown's Hotel."

"Brown's! How funny," Anne chipped in. "That hotel was founded by my grandfather's valet and my grandmother's maid."

"Life is full of coincidences, I find," the countess said.

Byron Ockham broke in: "I want to know more about this man who's been taken for desertion. This old friend of mother's."

Pierrette hesitated. It would be in the papers, so there was no safety in secrecy. "A fellow called Simeon Price. He went down with the HMS *Birkenhead* in 1852, and was thought to be missing. He's a good man, and has been kind to me."

"What drives a man to desert, I wonder?" said the countess coolly. "To turn his back on his duty. In the heat of battle, I can understand it. Cowardice is a powerful force. But to simply walk away?"

Byron's face was like stone. He addressed Pierrette as though the countess were not there. "I'll do what I can to help your friend. God help me, I'll even talk to father if I have to."

Ada's absent husband, the army colonel. Why hadn't Pierrette thought of going to him? There was hope, there were things she could do. She just had to keep her wits, and her knives, about her, and not look down.

Pierrette sat on a chimney stack, dangling her legs and kicking her black button boots. Brown's Hotel across the street was a five-story wall of little windows, each with an iron railing at its base. An easy building to climb in and out of. And she was dressed for climbing – or at least, as dressed for climbing as she could be while still being presentable for coffee with a countess. She would have preferred to have worn her darling mauve dress and her hoop crinoline, but there was a strong possibility that this invitation was a trap. The tearoom at Brown's was a public place, and she had her trusty Laguiole knife in her pocket and her revolver in her reticule. Even so, before she even went in, she preferred to know where all the exits were, and she wanted to be able to reach them in a hurry.

So she had borrowed one of Lizzie's more artistic dresses, so she could appear to be deliberately scoffing at fashion rather than unable to afford it. It was pale golden silk, buttoned down the front and embroidered with a floral pattern in white thread. It was too long on her, and Pierrette was afraid she did not look the slightest bit ethereal. But the dress had a loose skirt, gathered a bit in the back, that hung without the need for a hoop crinoline. She wore her corset with Ada's notes inside, and the heavy mourning necklace Nell had given her with the secret powder, both because it was her only jewelry and because one never knew when one might need to breathe fire. She'd walk through those fine hotel doors as though she was too good for them, and sit down with this countess and find out how she knew Oscar Kane.

Pierrette took a deep breath, pushed herself down to the roof edge, and swung down over the gable roof so she could descend to the street.

Two strong arms wrapped around her legs and pulled her inward. She knocked her head on a windowsill, and her world went black.

When Pierrette came to her senses, she was sitting in a wooden chair. Her arms were tied behind her, and her ankles were restrained against the chair legs. She was in the corner of a small room. The only other things in the room were a cold, empty fireplace, a round mahogany table, on which both her knife and gun were lying, and two people. There was a big man she didn't recognize, standing by the door. He had a scar on his face, horizontally across one cheek. Sitting in a chair much like her own was Countess von Visler.

"We know how Assassins think, you see," said the countess, lightly, as though they were drinking their coffees after all. "The best way to stay ahead of you is to think like you."

"I'm not an Assassin," said Pierrette.

"Perhaps not yet, but you've certainly been trained by one. Simeon is always scrupulously careful. He would teach you to come early, to understand the terrain. He would teach you about the value of staying up high. All it took to trap you was to identify the best vantage points, and make sure that all but one of them were covered in copious amounts of pigeon shit."

The countess smiled the smile of a friend.

"Kane must have access to a great deal of pigeon shit," Pierrette spat back.

"Kane is not your concern." The smile vanished, and the countess picked up Pierrette's little revolver, examining it idly. "Some years ago, he had you in his grasp, but he decided you were of no consequence, because he sent Hennighan here to search your room, and found nothing. Back when he thought Hennighan was working for him. Back before he realized that everyone works for us eventually." She paused. "Or they die. Sometimes that happens."

Hennighan. Pierrette looked at the big man with the scar, and remembered Tillie, in Vienna, saying a man with a scar had asked about Pierrette and Simeon Price. She shivered.

Everyone works for us eventually. So the countess was a Templar.

"And all along, you were the real treasure. You knew Ada Lovelace in her final years, when her genius was at its most acute. I was young when you first turned up, and distracted. But now I know that you came to Simeon for a reason. You have information, or you know where it is. Either way, what I need is inside your head." The smile returned, less friendly this time. "And perhaps, inside Simeon's. But we have Simeon where we can get at him. And now we have you."

Pierrette didn't like the way the countess kept referring to Simeon by his first name.

The countess put down Pierrette's gun, then picked up the Laguiole knife and opened and closed it a few times, appraisingly. She tested the blade against one fingertip.

Then Countess von Visler stood up. With the knife still open, she advanced. Pierrette pulled herself up, trying to stand, but the chair was heavy, and she only succeeded in banging it on the floor. If there was anyone else in the building, perhaps they'd complain about the noise. It didn't seem likely. The countess seemed to be a woman who prepared for such eventualities.

It took a long time for the countess to decide where to make the first cut. With the tip of the blade, she lifted the chain that held the mourning necklace. A weapon that was useless without a fire. Pierrette stared back at her, trying to calm her breathing and her heart, to give herself the best chance of fighting back. She needed to think. But it was hard to think when the knife – her own knife – was tracing a line along her jawbone. She hardly felt any pain, but she felt blood trickle down her neck. Lizzie's beautiful silk dress would be stained.

Out of nowhere, the countess stabbed her. Right in the ligament between her left armpit and her breast. Close enough to the heart to make Pierrette believe, for a moment, that she was dead or dying, but far enough away to make sure she wasn't. A jagged sound escaped her throat. She was not used to being afraid. Simeon hadn't trained her for this. He should have trained her for this.

Her side was warm and wet. Damn damn damn! Would the blood soak right through the corset and into Ada's careful notes beneath? She really should have made a copy after all. How confident she had been that the papers were safe as long as they were with her. God knows how faded and smudged they were by now. For years she had carried them, and they had never done anyone any good. She had never found anyone she could trust to interpret them, to stop the Magus. Pierrette had only succeeded in keeping them away from him… only for the Templars to destroy them with her own blood, if this kept up. Would they even know she had them about her all this time? Would they strip her body and sell the corset to a rag merchant in Petticoat Lane, who would never know what it was? The thought would have been funny, if it didn't involve Pierrette's corpse.

"You want to know what's in my head," Pierrette said. Her voice sounded strange.

"And you want to tell me," the countess said, standing back and tapping the flat of the knife against her palm.

"If you give me a pen and paper, I'll write down what I remember. I don't think there's anything to it. The ravings of a dying woman. If you want it so badly, it's yours. Just get me something to write with."

The countess smiled again, and this time the smile was that of a predator. "A very nice try. I won't be untying you. What you know, you can tell me, word by word. We have time."

Pierrette hesitated, thinking fast. "There's a figure she used to draw. I don't know how to describe it. It–"

The knife came out of nowhere, and slashed the orange silk from shoulder to waist, diagonally across Pierrette's body. It snicked her flesh near her collarbone, but it snagged on the corset and tore. The countess seemed surprised; she calibrated the depth and force of every cut so carefully. She put her head on one side and looked at Pierrette, who had tucked her head down to look at the corset.

The knife clattered onto the table. The countess's perfect fingernails pulled the torn silk away and plucked at the piece of exposed paper revealed inside the cotton corset.

"Oh, you clever girl."

CHAPTER TWENTY-FOUR

Simeon Price was a model prisoner. Even before the prison doctor cleared him to work, he volunteered for it, picking oakum to make ropes for ships. It was something to do, and it kept him strong. He ate every drop of gruel and every bite of hard potato. Sometimes there was bread and treacle, or a hunk of meat or cheese. As soon as he was able, he walked on his own to chapel, using his arms and the walls to take the weight off his leg as much as he could. In the exercise yard, he grimaced but kept pace with the other men, round and round with his hand on the walls. In his cell, he paced, despite the doctors' orders to rest. He wasn't allowed a crutch, so he made do. And he did get stronger, week after week.

Once, after night fell and he was in darkness, he forgot himself, and started to sing "A Parting Glass". There was soon a rattle of bolts, and the guard came along to threaten him with the punishment cell. No singing, and no whistling.

Halford said the court martial would be early in the new year, perhaps January or February. The upside of that, Simeon thought, was that his leg would be healed enough by then for him to make his escape from the courtroom. The downside was that Kane could go anywhere in the meantime, and Pierrette was out looking for him totally on her own. Halford had delivered his message, and brought him one back, laughing about the smoke bombs and telling Simeon not to worry. Easier said than done. He'd asked Halford to check up on her, but on his next visit to the Rossetti rooms, a pale and ailing Lizzie had shown him a two-sentence note from Pierrette, saying that she had had to travel to Dublin and apologizing for not saying goodbye. It had appeared under the Rossettis'door, without an envelope, address or stamp.

Dublin? It could surely only mean that Kane had gone home. But why? Simeon read Pierrette's short letter over and over. It looked like her handwriting, but it seemed odd. Rushed, perhaps. He held it up to the light to look for invisible ink, rearranged the letters in his mind to check for code. Nothing.

He had to trust in Pierrette now. Truth be told, he'd taught her everything he could. The rest was up to her.

Two weeks before Christmas, Prince Albert died. Halford assured Simeon that the cause was typhoid fever, that there was no doubt at all that it was natural, and seemed taken aback by Simeon's concern for the queen's husband. Across London, the shops were closed and parties were cancelled. In prison, the guards wore black armbands. The parish provided roast beef and vegetables for Christmas, with plum pudding for dessert. The prisoners did not mourn.

The year 1862 came in, and the wraps came off Simeon's leg. The skin was pale and clammy, and his leg didn't feel quite right, but so long as it would hold him, he was happy. He wanted desperately to run, to feel the ground speeding beneath his feet, but the only exercise allowed was walking round and round like a pony tied to a mill for a half an hour once a day.

Even in the bowels of the *Birkenhead*, his hammock banging up against others, Simeon had never minded close quarters. But now he felt a constant, low panic. His years as an Assassin had given him a fondness for being able to climb up and get a good look at things. Now he felt like one of Kane's pigeons, looking through the bars of their cages at a window's worth of sky.

When the prison doctor pronounced Simeon fit to withstand potential corporal punishment, they dressed him in a soldier's uniform and took him out into a bright and chilly morning. It was barely a mile from Millbank Prison straight north to the Horse Guards building where the court martial was to be held.

Two officers flanked him, a strong hand on each of his arms, as they walked in. They hadn't tied his hands, to his surprise. But Simeon did not jerk his elbows and run, though the impulse was strong. He'd had plenty of time to think about this in recent weeks, and had decided that he should allow Halford to try his quixotic scheme. Simeon would make his escape after it failed. He had sworn not to take the blood of an innocent, and that meant not taking blood in self-defense unless it was necessary, unless there was no other way.

In truth, however, he was quite sure that soon there would be no other way.

In a wide room, with a gold and red carpet and carved chairs, sat the judge advocate and the seven officers who would judge his case. Simeon had not been in the company of this many soldiers in a decade. There was Halford sitting behind a table, and a few other men he vaguely recognized from the *Birkenhead*, though he couldn't remember any of their names. There were a few men in uniform he didn't recognize at all, in the back rows, along with a few women and men in civilian dress.

"Journalists," Halford whispered in his ear. To Simeon's startled glance, he said, "Because of HMS *Birkenhead*. Makes you interesting. And there are always a few curious onlookers at these things."

Frowning, Simeon scanned their faces. At the end of the row was a woman in a deep red dress, with a black veil dropping from her hat. She looked up at him and smiled.

She was ten years older, more confident, more beautiful. But it took him no time at all to recognize Countess Konstanze von Visler. The Templar. Here in London, at his court martial. He'd had no doubts that Kane was behind his arrest, but he hadn't been sure whether Kane was working with the Templars. This seemed to clinch it. Whether Kane was a traitor or a double agent who'd been turned or something else, he was not merely a rogue Assassin. He was aiding their mortal enemies. Perhaps he always had been, right back to Vienna, or even before. The question was, how long had Kane known, himself, that he had been doing so?

But that didn't matter now. First there would be another reckoning.

At Halford's urging, Simeon walked, slightly stunned, to the front, very aware that he still had a slight limp. The judge advocate asked if he objected to the presence of any of the officers on the board.

"I would have to know them to object to them, sir."

The judge advocate grunted. The court was sworn, the prisoner pleaded "Not guilty." He sat beside Halford, straight as a knife.

The prosecution began, with a long speech about the courage of the men who went down to the bottom in what, to Simeon's annoyance, the prosecuting officer referred to as "the Birkenhead Drill."

They called a witness, and Simeon looked upon the face of Lieutenant Grimes. He was older, now Major Grimes, and had a small scar over one eyebrow, but he still wore the same sneer he'd worn when he told his men to beat to quarters. He informed the court that the troops had shown what England and Her Majesty's Empire was made of. They had obeyed their orders to their last breath. But Simeon Price had chosen otherwise. In a moment of crisis, he had acted with extreme selfishness and cowardice, putting his comrades and civilians, including women and children, at risk. No, Lance Corporal Price seized his chance to desert. He dove overboard, despite the danger of swamping the lifeboats, and let the world believe he was dead.

Halford had a question. Did Grimes see Price cause any harm to the lifeboats or to the men on the ship? Grimes said he had not been paying attention, as at that moment he had been making his own peace with the Almighty.

"And yet here you are," Simeon said.

There was rustling all through the room, and the judge advocate glared at him. "Does the defendant wish to question the witness?"

Simeon coughed, and deliberately did not look at Halford's face. "I am curious to know whether Major Grimes was among those court martialed after the wreck for the actions that led to the deaths of all those men."

Grimes's face twisted up, but he held up his hand to stop the prosecutor's objection. "Those were naval officers, and all were acquitted."

"Because the men who ran that ship onto the rocks had already paid with their lives," said Simeon. "But the men who told other men that their lives were worthless, the men who panicked and took solace in discipline, in regulation, over compassion and common sense–"

The judge advocate attempted to interrupt him, but Simeon carried on.

"You speak of the spirit of the *Birkenhead*, Major Grimes, but that spirit was only necessary because every single man in charge was utterly incompetent. We are very good at this game in England, aren't we? We create a disaster and then we applaud ourselves for how well we bear it. No, that's wrong. I misspoke." The judge said something, but Simeon interrupted again. "Some create the disaster. Others bear it."

Corporal Halford's expression could no longer be ignored. Simeon fell silent. The other man started in on his defense as though Simeon hadn't spoken. And Simeon kept quiet, out of respect for Halford and all he'd done. He had had every intention of staying silent through the whole thing, but then he'd had to listen to Grimes.

He didn't turn to look at the countess, to see what her reaction might be to all this.

Halford called witnesses: three men Simeon might have passed on the street with barely a second glance. He had been less observant in the days when he'd known them, but they remembered him. They told a rather different story about the last moments of the *Birkenhead*: how Simeon Price had been seen rescuing drowning men from below decks, below the rising waters, at great personal risk to himself. And from another man, wounded and retired now, the court heard that in 1850, before the *Birkenhead*, Simeon had stood his ground in front of a mob in Ireland that threatened government storehouses. Simeon wouldn't have called them a mob himself. He remembered that day very well, though he still couldn't remember the night in the pub that followed. He wouldn't have said that he had stood his ground, either, or that it had taken any particular courage, given that he was the one with the rifle and bayonet. If those starving women hadn't torn him to pieces and taken what they needed to feed their families, it was not to Simeon's credit, and maybe to his blame.

What would he have done, if they had tried to get past him? The thought had plagued him even then. He was on trial today for cowardice, but the night he'd truly been a coward was the night he stood between hungry mothers and the government's food, holding a gun. That night he'd been a good soldier. All of it was rotten, top to bottom.

There was silence in the room, and he realized he'd stopped paying attention to the testaments to his supposed upright character. Someone had asked him a question.

"Could you repeat that, please, sir?"

The judge advocate frowned, his temple wrinkling under his wig. "Do you give consent for Corporal Halford to provide the defense statement on your behalf?"

Simeon's thoughts rolled like the ocean. That was certainly

the plan. Halford was ready; he had a stack of papers in his hand. He was going to tell the court that Simeon had suffered from amnesia, a job that would now be more difficult because of Simeon's outburst about the leadership of the *Birkenhead*. Simeon remembered well enough. That night, on the ship, he had chosen not to be a coward anymore.

Simeon stood up, walked to the witness box, and asked to be sworn in.

Halford sat down again, his face a storm.

After he had sworn to Almighty God, Simeon began at the top.

"I was recruited in 1847 by a man who bought his commission for a sum of money that most Londoners will never see. A sum that would change their lives. That man knew nothing about how to keep the peace, stand for justice or protect the innocent. He'd never been taught any of those things, because there was no one to teach him. Nobody else around him knew either. They taught him how to shoot, and how to bark at another man, and how to bear up and do one's duty. They taught him what England expects of an officer and a gentleman. Fair enough."

He looked at Corporal Halford, whose face now showed only blank resignation. At the countess, who looked amused, damn her. Simeon carried on. Nothing else to do, now. "But where I come from, in that pub in Ealing, we learned those same things, too, because England expects exactly the same things from us, for worse pay. We already knew how to fight and how to bark and how to bear up. We accepted that we had to scrape every day to survive, because surely the men at the top, the men who were so rich they could afford to buy their own jobs – surely they knew something we didn't. Surely they understood how the world could work. Someone must have understood, because God only knows we didn't. Every day is hard in Ealing. It's hard everywhere I've ever been since. It's hard to feed your children, to keep them alive, to get them any kind of real education, to protect them from your own pain and fears. It's hard to know what the right thing is to do, and what honor looks like. People want to believe that someone knows what they're doing. And that keeps the men with the medals on top."

"Lance corporal," said the judge advocate, "this is not the House of Commons. If you have a statement to make in your defense, I'll ask you to make it."

Simeon swallowed, and said in a quieter voice, "What makes a man an officer is money, and money alone. So, when an officer tells his men that they must go down with the ship, that they should not even try to swim or find a bit of flotsam to cling to, what reason do we have to obey? When that man has shown no judgment or wisdom or even common sense? We–"

"Lance corporal!"

"We have sold our lives, and our honor, for a shilling."

There was quiet then, as though they were expecting him to say more, though a moment ago there had been banging and yelling at him to stop.

"In my defense," Simeon continued, calmly, "I can say nothing except that I was told to die, and I chose to live instead. From that day on, I would trust that my own judgment was as good as any other man's. I owed no loyalty to a creed that would have called me a hero for committing pointless suicide in an orderly fashion. Had I walked, all naked and sun-mad, to the nearest British Army office, I would only have been sent to Crimea to charge into gunfire to no purpose, or to India to slaughter women and children and old men.

"I do not regret my choice. I did the only thing that made a goddamned bit of sense. And if swimming among sharks until my lungs gave out, instead of meekly lying down and dying as ordered, if that makes me a coward, then call me a coward, lash me, kill me, transport me, but I will not, ever again, be anything but my own man."

The court paused to consider. Simeon was taken into an adjoining room with a few officers, including Halford. The moment to escape would be when they were transporting him, after the sentencing. It was always easier to take people by surprise in a crowded area when one was already moving, and the moment Simeon got out of their grasp, all he'd have to do was run. Presuming his leg didn't give out.

"I think there's a chance the character references will have saved you from the lash," Halford said gloomily, pacing. "But I couldn't guess as to the prison term."

"I am sorry, Halford. Truly."

"You might have warned me. I could have had you declared insane."

"It wasn't planned."

"And now I look a bloody fool, or worse, because they have my written statement of defense, with the whole yarn about you losing your memory. They'll have me up next, I don't doubt." Halford stopped pacing, looked at Simeon and said, "Well, there's nothing to be done about it now. I'll–"

The door opened, and an officer gestured. The board had made its decision.

"The board has decided in the case of Simeon Price, based on the testimony of witnesses to his character and actions at the time, and on the statement of defense provided by Corporal Halford, and on the unusual behavior of the defendant here today, that the effects of the shipwreck were sufficient to cause confusion and loss of memory, and that by the time Lance Corporal Price had recovered his senses, his term of service was ended. Let the record show that Simeon Price is not guilty of desertion and is considered discharged without pension as of the end of his term of service in the year 1857, now past."

It was a farce, or a ruse. Simeon looked at Halford, whose face was as shocked as Simeon's would have been, if Simeon let his shock show on his face.

"I'm free, then?" he whispered.

Halford shook his head in disbelief. "You are, but I couldn't begin to tell you why."

"I could," said a voice behind them, as the court grew noisy with reaction and bustle.

They turned to see a young man with a beard and a serious face. "Byron Ockham," he said, putting out his hand.

It took Simeon a moment to place the name. Ada Lovelace's son. He'd been a young child the last time Simeon had seen him, but now he was a man.

"My father, the Earl of Lovelace, is a colonel. He got me off when I should have been court martialed, and now he's done the same for you."

Simeon hardly knew what to say. "But why?"

"Why did my father do it? Because I promised him I'd be good. Or do you mean why did *I* do it? I should think that would be obvious."

Simeon was distracted by the sight of the countess leaving the courtroom in the crowd, her back to him. Why had she come? If it was only curiosity, she might have read about it in the papers. To rattle him, perhaps.

Another man came up beside them and asked to shake Simeon's hand. "You said it, sir," said the stranger, his face red. "You really said it."

"I think," said Halford, looking at the group of men gathered by the door, "that there are some old comrades in the room who would very much like to stand you a drink."

CHAPTER TWENTY-FIVE

Pierrette wiped some blood away from under her nose. She no longer wondered where the blood was coming from, or why. Sometimes she found it on her hands, a trace from one of the various wounds on her body. The one thing she did wonder was how long the countess would keep her alive, and whether Pierrette could get the one thing she needed before then.

In the first days of Pierrette's captivity, the countess would arrive once a day, in the afternoons, and ask her more questions about Ada Lovelace. After a few days, the reason became clear. As Pierrette knew well, the notes were not written in code, exactly – or at least most of them weren't. But they made no sense. Sometimes the sentences didn't even fit together coherently. There were references to names or objects thrown in haphazardly, like a kind of shorthand for Ada's thoughts.

"We have people among her friends and family," the countess said one day. "We will learn what we need to know, depend upon it. You can act quickly to save yourself, now, by helping us. The time is short."

And then Pierrette did what she did every day: she spat a string of unsavory French words at the countess, who left the room.

Then Hennighan came in and beat her up.

Every morning, the thug also brought her a single meal of gruel in a tin cup too flimsy to be much good as a weapon. It was not a comfortable existence. Pierrette had no water other than a cup of stinking stuff in the morning and before bed. She couldn't wash, and while she'd never been one for frequent baths, a rag and basin would have been very welcome. Worst of all, it was very cold. She'd twice asked Hennighan for a fire in the room. The request was denied. There was a stove on the floor below, and a pipe that heated this room well enough. Did the mademoiselle think she had crossed the road and was staying at Brown's?

The day after that conversation, Pierrette woke up light-headed but clear in her mind. Hennighan brought her cup of gruel, and she slurped it quietly and thought. Simeon had taught her that observation was survival. So she would observe. She made a long list in her mind of everything she knew, every fact or pattern she could discern. The first problem was that she was chained, her arms to the fireplace and ankles to the table, so she had to sleep between them on the floor.

She stayed defiant during that day's conversation with the countess, but deliberately let her voice break and her hand shake. During that day's beating, she broke down and sobbed.

The following day, when the countess came again, Pierrette said, in a small voice, "I would like to help. I knew Ada, and perhaps I can make something out of it if I try."

She was placed back in the chair, her ankles tied to it. She had her arms free so she could write, but the countess sat opposite her in the chair near the fireplace with her back to the door, a gun in her hand. Hennighan stood a few feet behind Pierrette's chair with his back to the window. To her surprise, the countess gave her access to Ada's notes. It was not a copy, but the actual papers that had lived for so long in Pierrette's corset, re-sewn roughly into a book between black cardboard covers. Not that there was much Pierrette could do with it all. The countess handed Pierrette some sheets of cheap paper and a few dull pencils.

The first day, Pierrette used up all ten sheets of paper, writing at length, then crossing huge sections out and writing over what she'd written. She included one true and useful interpretation, though, surrounded by black scribbles: where Ada had written "evening harmonies", that was a reference to a family joke that everyone's singing improved after their glass of port, and it meant that something was working well. It was a small amount of good faith, to gain what she really wanted. Pierrette had never been a good liar, but she knew how to act a part.

For days, this kept on, and she was patient. Pierrette gave up bits and pieces – she just hoped none of it would prove significant enough to let them build whatever weapon the Templars hoped had taken shape in Ada's strange imagination. She went through stacks of paper, a dozen pencils (all trimmed for her by the countess, using Pierrette's precious knife) and nearly all of a crumbly rubber eraser.

The beatings did not stop, but they became sporadic, and usually lighter. This was almost worse, as she never knew what the day would bring, and she found herself hoping that a particularly clever note, or a polite demeanor, would earn her a reprieve. On the bad days, she wondered why, and all she had to examine was her own behavior. It was easy to forget that she was acting, at first. After a while, she understood that she wasn't.

One night, she couldn't sleep because of the cold. Just what she had been waiting for. She was exhausted but smiling grimly when a bright, clear dawn broke through the window. The thug arrived with her gruel. Then the countess came, and Pierrette set to work, her ankles tied to her chair as always. She worked hard, but made mistakes and dropped her pencil. Her nose bled, and there were bloodstains on the worn-down nub of her rubber eraser. Her fingers were red with streaks of her own blood, and with cold. She blew on them for warmth.

"Why are you stalling?" the countess said, with soft curiosity. "The cold doesn't bother you that much, I know."

"It's not usually *this* cold." Pierrette caught herself being defiant, but she didn't alter her expression. "I simply can't write with my fingers frozen. If we could have a fire…"

The countess said nothing.

Pierrette coughed. She took refuge in the truth, risking it because what was before her in Ada's notes had nothing to do with weapons. "There's something in here about a temple, and given what I know about Ada's private references to parts of England, I'd say this was in Bath. There's a section about lines converging, coordinates, and an artifact – different bits of code words. I think I have it but I need to work it out, and my fingers–"

The countess held up her hand to tell her to stop talking, and then gestured for Hennighan. He left the room, coming back with a few logs.

Pierrette was patient.

She was midway through a sentence, and the fire had warmed the room, when she absent-mindedly lifted the mourning necklace to her lips, lifted her chin, and blew.

The yellow powder drifted in the air for one moment before it became a bright orange cloud of fire, with the center half a foot at most from the countess's head. The countess was out of her chair, making a noise like nothing Pierrette had ever heard pass her lips. Hennighan was quickly at her side, pulling her away from the fire. The dust lasted a few seconds at most, and then it was gone, but by then the countess's puffed sleeve was ablaze. Pierrette had already reached across the table, grabbed the knife and the book, and slashed the ropes that held her ankles.

Hennighan lunged at her. She snatched up the chair and kept to the plan, though it was tempting to try to run her knife through his ribs. But there were two of them, and there was still a gun in the countess's hand.

The countess screamed in frustration and fired a shot, just as Pierrette was lifting the chair to break the window. The shot went through the glass, making a nice target for the chair. With all her strength, diminished though it was after all the time spent in chains, she smashed the window, and then threw herself through it, ignoring the sudden rush of warm blood from a dozen cuts. She knew the angled roof below the window would break her fall, but it still hurt when she rolled down the tiles, then hung by her fingers, dropping to land hard on the pavement one story below. It was what Major Wallin would have called a good fall; she had her knees underneath her, and it hurt like the devil, but nothing was broken. Another shot came from the window as she pulled herself up and ran, very shakily, into the nearest tobacconists, and then out his back window, and into an alley, where she stopped to retch blood, before dragging herself up onto a window ledge, then to another, then up to a high rooftop.

She made it a fair way down the row of houses when her strength finally gave out, and she curled up in the lee of a smoking chimney. She hoped they hadn't seen which way she'd gone, but even if they had, she could go no further. Pierrette stayed there for a long time, shivering and bloody, her arm wrapped around Ada's notebook, while a busy London evening unfolded beneath her. She must have slept, because sometime later she looked up into the very surprised face of a young chimneysweep.

CHAPTER TWENTY-SIX

The Red Lion in Holborn was a favorite haunt of Dante Gabriel Rossetti. He liked the history: according to legend, Oliver Cromwell's exhumed body had been stored there overnight on its way to be hanged. It was near the Rossettis' old flat on Red Lion Square, and now it was halfway between his new rooms next door to them at Blackfriars, and the Working Men's College at Great Ormond Street where he taught.

So the Red Lion was the first place Simeon went, after the landlady at Blackfriars caught him at the door to say the lady was indisposed and the gentleman was out. He wanted to know everything he could about what might have sent Pierrette haring off to Ireland, and where in Ireland she might be. And then he would board the first ship to follow her.

Byron Ockham's working of miracles hadn't stopped with his acquittal. They'd given him back his hidden blade, his Italian knife, his revolver, his old clothes. It was all there, though his stone-colored cloak, a gift from the Paris Assassins, had a tear down the middle. Simeon carried it over his arm as he walked

302

through London's narrowest and darkest streets, out of habit. He came at last to the Red Lion, on a wide open street corner, lamplit in the cold evening.

Inside, it was busy, and noisy. Good. Rossetti was there, and the man looked exhausted. His dark curls hung long behind his ears. Perhaps it was the lighting from the few paraffin lamps in the pub, but there were dark circles under his eyes and a sheen on his high forehead.

Still, the man smiled a welcome when Simeon sat down. Rossetti slid down the bench from the group of people he was sitting with, and shook his hand.

"I had a feeling you would find a way out," Rossetti said. "Good for you."

"I'm told Pierrette went to Ireland," Simeon said without preamble. "Did she tell you anything before she went, about why?"

"She did not." Rossetti lit his pipe, with shaking hands. "Very unpredictable, your French girl."

Simeon tensed as someone approached him from behind, but it was just a man with soldier's eyes and a pint of dark beer in his hand. "For you, Mr Price, from the lads, if you'd like it."

He twisted to see a group of men sitting on stools at the bar, all looking at him. They each touched their hat brims to him, and he nodded back, uncomfortably.

"How do they know who I am?" he asked no one in particular.

The man who'd brought him the drink said, "We all followed the case in the newspapers. There were drawings."

Simeon shook his head. "Christ. They must have been very good drawings."

Rossetti gestured with his pipe. "You do rather have the

distinct look of a man who just got a reprieve from the lash and isn't sure how to feel about it. That probably helped them."

"I know how I bloody feel about it all right," grumbled Simeon, turning back. The man who'd brought him the beer had retreated, but he had had a face Simeon trusted. He took a sip; it was bitter, and strong. He took another.

"Well, so do they, it appears," Rossetti said. "You can enjoy celebrity as well as freedom. What will you do next?"

Rossetti and his wife had never asked many questions about what it was that Simeon did for a living. They seemed to have assumed it was something to do with the circus, and something illegal. Not far off the mark, really.

"Take the next ship for Ireland, and find Pierrette."

"Oh, she's back, didn't you know?"

Simeon froze with the glass halfway to his mouth. "Back?"

"Didn't bother to tell you, I suppose." The artist grimaced. "I was out – teaching – and apparently Pierrette came in through the window and nearly scared Lizzie half to death – which wouldn't take much, the state she's in. We lost our hopes for a baby, again, just before Christmas, and she's not at all well."

"I'm very sorry to hear it. What did Pierrette say, do you know?"

Rossetti narrowed his eyes at him. "I wasn't there. Lizzie said she looked rough, terribly ragged and thin. She said something about wanting Lizzie to know that she was all right, which was odd given that we had no reason to think she wasn't, until she came climbing in through our window. It gave Lizzie such a shock that I had to put new locks on the windows and set Mrs Burrell at the front door to turn visitors away."

"Yes, she's still following those orders." Simeon thought

furiously for a moment. "So, Pierrette is back in London." Or perhaps she had never really left.

One of the women in the group Rossetti had been sitting with leaned closer to them. "If you see her, Mr Price, could you possibly give her a message for me?"

He leaned toward the woman, the better to hear her over the noise of the pub and to make sure they weren't overheard, so close that his temple nearly brushed the jaunty straw hat on her head.

"Do you mean Pierrette?"

"Yes, indeed. I'm Fanny Eaton. We met several weeks ago – Miss Arnaud and myself, I mean. She was looking for an Irishman. If you see her, do please tell her that he's gone to Bath."

Simeon nearly fell off his chair. "The Irishman? You mean to say our bloody Irishman's gone to Bath?"

"Yes, well, you see… My old man drives a cab, and when I heard about Mademoiselle Arnaud going off to Ireland so soon after she'd been asking about this bloke, I says to my James to be on the lookout for the fellow she described. Then just yesterday, James said he drove an Irishman wearing a waistcoat made to look like peacock feathers, and another man with him called him Kane. They were taking a train for Bath."

He stood up. "Thank you, Mrs Eaton. That really is most… Rossetti, you'll excuse me… I have to…"

Rossetti waved him away, pouring the rest of Simeon's beer into his own glass.

Simeon stepped out into Holborn Street. Light February snow was swirling around the streetlamps, and the evening was young enough that the street was still busy, the hooves of carriage horses beating in time to the chatter from the pub. His head was reeling. Which way to go? He had to get to Bath, but could he trust that Pierrette was safe in the meantime? For that matter, maybe Pierrette had learned of Kane's movements herself already and was on his trail. Maybe he'd find both of them there.

He sighed, took a step forward, then stopped again. High over his head, someone whistled, long and low. A familiar set of notes.

He looked up – and saw a silhouette he knew, sitting on a stone roof gable three stories up, and dangling her feet as though she were a child playing on a bridge.

"Your movements are predictable, old chap," Pierrette said around a bite of fish paste sandwich as they sat together on the ledge. "I knew where to look for you. So would they."

He was so glad to hear her teasing him that he couldn't keep from smiling.

"First of all, my girl, thirty-five is not old. Second of all, I wouldn't have had to show my face at the Red Lion if you had bothered to tell me where you were." He kept his tone light, but he glanced at her from time to time, as casually as he could. He was troubled by the look of her. She was thin, and her face was puffed and bruised on one side. She had a not-quite-healed scab on her jawline, and the way she moved, wincing sometimes when she twisted, suggested another injury. Maybe even a cracked rib.

"I met a rich lady at a party, and the next day, without even asking, she grabbed me, tied me up, and made me talk all about Ada for what seemed like weeks. There you have it."

"A rich…" Heat rose up his neck at the realization. The witch had been sitting there in his court martial, smiling at him, and all the while she'd had Pierrette imprisoned somewhere? "Countess von Visler?"

"Ah, you know her!" Pierrette said drily. "Lovely woman, charming, very good with a knife. Possibly now singed a little, just around the edges." She smiled weakly at him. "I still haven't been able to use a smoke bomb, but I did get to use something close."

"Is she–"

"She's very much alive, I'm sad to say. Or she was a few days ago. It took me a little while to get my bearings, and then I heard you'd been freed, and here we are." She patted the satchel on her lap, tightly strapped around one shoulder, which had also held the sandwiches. "And here's the damned book. I think we should burn it, you know. But then every time I go for a match, I think, ah, but maybe there *is* an answer there that will help us figure out what they want, or where they have gone to."

"Kane's gone to Bath, apparently."

A sharp inhalation, then, "One of the things I told the countess was that Ada had written some nonsense about Bath. And it was from the notebook, Simeon. I had to feed them plausible things. Or I thought I did. Oh, that was a mistake. I don't know what they're looking for, but it can't be a coincidence."

"It's all right. We'll find him and put a stop to this." He threw the last bit of his sandwich to a pigeon, a good English pigeon, with no discernable neck and nothing tied to its leg. He pulled his cloak tighter around him, against the chill of the night.

"Your cloak is ripped," Pierrette said. "Give it to me and I will mend it."

"I'm a soldier, Pierrette. I can work a needle and thread."

"Huh, I've seen your mendings."

"Hmph." She was clever, he had to admit. The corset had kept the notes safe for years. "I wonder what Ada would say, to know her thoughts had caused us so much trouble."

"I think they caused her more torture than anyone else," Pierrette said, with pain on her face. She'd been the one with Ada in her last moments, Simeon reminded himself. While he'd contented himself with sending brief letters, soldier's dispatches that said little and asked less. She must have been getting the same sorts of letters from her son, Byron Ockham, at the same time. And it was young Ockham, another deserter, whom Simeon had to thank for his freedom.

"You know, we're always one step behind," Pierrette said. "Off we go now to chase him to Bath, and maybe it's another trap. Maybe they'll get you for good this time, Simeon, and me too. I don't suppose your mysterious Ghost could help us? Are there Assassins in Bath?"

"I've made inquiries," said Simeon. "I don't think we'll get much help from that quarter at the moment. They're busy. Being kept busy, maybe. The Templars have influence in every part of London, and I don't doubt that's true in Bath as well. I think we're on our own."

She shook her head. "We're very good, but we can't win if we're totally outnumbered. I have friends who are willing to help."

"Lizzie is ill, Rossetti said."

"Not Lizzie." She paused. "The Aurora Troupe."

"Circus performers? Christ, Pierrette, we have enough to worry about without endangering people who have no idea how to fight."

"They may not be soldiers, but I know a man who can shoot a shilling off a wall, and a woman who can jump six feet from a moving horse. I was not a fighter myself when I saved your life the night we met, remember."

"Saved my... oh, never mind. All right, if they won't get in the way." He could see in her face that she loved her friends, that she trusted them with her life, and would lay down hers for theirs. Which was the one thing he had missed from the army, the thing he had sought when he made his way to Vienna. The thing Kane had so long denied him. Brotherhood.

He thought of Sawyer Halford, of Byron Ockham. Of the brotherhood he'd been granted without looking for it. He thought of the group of soldiers drinking in the pub below, who had stood him a drink because of what he'd said in the dock.

"I think I might know some people too," he said.

Chapter Twenty-Seven

Simeon perched at the top of the bell tower of Bath Abbey. It was one of those evenings when the clouds seemed to catch the light from the streets below and hold it, so everything had a weird orange cast. The first time he'd ever climbed a cathedral, he'd watched the clouds rolling away beyond Vienna, into a wider world that seemed endless. Tonight, he could hardly see to the end of the road. He could just make out an unusual vehicle coming down the London Road: a red covered wagon with TWICE PATRONIZED BY HER MAJESTY THE QUEEN written in bold golden lettering on a sign above the driver. The driver was a small woman, whose blonde hair caught the light where it peeked from under her hat. She was guiding her horses expertly on the slick road. One of Pierrette's circus friends; she had probably driven chariots.

Simeon had come on ahead by train with Halford and Ockham. Halford, he had approached to ask if he knew any stout men who might want to make a little money in some business that might not be quite according to Queensberry

Rules. When Halford had insisted on coming, too, Simeon had argued. He'd already put his friend through enough; getting caught in a fight could get him a court martial of his own. He had a wife and child to think of now. But Halford had simply asked whether he thought this was a man worth fighting, and Simeon had had to say that yes, he was, and that was it.

Ockham had given him a bit of a twinge, too. This was Ada Lovelace's son; Simeon should really be trying to keep him safe. But Ockham seemed determined to taunt death in bottles and bar brawls alike, and even if his mother wouldn't have understood, Simeon did. Ockham was strong and smart, and he might as well fight something other than whatever specters followed him.

In his most hopeful moments, Simeon had even thought that with these two at his side, he might be able to deal with Kane before Pierrette and her circus troupe arrived. But he'd spent too much time sniffing around the city to find the place like the one described in Ada's notes. The area Pierrette thought it described was just a jumble of old hotels, where old ladies stayed when they came to take the waters. He had followed his nose through every musty tearoom and left-luggage closet and narrow brick alleyway, and found nothing. And no sign of Kane.

At last, he'd climbed the abbey that morning, and sat staring out for a while, just letting the patterns talk to his mind. And after a while, as it should, it all came clear. First, he noticed two men carrying shovels in a back street go through a small wooden door into an alley that he knew went nowhere, and then an hour later, he spotted Kane himself. He was wearing a top hat and a greatcoat. He walked into the alley, and didn't walk out again.

He'd let himself down to the ground, set Halford and Ockham to discreetly watch the alley exit. Then he'd ascended the spire again, to watch the city for other patterns, for anything he might have missed.

The men with the shovels meant two things: Kane was here looking for something, just as Pierrette had suspected. And it meant that Kane was not alone.

For ten years, Kane, the Magus, had used him or evaded him. It ended here, tonight. He'd had a telegram from Henri Escoffier, in France, telling him that the Assassins of Paris were satisfied that Oscar Kane had betrayed the creed. He had offered help, if Simeon could watch and wait. But Simeon had watched and waited long enough.

On the way down the cathedral, the wet stone scraped his palms and his leg ached. But he was free. He could soon slip into any shadow and live out the rest of his years anonymous and alone. A sweet, easy oblivion, a life free of duty. Never killing again, never losing anyone again. Never betrayed or betraying. No more relearning the lesson he knew very well: that sworn allegiance was no guarantee of honor. In the end, all there was in the world was a man and his conscience.

And if he slipped into the shadows, his conscience would slip in with him. Honor wasn't something a man could have on his own. Honor only existed where people tried to do something good together.

He walked out of the churchyard and into the street, to greet the red wagon. They were around the corner from the entrance to the alley, hidden from view. Pierrette burst out of the wagon's door in her dark brown cloak, and with a stone-colored bundle in her hands.

"Is that my cloak?"

"Good evening to you too. Our journey was very smooth, thank you." She shoved it into his hands with a grin.

He opened it, and saw that the rip was mended, but it didn't look seamless. In fact – he held it up to the light from the wagon's lanterns – it gleamed. Gold thread. It ran all along the repair, and around the hem and the peak of the hood. Not the most practical addition for a cloak that was meant to keep its wearer from being noticed, but it was kind of them to try.

"Nell did it," Pierrette said. "She's back in London minding the shop, but she did that before we left."

Simeon had heard many tales about Nell in his time. And minding the shop was important, since he had convinced Pierrette to hide Ada's notes there, under a pile of circus props. He knew the Robinsons had given their permission, and were happy to help, but Pierrette hadn't been happy about the idea. Simeon had convinced her that the Templars would assume Pierrette had kept the notes on her, as she had all these years, and that the safest place for them was far from here, but he knew Pierrette was uneasy about it.

He joked: "And was it Nell's idea to choose something other than plain thread?"

"You ask for help from a circus, you get circus help," said Pierrette with a shrug. She pointed to the tiny blonde woman in the driver's seat. "This is Tillie Wallin, the best equestrienne in Europe. And this"– she took the hand of a man with dark skin and gray hair as he climbed down from the wagon – "is Hugh Robinson, strongman and knife thrower. And this is Ariel Fine, who can walk upon a spider's web."

Ariel took Simeon's hand with a grin. "More to the purpose,

I once knocked two men's heads together when they tried to harass a friend after a show, cocked them out clean cold, the pair of them. We take care of each other, always. Just point me to the man who took Pierrette away from us."

That would be me, Simeon thought, but did not say.

In the shadow of a dingy brick wall, Byron Ockham stood with his hands in his pockets, a cigar glowing under his black fisherman's cap. On the other side of the little door that led into the alley, Sawyer Halford stood at attention, but out of uniform today. When he saw Simeon and his friends approaching quietly down the back street he smiled.

"No one's been in or out," Halford said softly. "Unless there's another exit."

"I don't think there is," said Simeon, who'd spent a long time watching from above. "But we'll learn soon enough." He turned to Pierrette. "He'll think he has me in a trap again. If I don't manage to prove him wrong, it'll be up to you. This alley is yours. Set everyone up where you think they're best – I'd say your people high up, leaving Ockham and Halford down here. Guns drawn."

Simeon had missed this alley on his searches for good reason. It was a narrow horseshoe of brick walls, with no doors or any other obvious exits. The one feature was a large, plain wooden box with a lid, up against a wall. The box looked like any other coal bunker, and that was probably all it was. But Kane had come into this alley, so he must have exited somewhere, and Simeon had been watching the rooftops from above. It was the only thing to try.

His suspicions were confirmed when he tried the lid: it

seemed to be locked from the inside. Simeon tried to pry one of the planks, and it strained but didn't budge. He was looking around for something to use as a crowbar or an axe when Hugh Robinson came up and took one end of the lid. Simeon took the other, and together they yanked it until it splintered in half.

"Thank you, Mr Robinson," said Simeon.

"I'm Hugh to my friends, and to Pierrette's," he answered, staring down into the box. "Shall we go in?"

"I'll investigate, and report back," Simeon said. "I think Pierrette may need all her friends up here, Hugh."

There was no trace of coal in the box, and there was no bottom that Simeon could see: just blackness going down, underground. He put his hands on the edge and swung over, then hung there for a minute in the darkness, trying to get a sense of where the bottom was. Pierrette had got herself nabbed doing something like this. Oh well. Let this be his last leap of faith during the lifetime of Oscar Kane.

It wasn't far at all, and his leg managed it without pain – or without extra pain. It always ached a little these days. There was just enough light from the opening above to get his bearings. A small, empty room, with a packed dirt floor. A long ladder, lying on the ground. He propped it up again so that it reached almost to the top of the box above, in case he needed to get out quickly. Leading away from the room was a narrow tunnel, just wide enough for a man to squeeze through.

He thought of Kane's waistcoats, and whether he'd lost any buttons. But it was only a few steps, and then he came out into a wider passage. Roughly dug steps led downward between dirt walls, and there was a blueish light coming from the bottom.

Simeon paused just outside the entrance to a circular room, lit by arc lights in glass globes, hooked up to battery cells of some kind. The room was enormous, dotted with broken pillars of stone and square holes dug out of the earthen floor. A scaffold supported a rickety walkway that led to another layer of archaeology carved out of one wall, and then across to the massive herringbone stone wall at the end. There were sections cut out of the side walls that might have been alcoves or corridors; they were too shadowed to tell. The last thing he noticed was Kane, sitting cross-legged and straight-backed on a chunk of masonry right in the middle. His white shirtsleeves were rolled up. Without a jacket on, his holster was exposed, along with the two guns in it, flanking a dull gold waistcoat that just caught the light from his arc lamp.

"One principle has guided me, for more than a decade," Kane said aloud, as though continuing a conversation. His voice echoed in the great room. "One unshakable belief. That Ada Lovelace was right. About everything. About you, certainly. About the potential of the Analytical Engine. Even about her predictions at the racetrack; I can't believe she would lose that often unless there was some factor she didn't know. Couldn't know. The races, I'm sure, were rigged. Maybe they were even rigged for the express purpose of impoverishing and embarrassing her. There were many people who took an interest in her life and ideas. Not just me."

"She was right about you too, eventually," Simeon said.

He expected a retort, but Kane only said, "That she was." He had something in his hands; something round. A weapon? Too small to be an Orsini bomb. It looked like it was made of stone. He tossed it lightly in the air. "Ada did get something wrong, but it used to be right, and the Templars know why. Like the horses."

"You've lost your powers of intellect in recent years, Kane." Simeon walked forward, into the circle of broken pillars. He kept his gaze on Kane but his attention on the shadows.

"Right again, Mr Price." He held up the thing in his hand, and Simeon braced himself for a blast, an attack, something. "This is just a clay ball. A decoy for me to find, and it did take me some time to find it. If there was ever an Eye here – and knowing Ada's tendency to be right, I suspect there was – the Templars found it themselves, long ago. Or they knew it was long gone. They traded me plausible information that they knew it would take me several days to disprove. Perhaps they hoped that I'd believe it a mistake, even then. Perhaps they hoped I'd continue to serve their ends, sending off idealists to botch assassinations, to frighten governments into hardening their laws."

Simeon took a step closer to Kane. "Then you know that they've been using you."

Kane looked almost insulted. "Well, that's been obvious for a long while, hasn't it? And I've been using them. Finding out what they knew. Trading information, but always getting the better bargain in the end. Today, I admit, was a setback, but I only lost a few days."

Another step forward. "You can't fight for freedom while working with the Templars to make governments so afraid of the man in the street that they keep the man in the street from ever being able to draw a free breath. You can't be an Assassin and work for that."

"They're playing their game. And I'm playing mine." Kane smiled at him, a real smile, one of the very few he'd ever given his student. "You know full well that the more they push the kings of the world to show their true colors, the sooner the people will push back. Their schemes are immaterial, and we can't prevent them in any case. What matters is that we will stand ready on that day. We have to arm ourselves, Simeon. With all of the many devices in Ada Lovelace's notebook."

"Pierrette escaped, and took back the notebook," Simeon said. "Then she burned it."

He couldn't tell whether Kane swallowed the lie. He'd convinced Pierrette to leave Ada's notes with Nell Robinson back in the shop. Nell had been eager to help, and there hadn't been a safer place to hand.

"If she really did burn it," Kane said, "then we'll design our own. I've made great strides in the last few years, Simeon. Working people will never again be weaker than the people who try to rule them."

Simeon noticed the use of his first name. He also noticed the way a shadow shifted near one of the openings in the dirt walls. They were not alone. The men with shovels he'd seen earlier. They must be here, and they would almost certainly have something more than shovels in their hands by now.

"Janos Libenyi was a working man," Simeon said. "Felice Orsini was a working man. You used them, the way you use your men standing here, waiting to kill me. This time, it won't work."

"Oh, how you disappoint me." Kane drew one of his guns and fired.

The shot would have gone through Simeon's liver, or perhaps his kidney, had he been half a second slower. He threw himself to the right, but that took his blade farther away. He tapped the mechanism and it slid back into the gauntlet, before drawing his own revolver. A new gun that Kane had never seen before, whose idiosyncrasies he did not know.

Another shot grazed his shoulder, and it stung. First blood.

Simeon fired back, but Kane ducked behind the chunk of masonry and the shot hit it, blowing chalky dust into the air. Kane's two men were also shooting now at Simeon from the shadowy alcoves; as the shots rang, he dove for shelter himself, behind a pillar, before straightening to take aim again.

From above, he could hear shouts, and the ring of another shot. Pierrette and her friends in the alley had their own fight, it seemed. Damn it.

"You always insist on isolating yourself, don't you, Simeon? I offered you brotherhood. Friendship. A chance to be great, to step out of the shadows at last. You've always been afraid of your potential. But I'm not afraid of it. I know exactly what you can do. You make people loyal to you. Not something I'm very good at, I admit. But I am good at guessing what people will do next. I knew the French girl would cling to you, because she always does. And I also knew that a man who deserted his comrades would run behind that pillar once the bullets flew."

Simeon just caught sight of a rope loosening from an iron hook on the ground, before a crack in the stone slab under his feet opened, and he fell. Hard. His injured leg crumpled beneath him, and every ugly word he'd ever heard on board ship flew through his mind, and some of them out of his mouth. Kane had led him into yet another trap.

He was in a narrow hole with earth walls. As he scrabbled for something to grab, a bullet from above narrowly missed him.

Christ, he was done for. Not even a bad shot could miss him twice, trapped down here.

Another shot rang out, and then the hole went dark, as the bulk of a man fell into the hole on top of him, knocking Simeon to his knees, his legs buckling. The man was gasping, with a hole through his neck, and his blood ran through Simeon's fingers as he tried to push him off. He grabbed the man's arms, to make sure the ruffian couldn't stick a knife in him, but in a moment it didn't matter, as he was dead.

And he could hear Pierrette above, screaming a barrage of mocking French at someone. The ring of her Apache revolver – it was a wonder she'd made such a good shot with that; it had a terrible aim. But she liked it because it folded into a knife or knuckle dusters. She liked it because it was a trick. And here was another: a length of rope, and Pierrette at the top of it, urging him to hurry up.

There was a loop tied in the end of the rope. He put his good foot in it and then with her assistance hauled himself up as best he could, breaking open calluses old and new. He clasped her arm as she pulled him to the surface.

Half a dozen of Kane's men were scattered throughout the room; some of them must have followed Simeon's friends down from above. Halford was pinning down the two nearest to Simeon and Pierrette, to give Simeon a chance to get out of the hole. Robinson was in a shootout by the entrance. Out of the corner of his eye, Simeon saw Ariel running along the makeshift walkway under the ceiling. They leaped onto the back of one of Kane's men, and a knife flashed at his throat.

Kane himself was crouching behind a ruined pillar base and shooting at someone unseen. Wait, where was Ockham?

Or was it another of the circus troupe? Simeon leapt towards them, his own gun shaking a little as he got his legs under him. He got off a shot and saw Kane retreat to the far side of the pillar.

In that moment, he saw who Kane had been shooting at: Ockham, lying on the ground with blood trickling from his hand, his gun on the ground. Kane stepped out, his blackthorn shillelagh in his hand. He swung it at Ockham's head, and it connected with a horrifying sound.

Ockham writhed, his hand to his bloody head, but he waved his left hand in a weak but unmistakable message: go get him, don't worry about me.

Simeon wheeled, looking for Kane and trying to get a sense of how many of his thugs were still standing. Tillie Wallin, the blonde woman, had somehow got herself up to the top of a broken pillar, and threw a knife into the chest of one of Kane's men. And there was Kane: he aimed his gun at Tillie and pulled the trigger, but his gun was out of bullets. As he reached into the holster for his second, Pierrette came up behind him and plunged the short knife of her Apache into his back.

It was a small blade, serving only to make Kane twist like a fish on a hook, reaching around for Pierrette, but she had her wicked Laguiole knife out by the time he did. She thrust upwards toward his jaw, but his knee came up and knocked her elbow. Kane grabbed the knife out of her hand and held it to her neck. He pulled her backwards by the arm, glancing at the stairs out of the chamber. When Kane saw Hugh Robinson approach him from that direction, he shifted course, and made for the steps up to the walkway on the scaffold.

Simeon planned to leap on Kane, but a bullet spat by, and

he dove aside instead. Halford came up behind the man who'd been shooting at Simeon and twisted his neck, and he fell down dead. There was a look on Corporal Halford's face that Simeon did not want to witness.

Simeon aimed at Kane but couldn't trust his bullet to hit the mark and not Pierrette, as she wrestled and struggled with him; she wasn't as deterred by the knife at her throat as he seemed to expect. Kane might have killed her then, but he clearly wanted her alive. Maybe he thought she would lead him to Ada's notes, or perhaps he wanted power over Simeon. As he pulled her back into the depths of the chamber, toward the walkway steps, Kane kept Pierrette between himself and Simeon, a hostage and a shield. She kicked at him and screamed, but the rest of them stood frozen, guns drawn.

There was one henchman left fighting for Kane, and he wasn't fighting. He stood for a moment, looked around, then ran past Hugh and Tillie to the stairs, gambling that they wouldn't go after him. They didn't. Their eyes were all on Kane.

Kane was dragging Pierrette up onto the walkway where Ariel Fine had been running a moment before. And Ariel was now up on Hugh's shoulders, ready to leap up and intercept Kane. What could Kane be doing up there? Unless there was another exit after all. That shallow dig… maybe it had a secret door of its own. Kane would only need a split second to push Pierrette away – or worse – then make his escape. Then they would be back where they started.

Simeon ran for the steps. He'd have to shoot, but he'd get closer first. Give himself the best chance of hitting Kane without–

Out of nowhere, a lasso settled around Kane's shoulders.

The rope Pierrette had used to free Simeon. Ariel had thrown it, from up on Hugh's shoulders. Kane, caught, dropped the knife. But before Ariel could pull on the rope, someone barreled into Hugh, and he and Ariel both fell to the ground. The last of Kane's men, the one who'd run to the door. He'd seen his chance and come back, damn him.

Simeon yelled at Pierrette to get down, to get away.

The rope end swung freely, and Kane put his hands to the lasso to free himself.

Then Pierrette grabbed the rope and leaped backwards off the walkway.

Kane, still caught in the lasso, staggered to the edge, and the wood strained under the weight as he planted himself. Pierrette dangled from the rope end. A clear shot at Kane at last – but if Kane fell, he'd let Pierrette drop too. It wouldn't kill her, from that height, but she'd be lucky not to break anything.

Simeon took aim, his finger on the trigger, hesitating for a moment.

Kane was staggering, fighting to keep his balance. Pierrette – good God, she was swinging back and forth, as if she were in one of her hoops in the circus. She wanted them both to fall.

The walkway swayed too, then buckled in the air.

It happened before Simeon's next breath, but between Kane tumbling off the edge and the double thud of Kane and Pierrette hitting the ground, there was an agonizing eternity. Simeon tripped, righted himself, took the steps down again two by two, then jumped the last few feet.

The walkway groaned then sprang back, pieces of debris falling all around.

Pierrette was wincing, holding her ankle.

"I'm all right, I'm all right," she breathed.

Kane was in worse shape. He was lying flat on his back. He was trying to say something, but he couldn't get enough air, and just coughed bloody froth.

Simeon checked the man's hands for weapons, then knelt beside him.

The walkway collapsed around them. Dirt flew up and stung his eyes. Simeon could see Halford pulling Ockham by the shoulders. Kane's man, the one who'd taken down Hugh Robinson, was running too. Yes, they all had to get out. The walls were crumbling; those wooden struts had been holding the whole chamber in place.

"All of you go," Simeon yelled, choking on the dust. "Go!"

Pierrette dragged herself to her feet, limping, but waiting for the others to file out through the dirty air.

"Don't—" whispered Kane at last. Simeon hadn't expected him to beg for his life. He grimaced.

Loose soil and stones from the dirt walls were rattling in around the breaches where the walkway had been.

"Don't—"

"They're all out!" Pierrette called. "Time to go."

"Don't be *weak*," Kane finished.

Whether he was talking about the Templars in the years to come or the job Simeon had to do now, it didn't matter. He didn't need Kane's advice and wasn't asking for it. Simeon cradled his mentor's head steady and drove the hidden blade into his neck. Blood sprayed the gold waistcoat and drowned Kane's last ragged breath. A quicker death than he deserved, but Simeon had given up on the idea of justice a long time ago.

Simeon hastily dipped a calling card in the blood of his mentor, before he let Pierrette pull him away and out, and the walls rushed to fill the ancient void that Kane had found beneath the city. It buried Oscar Kane, and it buried the last of the ordinary working men he'd led to their deaths.

Chapter Twenty-Eight

Pierrette took the train back to London with Simeon. They had much to talk about. Halford stayed in Bath to look after Byron Ockham in the hospital; the doctors said he would live, though he might not make a full recovery. What a partial recovery might mean, no one seemed to know. Pierrette and Simeon had been in the waiting room at the hospital, the morning after the fight, when Simeon had sat bolt upright and gestured at the newspaper that he had been reading.

He had handed it over to Pierrette without a word. The headline read: "*Death of a Lady from an Overdose of Laudanum*". The lady in question was Lizzie Siddall.

The Aurora Troupe were going to stay in their wagon outside Bath for a few days, to rest and heal their wounds, before making the slower journey back. Arriving in the capital, Simeon and Pierrette went first to the Robinson's shop, to tell Nell everything that had happened, and reassure her that everyone was all right and would be home soon. Pierrette insisted on retrieving Ada's notes again too. She couldn't rest easy with them beyond her reach.

Then she and Simeon went to the Rossetti apartment to offer whatever comfort they could to Gabriel. While Simeon went next door to his old rooms to find something to wear, Pierrette found Gabriel surrounded by friends and family, stunned with grief. Lizzie's body was still in the apartment, for her friends and family to pay their respects.

In her own little room, Pierrette had a black dress among her belongings, still folded in the small dresser, that she changed into. Ada's book was still with her. She didn't have time to cut it up and disguise it, and didn't want to leave it in her room. So she borrowed a deep violet velvet drawstring bag of Lizzie's, one she used to use to put her costuming things in when she went to model. The notebook fit inside it well enough, and purple was acceptable for a mourning color. She put the now-empty mourning necklace into a drawer with her linens and pulled out an old locket that had been her mother's. It was empty too; if her mother had ever had something worth remembering in here, it was long gone.

On a whim, she went back into the sitting room and quietly asked Gabriel whether she could have a lock of Lizzie's hair to go in it. The artist, his eyes wild and dark-ringed, merely nodded. Simeon had arrived, now in his dark suit, and was sitting with one of Gabriel's author friends, shaking their heads over a glass of whiskey each. Gabriel stood and led her to his painting studio, where Lizzie was lying in an open casket, close to the window that opened out to London. There was an older woman sitting in an armchair near the casket, with her head in her hands. When they entered, she stood up and went into the other room, without saying a word.

It was so strange to see her beautiful friend lying there, as

though Lizzie were merely sleeping. Her posture was like in
Millais's painting of her as Ophelia, but her eyes were closed,
her face at rest. Gabriel, beside Pierrette, was a mass of anger
and grief contained within the shape of a man, like a bomb.

There was gossip amongst her friends that Lizzie had left a
note pinned to her dress. That it was not an accidental overdose
at all. Pierrette ached to know – she was grieving Lizzie, too, and
wanted to understand – but she did not dare ask Gabriel about
it. And maybe it wasn't something that could be understood.
She had died from an overdose of laudanum, when all was said
and done. Perhaps the kind of pain she was dulling with the
stuff didn't matter.

Gabriel walked over to the dark window. There was nothing
for Pierrette to do but pull out her knife from her pocket and
snick a piece of hair away. It was the most astonishing hair, and
always had been. The color that fire wanted to be.

Pierrette was just closing her locket when she heard a familiar
voice: female, German accented.

She was speaking to someone in the sitting room, but near
the door.

"She is obviously able to take care of herself. She was never
in any danger with me." The woman's voice was as smooth as
silk.

"Everyone is in danger with you, countess." Simeon's voice,
just as smooth, and very quiet.

Pierrette's heart was in her mouth. Any moment now they
could come into the other room. Was her pet thug with her?
Ada's notebook weighed heavily in Pierrette's bag – Lizzie's bag.
If only there were a fire burning in this room! She'd throw the
damned notes into it, and happily.

The countess again: "Where is our mutual friend now?"

"Paying her respects."

"And the book?"

The Templar wanted Ada's notes, and it was obvious that she would stop at nothing until she possessed them. Pierrette would be caught again, she would be searched, she would be beaten, her clothes would be cut away. There was nowhere to hide them. She should have burned the damn notebook – she could have done it this morning, last night. Why did she always hesitate over this cursed object?

As the countess's voice drew closer, Pierrette did the only thing she could think to do. She swiftly pulled the notebook, still in its new cardboard bindings, out of the velvet bag. Then she tucked it down inside the casket, completely hidden under Lizzie's beautiful hair. The one place no one would look.

Gabriel, at the window, was silent. Had he seen? It wouldn't matter if he did. He'd think it was a remembrance. And maybe it was. Lizzie and Ada had not known each other well – they hadn't had the chance, before Ada's final sickness took her – but there was something about the girl from the hat shop that reminded Pierrette of the Countess of Lovelace. Perhaps it was their love of learning, the way Lizzie had read Tennyson on a butter wrapper and decided to write her own poems; the way she had been asked to model, but ultimately decided to paint. Maybe it was a fitting place for the notebook after all.

The door opened and Pierrette looked up to see Countess von Visler, clad in mourning black, her face partly obscured by a black lace veil.

"I have a gun," Pierrette said coldly.

"You wouldn't dishonor your friend by doing violence here today," said the countess.

"I wouldn't test that, if I were you," said Simeon firmly from behind her, joining them.

The countess smiled thinly, the movement just visible beneath the veil. "I only came to pay my respects. It cannot be easy to lose two old friends in as many days." She turned slightly toward Simeon. "We had a man among Kane's workmen, or bodyguards, or whatever they were. He reported back to me that you told Kane the book was burned."

"That's correct," said Simeon.

"And was that the truth?"

Pierrette said, "Would you like me to strip down here and show you? I don't have it."

The countess turned back, and the expression behind the veil was unreadable. "Not quite an appropriate form of entertainment for a wake, I think, not even in England. I will leave you, with my sincerest condolences." She held out her gloved hand for Simeon, who didn't take it.

After the countess had departed, they stood together in the corridor. Pierrette said, "You really shouldn't flirt with the woman who nearly killed me."

"I wasn't flirting. What you heard was me trying my best to keep things civil in our grieving friend's home."

"*Sounded* like flirting."

"I bow to your expertise. Listen, will you be all right on your own here? I want to get messages to the British members of the Brotherhood, and our French colleagues too. They need to know the Magus is dead, and they need to know all that we learned about the way the Templars were using him."

"You can tell them something else," Pierrette said. "You can tell them that if they will have me, I'm at the disposal of the British Council of Assassins, wherever it may be at the moment."

"You're not going back to France?"

She shook her head. "I want to stay and help the Aurora Troupe get back on its feet. I owe them that much. And Britain is going to need all the Assassins it can get, judging by the way the Templars seem to be running around freely all over London. Gabriel won't mind the company, either, if we stay on here for a bit."

Simeon was quiet.

"Ah. You're leaving, aren't you?" she said, but she already knew the answer.

He nodded just slightly. "My face is so well known in London now. Everywhere I go, people are trying to buy me a drink, or quote my words back to me."

"A terrible fate," she said, with a small smile.

"It is for an Assassin. I'm too recognizable here. See what kind of Assassin I am, now that Kane is dead. And you don't need me. The British Council will welcome you into the Brotherhood, I have no doubt."

She'd dreamed for years of becoming an Assassin, but she had always imagined that Simeon would be there with her when she did. But he was right. They both had a chance to see what possibilities life held, now that they had finally fulfilled their duty to Ada Lovelace. But Pierrette wasn't ready quite yet. She had more to tell him – not least, what she had done with Ada's precious notes.

She slipped her arm into his. "Well, if this is farewell, let's go out together to find your famous Ghost, and anyone else you want to get a message to. I'm sure you can handle London for one more night. We'll find some nice comfortable shadows."

ACKNOWLEDGMENTS

This book was written thanks to the patience and support of my son, Xavier, my mother, Cheryl, and my partner, Brent, who is beside me on every adventure, and to whom this book is dedicated. I thank my whole family for their unwavering love and encouragement. My thanks as well to everyone at Ubisoft who had a hand in creating this marvelous universe, to cover artist Bastien Jez, and to Marc Gascoigne, Gwendolyn Nix, and the whole team at Aconyte Books. I am so grateful for my wonderful agent, Jennie Goloboy. And to all my writer friends, my love and thanks.

About the Author

KATE HEARTFIELD is the Aurora Award-winning author of *Armed in her Fashion*, and the bestselling *The Embroidered Book*, a historical fantasy novel. Her novellas, stories, and games have been finalists for the Nebula, Locus, Crawford, Sunburst and Aurora awards. A former journalist, Kate lives near Ottawa, Canada.

heartfieldfiction.com
twitter.com/kateheartfield

WORLD EXPANDING FICTION

Have you read them all?

ASSASSIN'S CREED®
- ☐ *The Ming Storm* by Yan Leisheng
- ☑ *The Magus Conspiracy* by Kate Heartfield
- ☐ *The Desert Threat* by Yan Leisheng *(coming soon)*

ASSASSIN'S CREED® VALHALLA
- ☐ *Geirmund's Saga* by Matthew J Kirby *(US/CAN only)*
- ☐ *Sword of the White Horse* by Elsa Sjunneson

TOM CLANCY'S THE DIVISION®
- ☐ *Recruited* by Thomas Parrott
- ☐ *Compromised* by Thomas Parrott *(coming soon)*

TOM CLANCY'S SPLINTER CELL®
- ☐ *Firewall* by James Swallow

WATCH DOGS®
- ☐ *Stars & Stripes* by Sean Grigsby & Stewart Hotston

WATCH DOGS® LEGION
- ☐ *Day Zero* by James Swallow & Josh Reynolds
- ☐ *Daybreak Legacy* by Stewart Hotston